The cliff face bulged out, releasing a wave of pent-up slurry that knocked Ryan off his feet

His mouth filled with the stinking ooze, and he fought for his life, struggling in blind desperation to get back onto his feet.

The initial tide eased, and he managed to claw himself upright, fumbling for his shovel. He wiped his eye clear of the mud and looked around frantically for Dean. But the boy had vanished under the wall of earth, mud and water.

"Get help, Kate! Call the sec men. Need shovels here, now!"

The noise of feet rattled on the ladder, and someone bellowed orders, shouting for everyone to get out before the whole place caved in.

"There's folks trapped!" Ryan called, his digging fingers suddenly touching something soft and yielding, flesh within cloth. The one-eyed man scrabbled in the yellow muck, heaving out a limp little body.

"Leave him be," the sec man ordered. "We'll get him up top."

"I'll carry him," Ryan insisted, not even looking at the guard.

Ryan didn't see the rifle butt as it went crashing into the side of his skull. He recovered and reached for the sec man, his fingers clawing for the pale, staring face. But the M-16 swung down a second time, and he toppled into a dark chasm of unconsciousness.

**Also available in the
Deathlands saga:**

JAMES AXLER

DEATH LANDS

Chill Factor

A GOLD EAGLE BOOK FROM

WORLDWIDE.

TORONTO • NEW YORK • LONDON
AMSTERDAM • PARIS • SYDNEY • HAMBURG
STOCKHOLM • ATHENS • TOKYO • MILAN
MADRID • WARSAW • BUDAPEST • AUCKLAND

Once he rode with the rest of the cavalry.
Now he's keeping me company,
heading out together into the promised land.
With very sincere thanks for all his help
over many years in keeping the payroll safe from
the Apaches, this is for Don Day.

First edition May 1992

ISBN 0-373-62515-4

CHILL FACTOR

Printed in U.S.A.

Most of us would not be capable of taking the life of another human being, whatever the provocation. A minority might do it if sufficiently aroused. But there have always been and always will be, the mercifully small number of men, and women, who can kill. And kill. And kill again.

from *The Upward Spiral of Death*
by Hamilton Binder, 1903

Chapter One

The walls of the gateway were silvered glass, and Ryan Cawdor knew that they were back in New Mexico. The jump hadn't been too bad.

Outside the ruined redoubt the morning sun was breaking over the mountains to the east, throwing long shadows across the desert.

The companions managed to pick their way down onto the level ground without any difficulty, Doc Tanner and Mildred Wyeth helping each other over the steeper sections. Ryan was worried to see new tracks on the trail outside the military complex.

"Someone's coming," Krysty Wroth said, busily tying her hair back off her neck with a black bandanna.

The rising sun was in the youth's face, highlighting his dazzling white hair. There was no possibility of mistaking Jak Lauren.

He was riding a bay mare, spurring the horse on at a fast trot that turned into a dust-burning gallop when he spotted the little group of friends.

Krysty stared intently toward him as he closed the gap to a hundred yards. Her face was set like pale marble, and she reached out to grip Ryan by the wrist, hard enough to make him wince.

"Oh, no," she said, her voice soft and shocked.

Jak reined in the sweating, lathered horse, throwing himself from the saddle. "Heard your radio message. You hear mine?"

"No. What?"

The teenager's eyes blazed like chips of nuked ruby. "Dean."

Ryan stared at him, wondering what could have happened to his ten-year-old son. "What?"

"Taken."

"When?"

"Yesterday afternoon. Christina shot one of the gang."

"And?"

"Questioned him."

"Still got him?" Ryan was unable to control the anxiety in his voice.

"Died," Jak replied, as laconic as ever.

"Why didn't you ask him all—"

"Did. Slavers. North. Used gateway. Took Dean."

Ryan suddenly thought of the LD button—Last Destination. If this gang had jumped, then he could follow them. It wasn't all lost. Not yet.

"I'll go after them," he said. "Food and a rest, and then I'll go."

Jak nodded. "One other thing from wounded man. Before died."

"What?"
"Slavers' leader."
"Yeah?"
"Russian. Name Zimyanin."

Chapter Two

The corpse lay in a small barn to the east of the main house.

In warm weather it didn't take long for a human body to start deteriorating. Only a few hours and the eyes began to melt back into their sockets. The soft tissues of the mouth, nose and throat rotted next, along with the genital area.

The man had died around fifteen hours earlier and had been placed on an old door that stood on a trestle table.

It had gone through the brief period of rigor mortis and now looked relaxed, the skin darkening. The man was naked, head back, staring blankly at the roof beams above him in the dusty darkness. His hair was graying, cropped short, with an old scar seaming the side of the scalp just above the left ear.

He might almost have been asleep, if it hadn't been for the dreadful mutilations.

Christina had greeted them with a solemn pleasure, showing the way across to the barn. The strain of the last day showed on her face. She limped more heavily than usual, the built-up boot on her left foot dragging through the dust.

"Did you both question him?" Ryan asked.

Jak looked at his wife. "Both."

"Bullet killed him," Mildred said, leaning over to examine the dark-rimmed hole in the center of the man's chest, framed with the lacy pattern of dried blood. "Lungs. Can't have taken too long for him to die. Not just from that."

Jak nodded. "Knew that. Knew wouldn't live much. Had to find out where boy went."

The black doctor straightened. "Someone made it a hard passing for him. Carving knife, hot irons. Razor? Yeah, a razor. Needle by the eyes and through the end of his penis."

Doc coughed and turned away. "Think I'll go outside and get myself a smidgen of fresh air," he said. "Seems a tad humid in here. Just a little oppressive."

He went out, leaving the double doors ajar, so that a carpet of golden sunlight spilled across the straw and dust. It reached just to the foot of the makeshift table.

"I tortured him," Christina admitted. "Jak tied him so he couldn't move an inch. I made him go out while I did it. Best that way. Not a pretty sight what I did to the bastard."

There were rope burns around the man's wrists and ankles, and around his scrawny throat. The cords had been knotted so tightly that the pattern could still be seen on the skin, and blood had burst from under fingernails and toenails.

"You did right," Krysty said, touching the older woman on the arm.

"Once the boy's gone, one of the disappeared ones, you could search Deathlands all your life and never find him. Least we know more or less where he's been taken."

Ryan asked the question that had been tormenting him since Jak told him who the slavers' leader had been. "Did he say that they'd come specially for Dean? That this Zimyanin knew he was my son?"

Christina looked surprised. "No. Why should he? Man said they raided all around the Southwest and along the Big Miss River. Need them to work up north. Why should they have known who the boy was?"

"Long story," Ryan replied. "Tell us about the raid, and I'll tell you about Zimyanin."

She nodded. "Got a stew near ready. Must be hungered. Let's go in."

Ryan took a last glance at the tortured corpse. "How about him?"

"Bury tonight," Jak said.

THERE WAS little conversation during the meal. Everyone was too concerned with eating. Christina was an excellent cook. They ate beef stew, with potatoes and turnip greens, a rich gravy, flavored with herbs that she grew out in the trim back garden. There was fresh-baked cornbread and some blueberry muffins with butter and peach preserve.

Doc leaned back, his chair grating on the floor, and sighed. "Upon my soul, my dear young lady, but that was a feast fit for a prince. My sincere compliments on your culinary skill."

Christina smiled, almost for the first time since their arrival. "Why, thank you, Doc. My mother used to do her best, but..." The smile vanished like the dew off the morning prairie, and the sentence trailed away into stillness.

J. B. Dix filled the silence. Wiping a dribble of melted butter from his stubbled chin, he looked at Christina. "Tell us about how they came at you."

WITH OCCASIONAL interruptions and additions from Jak, she told them what had happened. Sleeves rolled up, elbows on the table, Christina kept it short and simple.

Dean had been checking fences, riding a pinto pony. He'd carried a small .22 hunting rifle in a saddle holster. Christina had given him some bread and bacon to carry him through the morning, with a canteen of spring water.

"No danger," Jak said. "Not been any trouble for long time here."

Ryan nodded. "Hell, I know that."

Jak had been working on a broken blade off the main windmill, up a long narrow ladder, and Christina had been salting down some pork in one of the sheds.

"Fine day. Few clouds to the south. Saw an old miner with his lame burro on the trail. See him every few months. He didn't stop."

Ryan interrupted her. "Could he be a scenter for these men?"

She shook her head. "No. Old Josiah couldn't pull the wings off a dead butterfly. About an hour after he passed I saw the dust."

There was a silence. Mildred reached and poured herself a mug of coffee-sub from the blue enameled pot. All of them knew that the sudden appearance of strangers on the road in Deathlands could mean instant trouble.

"Was higher. Saw better. But can't make out too good in bright sun."

Being an albino, with death-white skin and pink eyes, Jak had never been able to see very well in a strong light, though he saw better than most in semidarkness.

Christina took up the story again.

"Dean was spurring his pony, about a hundred paces ahead of them."

"How many?" J.B. asked.

"About fifteen. Maybe twelve. Maybe twenty. Broken land like all over here...can't be certain of the numbers."

"Armed with..."

She looked at J.B., who'd taken off his glasses, wiping dirt off them.

Jak answered. "Haven't got your cunning. Only heard long guns. One we caught had small-caliber hideaway blaster and repaired carbine."

"What kind of discipline did they have?" This was a major question, and Ryan waited for the answer. There were enough gangs of raggedy killers all over Deathlands. They rose like a foul growth of weeds and generally didn't last more than a few weeks before they perished, months at the outside.

"Good. Skirmish line around house. Tried long enough. Pulled back. Tried to get wounded man. Too close. Left him."

"Yeah. Go on. How about Dean?"

"They shot his pony from under him."

Christina finished the brief story. "After they took Dean they came and tried for us. By then Jak was in the house and we had the firefight shutters up. One we shot—"

"*You* shot," Jak contradicted, unable to hide his pride. "Better'n me with long blasters. Knocked over in dirt by corral fence."

"Thought I'd chilled him clean." Christina smiled again. "Went over, legs kicking, like a brain-dead gopher. Think I hit a couple of others. Jak found blood after they'd gone."

He nodded. "Pool. Drag marks in grass like hauled off."

"Can we see what he was wearing and carrying?" J.B. stood.

"Out back. I'll tidy up in here."

"I'd be honored to be allowed to lend you a hand, Mrs. Lauren," Doc offered.

She blushed. "Not many call me that, Doc. But I'll take you up on it." She glanced at her teenaged husband. "Mebbe teach him a lesson in manners."

Jak got up hastily, nearly knocking his chair over, not meeting his wife's eyes. Mildred and Krysty also decided to stay in the house to rest, leaving J.B. and Ryan to accompany Jak outside into the baking heat.

Their boot heels crunched in the dirt, and the wind blew a ball of tumbleweed across the desert behind the homestead.

"You and Mildred together, J.B.?"

"Category of my business, kid."

"Don't call me 'kid,' old man."

All three of them laughed. "Old jokes are still the best," Ryan said, grinning.

THE CLOTHES AND BLASTERS were piled on a bench in a pitch-roofed shed. The wind tugged at the door, and Jak slipped the catch to close it.

Ryan picked over the blood-soaked pants and shirt, while the Armorer glanced at the rifle and the tarnished handgun.

"These are all thermal-lined!" Ryan exclaimed in surprise.

"Yeah. Some fuckers carried big coats. Like come from real cold place."

"Man you caught say where?"

"Didn't know. North. All said. Christina tried real hard to keep alive, but fucking weak from bullet."

"Dreck blasters," J.B. said. "Hideaway was once Model 87 Beretta. Looks like it'd blow your hand apart if you pulled the trigger."

"Long gun?"

"Old Marlin bolt-action. Seven shot. But it's been chopped around so much there's not much left they'd have recognized up in New Haven." He saw that Ryan and Jak looked puzzled. "Where they made them."

Ryan held up a woollen cap, showing it to J.B. "Recognize this?"

There was a badge on the front, a small, hand-beaten circle of silver.

"Russkies. They wore something like that."

Jak nodded. "I told Christina about that time in Moscow. You remember Zimyanin?"

Ryan nodded.

He remembered Zimyanin well enough.

They'd met Major-Commissar Gregori Zimyanin twice, once up in the wilderness of Alaska and once in the muddy roads around Moscow. He worked for the Security Section.

He was one of the strongest men that Ryan had ever met, with the bursting muscled look of someone who worked out every day and kept himself needle-sharp. Zimyanin wasn't very tall, as Ryan recalled, not much over five foot six, but stocky. He was totally bald, with a face badly marked by smallpox, and he'd worn a long, drooping mustache then.

The man had carried a Makarov 9 mm pistol, the PM model. And Ryan also remembered the long Dragunov sniper's rifle. By a quirk of the lords of chaos, it was an exceedingly rare weapon, yet it was similar to that used by Ryan's most bitter enemy, the late Cort Strasser.

Zimyanin had learned passable English between their two meetings, though it was archaic, making him sound like Doc Tanner on a bad day.

It had been a freakish accident that had led to Ryan being indirectly responsible for the Russian sec man being in Deathlands.

Now this man, with his ready smile and his strangler's hands, had Dean Cawdor prisoner.

"Will he know who boy is?" Jak asked the question as they walked back toward the house.

"Hope not," Ryan replied.

Chapter Three

"My responsibility."

"Dean is Ryan's son, not ours, Jak."

"Know that. But Ryan left with us."

Freed of the weight of the heavy surgical boot, Christina stretched, relishing the cool linen sheets on her naked body.

"It wasn't our fault, Jak. They know that. Let them go after him."

In the dim light, she could see the magnesium flare of her young husband's white hair. He was shaking his head.

"Sorry, Chris. Real, *real,* sorry."

MILDRED REACHED DOWN over the short hairs of his chest and across the flat muscular wall of his stomach. She finally found him, cradling him, bringing him gently to readiness.

"What's this, John? I can't stand the way you keep bothering me with your incessant demands."

He chuckled, rolling onto his side, allowing his own fingers to work their way along the inside of her thighs, higher and closer.

She began to breathe faster. "One thing."

"What?"

"Before we get this boat launched into deep waters, I got a question."

"Yeah?"

"You going with Ryan?"

There was a momentary hesitation. "Guess so. If he wants me."

"That's what I thought." She began to caress him again. "I mean that's what I expected, John. I've got no problem with that."

DOC WAS SLEEPING on his back, on a truckle bed made up in a corner of the larder beyond the kitchen. He was wrapped around in the warm familiar scents and flavors of his own distant youth—the cheeses and the smoked ham, salted fish and cinnamon, and ginger and strings of dried chilis, red and green.

Doc had felt tired in Florida, tired of the oppressive heat, the pressure and the killing. The endless killing.

"So good to rest, Emily, with my head upon your bosom," he whispered.

His wife's face was in deep shadow, but he could just see the sunlight as it reflected off the crystal pendant that hung from her slender neck on a thin gold chain.

He held Emily's hand, closing his eyes. There was a moment of doubt and fear, that some creature would come gibbering from the valley of darkest night. But it was a kind, gentle sleep, and Doc smiled.

The old man was content in the embrace of his wife, nearly two hundred years dead.

IN THE BEST guest bedroom, its shuttered window looking to the south, Ryan and Krysty lay in each other's arms. They'd been talking quietly since leaving the others. Neither felt like making love, the desolate loss of the boy hanging above the bed like the naked blade of a sword.

Krysty knew that Ryan would go after Dean. It was a question of when.

"Who'll go with you, lover?"

Ryan had hesitated a long time before answering, making her think he'd actually fallen asleep.

"Can't say."

"All of us?"

"Probably better not. Not Mildred and not Doc. Going to be a serious knockdown bloody-bones fight."

"Me?"

Another long pause.

"Tell you what I think's going to happen in the morning."

She could feel the icy touch of fear, probing inside her mind. "What?"

"My guess is that Jak'll want to come."

"Will Christina let him go?"

"She won't stop him. He feels responsible for what happened."

"But he—"

He brought his hand to her face, hushing her. "Course he's not to blame. But he *feels* he is. Comes on down to the same thing. So, if he goes, then J.B. has to stay here. Take charge of the place."

"Christina won't like that, lover."

"Course. But she's not stupid. See how the wheel turns. Someone has to."

"So it'll be you and Jak. Alone."

"My guess, lover. No point saying I'm sorry or wishing we could all go. Be like wishing the pitcher of milk never fell off the table. Or the stray bullet didn't puddle the brains of the friend at your side. No point having regrets. Just go and do it and return here with the boy."

Krysty rolled away from him, lying on her left side, offering him her back. Ryan said nothing, waiting.

Finally she spoke again, her voice muffled by the pillow.

"One day you won't come back. I know I've said this before, and you're still here. You and me, lover, we're like two parts of one whole. Take me away from you, and I'm nothing. Same with you. I wake in the night and I lie trembling at the loss that'll come. You'll die, Ryan."

"We all will, Krysty. Until then, the man who sits down when he should be up and standing isn't much of a man."

She swallowed hard. "Sure, lover. Doesn't stop it from hurting."

BY MORNING all of the talking had been done. Ryan was second into the kitchen, smelling bacon sizzling in the pan and a pot of coffee-sub bubbling on the iron stove. Jak stood by, cracking eggs into a second skillet with one hand while stirring up a mess of hash browns with the other.

"Good to see she's finally got you to learn something useful," Ryan commented.

"Still work out with throwing knives hour every day."

"You happy here, Jak?"

The white face turned to him, the narrow eyes looking suspicious. "Joking?"

"Course not. Just that you seem content here. Good place and Christina's a good, good woman, Jak. You're lucky."

"Man makes own luck, Ryan." He concentrated on the eggs. "Over or sunny?"

"Over."

One by one the rest came down to join them. Doc was last, rubbing sleep from his rheumy eyes. "Oh, what a fearful sluggard and lagabed am I! Hope there's plenty of victuals left. I swear I could demolish a horse. Hooves and all."

"Only some pig and some hen fruit, Doc," Christina said, smiling.

Everyone could see that she'd been crying.

Ryan caught Jak's eye across the table. "When?" he asked.

The young man looked down at a small wrist chron. "It's just before seven now. Go at eight."

Christina looked around slowly, her eyes brimming. Then she pushed away from the table and ran out into the bright morning sunlight.

Chapter Four

J.B. had joined their council of war, agreeing that this didn't sound like the kind of mission where long guns would be needful.

"Get in close, skin on skin," he said laconically. "Best way."

He offered them the Uzi machine pistol, but both Ryan and Jak elected to stick with their own weapons, the ones they knew best.

Ryan had his 9 mm SIG-Sauer P-226 blaster. It held fifteen rounds and had a push-button mag-release, with a built-in baffle silencer. He had the trusty panga, its blade eighteen inches of honed steel, on his left hip. The slim flensing knife was snug in the small of his back.

Jak had four leaf-bladed throwing knives, hilts taped for perfect balance. They were hidden so well about his person that even Ryan himself wasn't certain where he had them concealed. On his right hip he still hefted the enormous satin-finish cannon, the .357 Magnum with the six-inch barrel.

They'd talked about what to wear.

The evidence was that the slavers had come from somewhere seriously cold. J.B. pointed out that the dead man had lost three toes off one foot with what could well have been gangrene from frostbite.

Ryan had his familiar old coat with the fur collar, and the white silk scarf, with its weighted ends, tucked inside the collar. Jak was wearing jeans and a quilted jacket, western working boots and a knitted cap in dark blue wool to hide his unmistakable hair.

"Wish I could do something about the patch over my eye," Ryan said. "If we run into Zimyanin I figure he'll probably recognize me."

Christina gave both of them a package wrapped in oiled cloth, which contained meat pies, savory and fresh, with some corn dodgers and strips of jerked beef. Each man had a canteen of water, drawn that morning from the Lauren's well.

It was eight minutes after eight.

A bay mare stood docilely in the shafts of the buggy, it's head down, munching its way through a heap of hay.

Jak kissed his wife, hugged her and climbed into the seat of the buckboard, picking up the reins and holding them loosely.

Ryan shook hands with Doc and J.B., embraced Mildred and looked at Krysty.

"Time to go, lover," he said.

"Gaia watch over you and bring you and the boy safe home again."

"Keep your back to the sun," J.B. said, grinning at Ryan as he offered him the old gunfighter's creed.

"Stay crucial." Mildred laughed. "And let's be careful out there."

Ryan clambered aboard the well-sprung rig, settling himself on the narrow seat, his coat across his lap. He nudged Jak. "Let's go."

The teenager whistled between his teeth, and the mare moved forward. The wheels clumped and rolled over the dusty ground as they headed along the trail toward the redoubt.

Ryan clung onto the rail at the side to save himself from being thrown off.

"See why they call it a 'buckboard,'" he shouted through gritted teeth.

He glanced behind, seeing that everyone was waving. Christina stood a little to one side, one hand on her hip. Doc had run a few steps after them across the cropped grass.

As Ryan waved to him, the old man called something. It was difficult to catch what it was above the noise of the buggy. It sounded like he was yelling "Shane!" but that made no sense to Ryan.

"YOU KNOW YOU DON'T HAVE to come all the way, Jak?"

"Yeah."

They were drawing near to the rusting radar dish that lay ruined in the sand at the foot of the crook-topped mountain.

"The horse'll take the rig back home?"

Jak nodded, reining in. "Sure. Nearest water. Just let her go."

Ryan jumped down, stretched his arms and shoulders. He picked up his coat and slung it over his arm. "Goin' to be a warm climb."

Jak slapped the mare on the flank and stood watching as it trotted dutifully off, retracing its own tracks toward the distant farm.

The trail was steep, open and unshadowed, baked by the rising sun. Jak led the way, light on his feet, Ryan panting and sweating behind him.

There was a temptation to drink from their canteens, but they both resisted it, knowing that dehydration was the greatest killer in the bare desert, knowing that once you'd drunk your water, the going could get bleak.

Finally they reached the crest, where a huge explosion had ripped away the entire peak and flank of the hill. A dark hole gaped there.

Ryan followed the teenager, standing head down, taking in several lungfuls of air. He wiped perspiration from his forehead, moving his eye patch where salt irritated the empty socket.

"See for miles," he said.

Jak ignored the view, peering into the pitchy blackness of the wrecked entrance. "Forward," he muttered. "Not back."

IF IT HAD BEEN a fiction-vid, Ryan would have found a clue that Dean had been taken there. Maybe his turquoise-hafted knife, a distinctive button ripped off his jacket, a rumpled piece of paper carrying a vital, scribbled message.

Life wasn't like that.

There were the marks of feet in the driven sand that coated the tunnels and passageways of the redoubt. Jak knelt down to peer at them, shaking his head.

"Tells nothing," he said.

When they eventually reached the gateway chamber with its walls of silvery armaglass, Jak showed an odd reluctance to enter it.

"Problem?" Ryan asked.

"No." He paused. "Yeah. Always hated jumps. Made sick. Dark-out in head."

Ryan hesitated, standing by the heavy door, looking back past the small anteroom into the main control area. "Best you go home to Christina and the others, Jak."

"No." He shook his head firmly. "Let's get jumping, Ryan."

He walked in and sat, his woollen cap gripped in his hand, and rested his head on his knees, back against the translucent wall. He attempted a smile, which was like the rictus of terminal agony on a death's-head.

Ryan pressed the button marked LD, stepped inside the chamber and pulled the door firmly shut behind him.

The lock clicked. He sat opposite Jak, adopting a similar position. He placed his coat to one side in case he was sick or suffered from a nosebleed. It was oppressively warm and humid inside, and he could feel sweat trickling down into the small of his back.

The metal disks that patterned the floor and ceiling of the mat-trans unit began to glow, and a faint mist appeared in the air. Ryan could hear a distant humming sound, and he felt the familiar, nauseous swirling in his brain.

"See at other end," Jak said, his voice stretched and plangent, coming from some other dimension.

Ryan tried to reply, but his jaw was locked and his head was filled with a churning, tepid mess of lead and molasses.

Darkness came.

JAK LAUREN'S LAST SENTIENT thought was a sweeping regret that bordered on panic, then he slumped sideways into unconsciousness.

And the dream began.

He was sitting in a small boat amid the swampy bayous of what was once called Louisiana, engulfed by the scent of rotting vegetation. Spanish moss drooped from the mangrove branches like the intestines of long-dead lepers. There was very little freeboard, the thick, muddy water coming within an inch or so of slopping over the sides.

Jak kept very still.

Water dripped all around him, each separate drop leaving a distinct hole in the swamp.

"Jak!"

He turned his head, very slowly.

"Jak, help me!"

He knew the voice, knew that Christina was in some deathly danger. There was a ripple of movement near the distant bank, and he glimpsed the serrated back of a huge alligator. To the right was another one, hooded eyes just above the ooze. The boat rocked from side to side and filthy water came slopping in, lapping at his bare feet.

The cry was repeated, the sound stifled by the oppressive branches that lowered around the teenager. Jak felt for his gun, but the holster was limp and empty. His knives had vanished.

"In the name of Jesus, help me, Jak!"

There was a fierce stabbing pain in his stomach, and he wanted to lie down. But he couldn't see for the snow that was drifting all around him, masking the sharp-fanged rocks and the lean wolves who paced hungrily up and down.

"Christina," he said, tears rolling down his narrow cheeks, mingling with the threads of puke that dribbled from his open mouth.

In the gateway chamber, Jak's skinny body began to go into convulsions.

RYAN WAS RUNNING through a great forest. Tall pines blotted out any glimpse of the sky, standing so close together that he had to twist and turn to make his way along the ill-defined and overgrown path. His feet were bare, bleeding, painful.

Somewhere behind him he could clearly catch the sound of heavy artillery, the shells screaming high above his head, landing with a distant crump far in front of him.

Ryan knew that he had friends all around him—the snow-headed boy and his limping wife, the woman with hair like flame and eyes like frozen emeralds, an old, old man who laughed at life. There was a black woman to his right. It was odd that he knew that, even though it was impossible to see anything through the surrounding trees.

And a pale-faced, short man in glasses. Ryan knew him.

"John." The sound barely broke the mist that flooded the gateway chamber.

He'd been sprinting along a narrow stream kicking his way through the polished pebbles, diving full-length onto a gravel beach, running the tiny stones, cold and wet, between his fingers.

"A living man," Ryan whispered.

Ahead of him he could make out the silhouette of a trestle bridge, way above the river. Sec men, wearing dark uniforms, lined the bluffs to the right and left, looking down at him.

A boy stood on the bridge, his hands bound behind him. He was a small, sturdy figure, with a shock of dark, curly hair. A hemp noose had been tightened around his neck.

Beside him was an officer in a slouch hat, gripping a brass-hilted saber. He was grinning down at Ryan, who stood knee-high in the surging stream far below.

"Bastard!"

The man lifted his hat, revealing a glitteringly bald dome. His mouth parted in a smile, his lips covering a luxuriant mustache.

As Ryan reached despairingly upward, the officer pushed the boy with the tip of his sword, toppling him into singing space where the rope tautened and his neck broke with a dry crack.

When Ryan recovered consciousness his eye was wet, his cheek streaked with tears.

And he realized that he was bitingly cold.

Chapter Five

Ryan's stomach was roiling as though he'd just eaten the worst bowl of dog chili that the foulest gaudy on the darkest part of the frontier could offer him.

He closed his eye again, trying to lever himself into a more upright position. The floor was icy cold, and he could feel the chill of the armaglass through his shirt.

Part of him wondered why some jumps were so much worse than others. Another part wondered if he was going to throw up.

It took a hundred heartbeats to regain some degree of control over his body. Finally, cautiously, Ryan opened his eye again.

His breath plumed out ahead of him, and he rubbed his hands together, hunching his shoulders protectively against the arctic cold. Remembering his first meeting with Gregori Zimyanin, it occurred to him that the jump might have taken him back into Alaska.

He searched his memory for the color of the walls of that particular chamber. A pale blue, with streaks of gray, he thought. Or gray streaked with blue. One or the other.

These walls were so dark a brown that they were almost black.

"Triple cold," he whispered, finding that his teeth were beginning to chatter.

Jak lay on the floor, across from him in the six-sided chamber. The boy was still, blood seeping from his ears and nose, bright scarlet against his ivory skin.

"Jak."

Ryan was suddenly aware of a very faint scratching sound in the gateway, like the claws of a small bird on a shingle roof.

He leaned forward, wincing at a shaft of pain through his good eye. He saw that the little finger on Jak's left hand was moving from side to side, nail scratching at the floor.

Ryan crawled over on hands and knees. He rolled the teenager onto his side, reaching into his open mouth to make sure that he hadn't swallowed his tongue. Gobbets of clotted blood splattered onto the floor. Jak moaned feebly, eyelids fluttering.

"Come on," Ryan said, trying to lift him into a sitting position.

"Fuck off." The words were spoken with no discernible anger or passion, Jak's voice flat and dulled.

Ryan propped the lad against the smooth wall, gently straightening his legs, then moved back to pick up his own coat and slide his arms into the sleeves.

"Want take my blaster? Only way is to pull my cold, dead finger off trigger. So…" Jak's voice faded away into total silence.

Ryan stood and steadied himself, closing his eye again as a spear of pain darted through his skull. "Jak, it's time to go. Freeze if we stay here too much longer. Get up, kid."

Not even the old taunt provoked the albino teenager. He still lay prone, fingers clenching. His eyes remained closed.

Ryan eased open the door of the chamber, peering out. His hand rested on the butt of the pistol in its holster.

There was a small bare room outside, and dark splashes and stains on the white stone floor that looked uncommonly like old spilled blood. Beyond that, the consoles chattered and lights flickered on the control units.

"Forgotten how bad jumps were."

Ryan turned around, seeing that Jak had managed to get up on hands and knees.

"Want help?"

"No. Thanks. Fucking cold, Ryan."

"Yeah. Freeze the balls off brass well-digger. Get your coat on."

The teenager managed to work his way upright, leaning heavily on the walls. He struggled into his coat and slapped his arms against his sides.

"If cold in here, what like outside?"

"Colder, I guess. Ready to move on?"

Jak sighed. Ryan couldn't decide if his face looked even more pale than usual. "Head's bad," he said.

"Want to rest awhile?"

"Don't know." Jak's legs suddenly gave out, and he sat in a floppy heap, very nearly rolling on his face.

"Jak! Fireblast!" Ryan stooped over him, not sure what to do.

"Sorry. Went black. Rest here. You go look around, Ryan."

"Sure. Keep your blaster handy. And do your coat up."

Ryan went out, careful to leave the gateway door partly open. Jak gave him a small wave of his hand as his friend left.

Ryan found a pile of clothes almost immediately, heaped in a corner of the control room, close by the main sec doors to the whole mat-trans section of the redoubt. The doors stood wide open, showing evidence of having been blown with ex-plas by a real expert.

There were heavy coats—many fur-lined—plaid shirts, warm boots in all sizes, woollen jumpers with roll necks, at least twenty pairs of winter gloves and several scarves.

Ryan guessed that it was a selection ready for Zimyanin's men as they returned from their slaving missions, and for their victims to save them from freezing to death in the first minutes after their arrival.

"Arrival where?" Ryan wondered aloud. He'd forgotten to bring the Armorer's pocket sextant to help find out just where they'd ended up.

Which reminded him to check his rad-counter.

He opened his coat to glance down at it and saw that it was way over from the green level, through orange toward red.

Hot spots were somewhere near.

At least they could make use of the extra layers of clothing.

Ryan picked out a mackinaw coat in dark gray and black plaid. It was thick and heavy, and looked to be about the right size for Jak Lauren.

He also took a couple of pairs of thermal gloves, thin enough to enable you to still operate a blaster, but warm enough to stop your fingers from freezing.

Before returning to the gateway chamber, Ryan stepped to the sec doors and glanced out. The corridor to the left was an instant dead end. To the right it wound along out of sight. The air was freezing, and the walls, floor and ceiling were all coated with a fine layer of powdery snow. The vid-cameras below the roof all seemed to have become iced up. Not one appeared to be functioning.

Jak was standing when he returned, but he was holding his head, his fingers pressed against his eyes.

"Feel . . . Head's worse than any jump before. What'd you find?"

"Good thick coat. Should go over everything else you got on. And gloves for both of us."

"Been out?"

"Looked into the passage through the main control room. They've been blown open. Haven't gone any farther. Bit of snow's lying." He handed him the mackinaw. "Oh, and there's some rad hot spots close by. Counter's near red."

Jak pulled on the plaid coat and whistled. "Better. Thanks." He managed a thin smile. "Be okay, Ryan. Walk it off. Any idea where we are?"

Ryan shook his head. The worrying thought had come to him that they might not even be on the North American continent anymore. Their one jump that had landed them in the heart of postapocalypse Russia had been a dreadful warning. And if there was a gateway in Russia, then there might be one anywhere else in the world.

Jak stumbled as they moved into the wide corridor beyond the control room. He quickly regained his balance, but Ryan had noticed. Noticed it and was worried.

He had known the young man long enough to have built up a profound admiration for his incredible agility and athletic skills. Nobody was more lethally acrobatic in close-combat fighting.

"Lot foot marks, Ryan."

In weather that was well below freezing, it was almost impossible—even for the most skilled tracker—to determine how long tracks had been made. Here there was also a faint breeze that kept the microscopic grains of snow in perpetual motion, like a shallow river of ice.

Ryan knelt and examined the marks, but the edges were blurred and indistinct.

"What are these?" Jak asked, moving closer to the wall. "Like bear? Double small. Cubs?"

Where there were cubs there was probably a mother bear. Ryan had seen mutie grizzlies that had topped eighteen feet on their hind legs, and it wasn't a sight he particularly wanted to see again.

"Could be cubs," he agreed. "Better walk real careful here."

THE REDOUBT HAD BEEN totally abandoned and stripped clean, probably even before sky-dark and the onset of the long winters.

Most of the lights still worked, showing that the trusty nuke generators were still ticking away, buried deep in the bowels of the complex.

As they moved along, the breeze noticeably fresher, Jak seemed to be recovering a little of his strength, though Ryan noticed him twice put his hand to his forehead and press it against his eyes.

"You okay?" the one-eyed man asked.

It wasn't simply a polite question. You didn't have polite questions about health in Deathlands. If you asked, it was because it mattered.

Jak stopped and looked at Ryan, his face showing the struggle.

"No," he said. "Head filled with snow. Very sick. Muscles feel like wet string." He paused. "Sorry."

"Can you go on?"

"Yeah. But not firefight. No."

"Mebbe we should try and find somewhere to hole up. Let you gather strength again."

Jak sighed. "Time's wasting." Ryan figured that this was probably one of Christina's sayings.

"Couple of hours?"

"Sure."

"We'll go on and try to find a shelter. If not we can go back to the gateway."

The boy turned away from him, eyes narrowing. "Something," he whispered, pointing down the wide passage ahead of them.

Ryan couldn't hear a sound, but he trusted Jak's heightened senses.

Both of them drew their blasters, flattening against the curved wall, one on each side. There was no cover at all.

Then Ryan heard it, a peculiar noise, snuffling, halfway between the cooing of a wood pigeon and the whimpering of a young puppy.

He glanced at Jak, who shrugged his shoulders.

The noise grew closer.

Jak laughed, holstering his Magnum. "Cuddlies." He shook his head. "Heard of 'em. Never seen. Double cute."

Ryan also holstered his SIG-Sauer, finding his own face breaking into a smile. He'd once heard an old man, singing in a gaudy someplace, talk about how people didn't like to eat "cute" food. Chickens were ugly. So were pigs. Kittens were cute, so nobody wanted to eat little kittens.

The cuddlies were cute.

There were three of them, about twelve inches long, with stubby little legs, covered in a coat of hair that was a mixture of honey and gold. They came scampering toward Jak, making tiny noises of pleasure and welcome.

The teenager started to kneel down, beginning to peel off his gloves.

Ryan wished he could have had an old vid-camera to record the charming scene.

The first of the cuddlies reached Jak—and sprang at his throat, ripping a gash with its razored claws that gouted bright crimson blood into the snow.

Chapter Six

"Fireblast!"

The second of the cuddlies had set its needled teeth into Jak's calf, just above the top of his heavy combat boot. The third was pattering amiably toward Ryan, its liquid eyes alight with the desire to butcher him.

Hampered by the thick plaid coat, Jak was struggling to knock the creature away from his throat. There was no time for either man to draw a blaster. Besides, the cuddlies were too close.

Ryan had to look to himself first.

The little furry animal was at his feet, poised on its muscular hind legs, ready to power itself up toward his face.

The panga whispered from its sheath, the haft filling Ryan's gloved hand.

"Fuck bastard!" Jak yelped, dancing away and kicking the second of the cuddlies from his leg. He was grappling with the one that still raked at his face and throat, clinging to the collar of his coat.

Ryan swung the eighteen-inch steel blade down in a curving blow, decapitating the creature. Its head rolled like a child's furry toy, its body plopping dead at his feet, blood trickling from its neck.

Instinctively the second of the miniature killing machines turned away from Jak and went whining toward Ryan. It dodged the first hacking cut from the cleaver, its claws skittering sideways on the powdery snow.

Nothing seemed to deter its murderous intentions, and it closed in on the man again.

Ryan feinted to slash, then turned his wrist, thrusting with the point. It caught the jinking beast through the side of its chubby stomach, penetrating clean out the other side.

There was a squeal of rage and shock from the cuddly, as it was lifted off the ground by the panga, its little legs kicking furiously.

Having got it onto the blade, Ryan was now faced with the problem of getting it off again.

Its jaws gaped, its forked tongue flicking toward him. There was a bizarre image of food being cooked on a long skewer over hot coals.

"Cute fucking food," Ryan grated, clenching his gloved left fist and punching the cuddly as hard as he could. He knocked it off the cleaver onto the floor, where he was able to slice its head off its body as it struggled to regain its feet.

Jak finally ripped the surviving creature from his collar and threw it to the ground. It scampered away down the corridor, its pretty fur matted with the boy's blood.

The youth's face was a mask of scarlet, the plaid coat sodden with blood, steaming in the icy cold. He ripped the jacket off, hands darting behind him, coming out with one of the throwing knives. By now Ryan had drawn his blaster, but Jak waved at him.

"No! Fucker's mine!"

His arm went back then flicked forward, his wrist snapping with the force of the throw. Ryan caught the flash of pale light as the leaf-shaped blade spun along the passage, striking the furry little creature through its nape, severing its spinal cord and leaving it dead in its tracks.

"Ace on the line," Ryan said appreciatively.

"Bastard!" Jak grinned at his companion, teeth like white pearls set in crimson velvet.

Then his eyes rolled upward and he slumped unconscious to the bloodied snow.

THE ANGLES of the corridor held small piles of snow that Ryan was able to melt in the palms of his hands and use to try to clean the teenager's face.

He'd suffered a maze of cuts and gashes, most clean-edged, some of them superficial. There was a longer, deeper one that ran along the angle of Jak's jaw, below his ear, another that just missed the corner of his mouth.

He'd come around in less than half a minute, wincing as the water touched the open wounds.

"Poisoned?" was his first word.

"Doubt it."

"Never heard cuddlies bein' killers."

"Me, neither. Keep still."

The blood had virtually stopped from all but the two deepest cuts. Ryan had torn a strip of cloth from the lining of the plaid coat, pressing it against the lips of the wound, trying to hold them together and check the flow.

But every time he took it away, the crimson began to seep again.

Jak tried to sit up, but Ryan made him lie flat and still.

"Keep watch for more fuckers."

"Sure." He had the blaster drawn and ready by his hand.

The boy lifted his own fingers and touched himself on the cheek, staring fixedly at the brightness of the fresh blood.

"Bad," he said.

"Not good," Ryan agreed.

There was a stretched stillness in the freezing corridor. To Ryan's great relief, there was no sign of any other cuddlies in the vicinity. Despite their diminutive size, they had a murderous passion for killing that would have made a dozen of them potentially lethal opponents.

The wounds weren't in any sense terminal, but they were severe enough to need stitching or clamping. The reality was that they might be facing some double-prejudice action in the next twenty-four hours or so.

"Not fit enough, Jak," Ryan finally said. "Best get back home."

"Another jump?"

"Yeah."

He almost smiled. "Think stay with you."

But they both knew he wasn't going to be able to remain there.

"Can't stop the bleeding."

Jak sniffed. "Tear more cloth. Use it on way home. Be fine."

"I know."

"Sure jump'll be home?"

"Sure." Ryan wasn't at all sure. It all depended on whether anyone else had used the gateway outward in the past couple of days. If they had, then that would be the last destination and that would be where the wounded teenager finished up.

IT DIDN'T TAKE THEM LONG to walk slowly back along the passage, through the large room that held all the master controls for the mat-trans unit, then on through into the gateway itself.

Ryan glanced behind them, seeing that Jak was leaving a clear trail of ruby drops on the shimmering whiteness. If there were many cuddlies left in the redoubt, it wouldn't take them very long to pick up the scent of spilled blood.

"Shall get in?"

"Sure. Get comfortable. Then give me the word, I'll press the buttons and then shut the door for you. All right?"

Jak took another long breath, shaking his head. "Don't know. Mebbe could—"

Ryan slapped him on the shoulder. "Mebbe couldn't, you stupe. Best for both of us, you going back to the others."

"Want blaster?"

"No, thanks. Go on."

"Luck, Ryan."

They shook hands quickly, the merest brush of skin against skin. Jak stepped into the chamber, then spun around. "Fuck that," he said, grabbing Ryan and hugging him hard.

Ryan returned his unexpected show of affection, feeling a slight prickling behind his eyelid. "Go on now."

He waited until the teenager was sitting, facing the doorway.

"Could be better if you lie flat. Sure it'll be okay the other end?"

"Want come see?" A single finger was raised, bringing a smile from Ryan.

The Last Destination control was pressed, then Ryan closed the door firmly, making absolutely sure that the mechanism was triggered.

"Watch your back!" Jak called.

Ryan was fascinated, never having been able to watch a jump from the outside of the gateway. The armaglass walls were unusually dark, but he went to press his face against them.

A great spark of static electricity slapped him across the side of his cheek with an audible crack, making him jump.

He could hear a humming, and there seemed to be tendrils of white mist billowing around, making it impossible to see anything, even to make out the slight figure of Jak Lauren.

A very bright light began to glow behind the armored glass. Ryan could hear a sound like a mighty rushing wind, becoming louder and louder, like standing in the path of a chem-storm hurricane.

It swelled, then began to fade. The light dimmed and he knew that Jak was gone.

And that he was alone.

Chapter Seven

Ryan had lost count of the number of redoubts that he'd been in. The Trader used to reckon that nobody in the United States, except the topmost generals, had ever known just how many had been built. He used to talk about what he called a "new cold war" that had begun close to the end of the century. The secret military complexes had been established in a variety of isolated locations, many of them in commandeered sections of old national parks, as well as some in cities. And one or two in other places.

He walked on, following the cold wind, his thoughts turning back to the Trader. The strange half rumor that he'd heard preyed on his mind—the possibility, however remote, that the Trader might still be alive, that his mysterious disappearance, clearly dying, might have been contrived. It wasn't possible. Ryan knew that. Yet nothing was impossible with the Trader.

"Over, under or around," Ryan said, shaking his head and smiling at what had been one of the Trader's favorite sayings. Perhaps that had been how he'd treated death.

Something that you found a way of defeating.

"No." That was foolishness. He knew it. Still, it couldn't be denied that the strange whisper that the Trader could be alive had made his own heart race.

Ryan thought back to redoubts.

Not all of them held gateways. He knew that from experience. But since they'd first discovered how to make jumps, back in the Darks, he seemed to have moved only through the mat-trans system.

Ahead of him, the wide passage was dividing, some fallen slabs of reinforced concrete showing what was probably old nuke damage, either direct from missile hits or indirect from earth shifts.

It felt strange to be on his own, with nobody to consult, no Krysty to ask what she "felt" around them, no J.B. to check his opinion.

He decided to check out the corridor that wound upward. The snow was thicker, drifted into neat piles against the walls, and it creaked under his boots. He stopped to wind his scarf over his nose and mouth. It was so cold that ice was forming in his nostrils, making breathing uncomfortable.

Ryan found more and more evidence of positive nuking damage. This redoubt had suffered some extreme prejudice at enemy hands, meaning it was probably a particularly important establishment. It clearly hadn't been neutron bombing, either, taking out life and leaving buildings. These must have been old-fashioned nukes that simply knocked the shit out of everything and everyone.

Walls were scarred, bare metal supports showing through in places, rust red. Huge chunks of ceiling had fallen, making it hard to scramble by. At one point a large arrow was daubed on the wall, pointing into the deeps of the complex.

The light grew stronger.

Ryan glanced at his wrist chron. It had been early morning when they'd left the New Mexico homestead. It took less than two hours to make the jump that had brought them to this frozen place, another hour or so on recovering and on the fight with the cuddlies. It should be close to midday.

"Fourteen hundred," Ryan said. Somewhere along the line a couple of hours had somehow gone missing. There were so many things about the mat-trans system that were inexplicable.

Less than a hundred paces farther on, Ryan found himself out in the open. He hesitated, keeping within the shadowed mouth of the cavern.

Here the damage was total.

There wasn't any way of being sure, but it looked to Ryan as though the redoubt had once extended a good deal farther. But there'd obviously been a number of direct hits by nukes, hitting the sec doors and demolishing them in explosions of almost unbelievable intensity.

Outside there was a day of fierce dullness. A leaden sky squatted over the surrounding mountains, leaking occasional random flakes of uncertain snow.

Ryan was high above a valley. A steep trail picked its cautious way down the flank of the mountain toward a frozen river at the bottom. Layers of mist sliced into each other, rendering it difficult to make out what was happening at the lower end of the narrow roadway.

There appeared to be some kind of industrial complex, with a broad highway running parallel to the river, and dark tunnels that vanished into the steep crags opposite.

Ryan shaded his eye with his hand, peering into the sighing depths two thousand feet below him, trying to make out what was happening. It looked like a mine, with several shafts. There was a number of buildings, some with smoke or steam billowing from them.

Close by the river there was what could be a spoil tip, covered in snow, but with a pale yellow streak running from it into the water.

"Sulfur?" Ryan said. "Could be."

There was a wide variety of mines scattered throughout Deathlands. Some of the older minerals, like gold, silver and platinum, were now of very little value. With scant industry, it was the older basics like coal, iron and lead that mattered. And sulfur was useful to make so many things, most notably explosives.

It was also, Ryan knew, in very short supply. If the scene below him was a substantial sulfur mine, then it would represent enough jack to turn a man into a baron overnight.

And if that man happened to be Major-Commissar Gregori Zimyanin?

THE MIST WAS THICKENING and the snow was beginning to fall with a more serious sense of purpose. Ryan looked once into the valley, deciding that he really didn't want to pick his way down that exposed trail. If it *was* Zimyanin, then it would be very surprising if there wasn't armed guards all over the place, probably with glasses, monitoring the area around. From above, it appeared that there was only one road into the site, though the head of the long box canyon had a faint track smeared across the sheer face at its end.

It would make more sense to try to get down into the occupied zone during the hours of darkness, which meant finding somewhere to hole up until then.

He retreated along the corridor until he found the place where it had split, turned and went along the second passage.

It dipped and climbed, with no side turnings and no doors of any sort. The lights were worse, with only one of eight working. Ryan was able to see that this was the way less used. There was little driven snow and only the faintest of boot marks.

Eventually even those vanished.

It was a puzzle why the corridor went such a long way without getting anywhere. Ryan guessed he'd walked over a mile, along a featureless tunnel.

When he glanced up, surprised to find no sec-vids at all, he spotted the height of the ceiling—and the heavy-duty brackets fixed there at intervals.

"Monorail wags," he said, his voice disappearing into the vastness below the mountain.

This wasn't a normal corridor like in other redoubts. This was a communication link between two totally separate sections of the military complex. In the days before the endless frosts there would have been little metal cars, suspended from an overhead rail, whisking personnel at high speed from one part of the redoubt to the next.

RYAN HAD WALKED for more than an hour. He was sweating, his coat unbuttoned. He'd noticed that the lights were getting stronger again, with nearly fifty percent of them functioning perfectly.

And there were bones.

In the four weary miles of passages there'd been skeletons of a variety of wildlife that had crept into the redoubt and died there, of either starvation or thirst.

Only one was human, the brittle clothes indicating he'd died many years earlier. And the manner of his passing was clear. The bones were entangled with those of a middle-sized bear. A rusting iron spear was buried in the hollowed rib cage of the animal, piercing the ragged shreds of hide.

Ryan stopped to eat, sipping sparingly at his canteen. He looked ahead of him, then back. It was impossible to tell which was which. Both looked utterly, blankly identical.

But Ryan knew. He'd been blessed since his early youth with an excellent sense of direction. He carefully corked the canteen and pressed on, past the heap of white bones.

It was another mile before he finally reached the sec doors.

By now, he guessed that he must have traveled almost through the mountain, well into another valley. Or, possibly, much farther down the present one. Either way, he was a long ways off from the mine.

And, probably farther away from his son.

"CLOSED," HE MUTTERED. "Fireblast! Got to stop talking to myself. The first sign of turning shithouse rat crazed."

They were massive vanadium-steel doors, running from floor to ceiling, with not enough room to get a gnat's wing through the gap.

Ryan closed his eye and sighed. It was a double bastard that meant he'd have to walk partway back and then find some corner to curl up and sleep.

There was a sign to the right of the doors:

Security Weapons Research Unit. Closed Access. Personnel Cleared C5 and Above. Must Carry and Show Passes at All Times. Warning! This Means You. Sec Traps Set. Termination Levels Apply. Project Styx Subordinated Overproject Whisper ComSecCa-WeaRes.

It was one of the longest notices that Ryan had ever seen, and one of the most meaningless, though he didn't like the sound of "sec traps," and "termination level" had a finite ring to it. Since he couldn't get in through locked sec doors, none of it mattered very much anyway.

"Bastard," he said quietly, banging his fist on the dark green door.

He was already turning away from it when he realized something extraordinary. The door had moved.

Ryan shook his head. Maybe the place was getting to him. He pushed gently against the cold steel.

It *did* move. Only a fraction of an inch, but it had definitely moved.

He leaned against it, using all of his strength. Silently the sec door began to open.

Half an inch.

An inch.

Six inches.

At two feet Ryan stopped pushing and peered through the gap, sticking out his tongue to try to taste the air.

It tasted stale but breathable, just what he'd have hoped for in a section of a redoubt that had been sealed off for about a century.

The light was much brighter inside. Ryan could see a kind of entrance hall, about a hundred feet across, with several smaller sec doors leading off it. All were shut.

The floor was patterned with zigzag black-and-white squares, with silver wire in between the large tiles.

Blaster in hand, Ryan slipped through the part-open doorway into the weapons research unit of the complex. Somewhere to his right, from a large black box with dancing green lights, he heard a faint click.

He moved forward, his boots ringing on the tiles. To his surprise, he found that they were made of metal. Somewhere behind the walls, in the utter silence, Ryan could hear a humming, swelling noise, becoming louder, sounding like a generator building up a powerful electrical charge.

"Sec traps," he said. "Termination levels."

Then, before his brain could make all the connections, the murderous booby trap detonated itself and exploded into terminal action.

Chapter Eight

Ryan's fighting reflexes had sustained him through thirty-five or so years in Deathlands. They'd carried him out of innumerable life-threatening situations. But what he'd also had was luck.

This time it was luck that saved him.

The patterned floor was simply a huge death trap, triggered by his weight. A massive jolt of electricity ran through the steel tiles, designed to fry anything and anybody.

The mechanism was a hundred years old, designed in the megacull times before the ancient Earth died. The nuke generator responded nobly to the sudden call on its resources, providing the surge of power. But the wiring had rusted and frayed, attacked by damp and cold.

Ryan was already starting to move, diving forward to try to get off the black-and-white patterns. His heart pounded with the bitter realization that he'd likely be too late.

There was a crackling and a choking stench of ozone and burning insulation. Sparks erupted behind him and around him. He felt the blast of electricity as it hit him, sending him spinning off balance. The breath was driven from his body, and every muscle went into a spasmodic paroxysm.

But the aged sec trap had malfunctioned before anything near full power had been able to lash at the intruder. It had still been enough to knock Ryan on his ass, leaving him shuddering and shocked.

"Fireblast!"

He lay on his side, the SIG-Sauer twenty feet away, near one of the sec doors. When Ryan tried to sit up he found that his left arm was jerking, the fingers opening and closing, all utterly beyond his control.

It took a quarter hour before he could stand. He staggered backward, whistling between parted lips, finding that his pulse was finally back somewhere toward normal.

He looked at the floor by the entrance and saw that some of the metal tiles appeared to have melted, and that thin tendrils of smoke were still snaking up from between them.

The box on the wall that had been gleaming with green lights now hung off at an angle, its interior blackened and charred.

"Terminal sec trap," Ryan muttered. "Wonder if there's any more like you."

His blaster safely holstered again, he made the rounds of the other doors, finding that all of them were securely locked against him.

All but one.

Ryan was puzzled why a double sec barrier should have been used for a single room, and why it had been left unsealed when all the others were triple bolted.

The room was empty, except for a huge dust sheet draped over something. Or some things.

Ryan grabbed a corner and pulled. The cloth disintegrated in his fingers, falling apart in a cloud of stinking dust. Coughing and blinded, Ryan staggered away, rubbing at his eye.

Blinking through tears, he tried to recognize what it was that stood on a low stone plinth. It was some kind of machinery.

He wiped his eye with the sleeve of his coat, finally clearing his vision.

He could now see there was a wide red line painted on the floor around the plinth. The word "WARNING" was repeated several times. A rectangle of white card, which looked as though it had been propped against the machines, had fallen over when he tugged the cloth away and now lay facedown inside the red line.

He looked up at the machines, fascinated by their strangeness.

"Droids?" he asked himself.

Five humanoid robots stood there patiently, legs slightly bent at the knees, arms dangling at their sides. They were no more than five feet tall, built mainly from rods of chromed steel. They gleamed in the overhead lights, untarnished by the passing of long, solitary years.

The heads were polished domes, with small crystals set in place of eyes. They were dull and lifeless. Below was the android equivalent of a mouth—a metallic slit, half open, with the hint of teeth within. Was there a sharpness there? It wasn't possible to tell.

The neck was tubular, articulated, like the small scales on the throat of a serpent. The chest was armored, broad, containing all the comp controls. Each arm was slightly longer than a human's would be, in proportion to its height, giving the robot the appearance of an orangutan, slouching toward eternity.

One arm ended in three digits. Two were like pincers, with honed edges. The third was a clubbing hammer. The other arm terminated in four sharp blades, their points winking like needles.

The droids' legs were a little shorter than those of a man, ending in flexible platforms, each tipped with shorter versions of the finger knives.

They were the ugliest creations that Ryan had ever encountered.

"Wouldn't like to meet you guys in a dead-end street at midnight," he said.

Ryan was about to turn away, but the fallen notice captured his attention.

Part of his concentration was focused on the quintet of stunted robots, and he ignored the red line and the warning painted on the floor. He stepped across it and bent to pick up the large card.

Far away there were five dark panels on a control console. One of them became illuminated with the single word "Activate." Another set of screens lighted up, and flashed "Genetic Recording."

The card was creased, the corners dog-eared and bent. The writing was covered in dust, and Ryan wiped it clear with his sleeve, his forehead wrinkling as he followed the faded printing.

It was headed with a single line in maroon capital letters: SEC HUNTERS.

Underneath there was an explanation, as though the five creatures had been exhibits in some sort of a military museum.

Developed in the late nineties using latest cybernetic technology, the sec hunters are the most sophisticated devices known to man, and are years ahead of any comparable machinery from the Eastern Bloc. They "sniff out" the genetic body pattern of their prey. Once locked on to that one individual, they will follow and destroy, even though it takes them to the ends of the known world. Nothing short of total destruction will divert them from their lethal purpose.

Ryan sniffed. At the back of his neck, the short hairs were beginning to prickle. He looked around the silent, deserted room, but nothing moved. Not even a grain of dust.

There were a few more lines at the bottom of the notice.

Warning: During test conditions on the sec hunters it is very dangerous to cross the marked red line. To do so may expose you to a potentially serious threat. If this caution is ignored and death, maiming or harm to personal possessions results, then the Government of the United States declares itself not liable for any, all or several suits for damages arising. In the event of accidental crossing of warning line IMMEDIATELY notify the nearest guard who will negate termination instructions to the devices. *You have been warned.*

Not much of that made too much sense to Ryan Cawdor. He dropped the card back onto the floor and walked a few paces away, looking up at the five motionless pieces of ancient machinery.

They had an air of menace about them that was unsettling. Ryan decided that he wouldn't spend the night in the same room and turned on his heel, walking out of the room, through the sec doors, back into the rest of the redoubt.

Behind him the stillness was unbroken.

For long seconds nothing happened. Then, in the empty silence, red lights clicked on in the eyes of one of the sec-hunter androids.

Chapter Nine

Less than two miles from his father, Dean Cawdor was getting himself ready for sleep.

He was tired and sore, his hands blistered, his lungs filled with filthy yellow dust. Dean kept coughing, trying to clear his throat of the ocher phlegm that threatened to choke him.

In the dormitory around him, the semidarkness was noisy with coughing.

Sulfur mines are hard on breathing.

The ten-year-old boy lay on his back, staring at the rocky ceiling of the cavern only a few inches from his face. He didn't cry. Dean Cawdor knew better than to waste his time on pointless weeping.

The past forty-eight hours would have been enough to reduce most men to helpless self-pity. Ryan's son had been devastated by what had happened, but he wasn't about to give in—not to anything nor anybody.

The slavers had come at him out of a clear day, without any warning. By the time he'd seen the sign of their dust, it had been way too late.

His Smith & Wesson 425, with its ten rounds of rimfire .22, had been safely, and uselessly, back on his bunk in the Lauren homestead.

They'd been brutally competent, but their hasty body search hadn't found the thin-bladed knife with the turquoise hilt sheathed in the small of his back.

They'd tied his wrists behind him with a slender thong of rawhide, then hefted him onto a horse on a lead rein.

The jump had been done, he thought, in two lots. The chamber wasn't large enough to accommodate the whole party, with their captives. There'd been four other prisoners with the gang, all male, all young. One was an Apache who spoke no English.

The leader of the raiders had tried to make him talk, but the handsome boy had shaken his head and spit at the man, who'd drawn a long knife and cut the Apache's throat from side to side, dropping him to the sandy desert to kick and bleed.

Once they'd arrived in the freezing redoubt, the prisoners had been hustled along, thrown warm coats and gloves to combat the bitter chill.

The march down into the valley had been slippery, with rutted ice along the trail. Dean had spotted the mine and caught the sour smell of sulfur. He remembered the yellow spoil heap from a similar operation in the east, when he'd been with his mother.

As they drew nearer he was able to appreciate the scale of the scene. There were dozens of men, and a few women, hauling tubs of raw earth in iron buckets along narrow rails. The guards wore a silver circle either on caps or on their chests.

Along to the left, hidden in the shadows of the three-tiered bunks, Dean heard someone talking in his sleep, chattering and trying to explain that his mother would be worried about him. There was the sound of a punch against flesh and the talking stopped.

The young boy was exhausted.

After they'd been brought to the wired-in compound, someone had come to inspect them, a short, very muscular man that Dean had guessed must be the leader of the complex. He'd had a drooping mustache and had once removed a fur cap to show a totally bald skull. His face was very badly scarred, as though someone had fired salt at his skin from a scattergun.

His eyes had roamed along the line, stopping when it encountered Dean Cawdor. Accompanied by one of the raiders, he'd stepped stiffly forward and paused in front of the boy.

"I would be grateful to know your name," he'd said.

Dean had hesitated a moment. "Goode," he said. "Will Goode."

"I am Gregori Zimyanin, Will. Have you and I ever had the pleasure of making each other's acquaintance? Your face is oddly familiar."

Dean had been bewildered by the man's odd, accented way of talking, which reminded him a little of Doc Tanner.

He couldn't have known that the Russian had originally taught himself the language from a book published in 1911, called *The English Tongue for the Benefit of the Russian Gentleman Abroad.*

The pockmarked man had tried again. "How old are you, Master Goode?"

That was a tricky one. Having seen what happened to the young Apache boy, Dean tried to guess what would be a good answer. He hadn't yet seen anyone who looked under about twelve, though he knew that he seemed older than his years.

"Thirteen," he said.

"Best you call me 'sir,' I think," Zimyanin said, smiling at him.

A hand, in skintight black gloves, had reached out and touched Dean's face. With an effort he'd avoided recoiling. Fingers and thumb had spread wide, gripping his chin, squeezing. Dean had heard the bones creaking, and a little blood had seeped from his gums at the man's strength.

Finally he'd let him go. "Watch yourself, Master Goode," Zimyanin had warned him. "There are those who would spread your lower limbs and attempt to penetrate you with their privy member. I do not permit that, but I can do little to prevent it. The lust that does not even whisper its name, as the poet had it."

He'd smiled again and patted the boy on the cheek, leaving him puzzled and frightened.

DEAN FELT HIMSELF SLIDING down toward sleep, welcomed after the rigors of the endless day. The work had been appallingly tough.

They'd been roused at dawn, counted and fed with ample bowls of hot, salty soup, then marched under armed guard to the nearest of the mines.

The boy's eyes closed, his memory of the next fourteen hours fading into a dismal blur.

His last conscious thought was to wonder if his father would know where he'd been taken.

Would he come after him?

"Ryan," he whispered.

Chapter Ten

"Dean," Ryan said.

He was sitting huddled in a corner of the corridor, some distance back toward the gateway, closer to the ruined entrance.

There was still no shred of real proof that his son was anywhere within a thousand miles of the redoubt, but if he wasn't down in the valley, working in Zimyanin's sulfur mines, then he might be anywhere in the whole of Deathlands.

The food that Christina had given them was delicious, though it was already becoming stale. Water wasn't a problem in such a frozen wilderness, so Ryan drank deeply from his canteen.

He lifted his head, leaning forward a little, straining his hearing. He tried to snatch again at the faint, elusive sound that had disturbed him.

Without any conscious movement, Ryan's right hand was on the butt of his blaster.

There it was again. Still only the smallest noise, far off, but in the overwhelming stillness of the stone sarcophagus it was unmistakable.

Ryan stood, the SIG-Sauer drawn, his back against the curved wall. It wasn't a good place to try to defend, and he decided to move out to the place where the passage divided.

The sound followed him.

Each time he stopped, allowing the echoes of his own movement to fade away, the distant noise was closer to him.

Ryan tried to analyze it: something that both clicked and scraped. Possibly a large bird.

That was a particularly chilling thought, to be pursued along the endless passage by some vast, mutated eagle, with a huge beak of bronze and claws like steel arrowheads.

He moved away faster.

When he went more quickly, the noise seemed to recede a little. And when he slowed, gathering breath, it came closer again.

There was an inexorable, worrying, ceaseless quality to the pursuer. Or was there more than one of them? Was it a flock of feathered avengers? It couldn't be birds. They'd have caught him now. Lizards? Snakes?

Whatever it was, it kept on coming, never altering its speed.

"Like a bastard machine," he said, as he stopped again for a few moments.

RYAN WAS OUT OF BREATH, doubled over with a stitch, wincing at the pain in his side. "Time to stop running," he panted.

He'd chosen to go toward the outside of the complex, halting as he neared the entrance. Outside it was snowing, the flakes drifting by on a gentle wind from the north. It was evening, the light almost gone. The tunnel was still dimly lighted by the remaining few ceiling lamps.

There was rubble everywhere, and Ryan picked a large pile to make his stand. He kneeled behind it, gun ready, waiting for his pursuer to reveal itself.

Clicking and scraping.

Whatever it was moved steadily along, keeping up a good brisk walking pace mile after mile, without once slowing or checking, following him as though an invisible wire linked them together.

The wide passage in front of Ryan curved slightly to the right, so that it wasn't possible to see what was advancing toward him. At his back there was another fifty yards or so of the package, then the open space above the endless, dark drop down into the valley far below.

Now the noise was much louder, so close that Ryan could pick out new, subtle shades and tones buried within it.

There was a faint creaking, or squeaking, like unoiled hinges on a door, the metallic scraping sound and a faint mechanical whirring. Ryan shook his head, trying to imagine what could be moving toward him around the bend of the corridor. It now cast an oddly distorted shadow in front of itself, from the brighter lights farther in.

"Come on," he breathed, steadying his right hand, holding the blaster in his left hand.

The floor was far more uneven, heaps of tumbled stone scattered all around. From the sudden slowing of the noises, it seemed as if Ryan's pursuer was finding it peculiarly difficult. The steps had become hesitant, less even.

The shadow still moved, growing shorter.

Ryan squinted along the barrel of the pistol, centering it chest-high, onto the middle of the wide corridor.

The sec-hunter android suddenly appeared in his sights.

"Triple fuck," Ryan growled.

The robot stopped.

In the half-light it looked less human than when it had been standing on the plinth with its four fellows.

The head was a mass of metallic planes, the ruby eyes reminding Ryan of Jak Lauren. It turned very slowly from side to side, almost as though it were trying to scent its prey. Its hands hung motionless at the end of the skeletal arms, the polished chrome reflecting the overhead lamps.

Ryan guessed what must have happened. The warning on the card, and on the floor, came back to him. Obviously he'd managed to trigger the sec hunter, allowing it to somehow lock on to him and trail him through the redoubt.

A droid like this wouldn't have much of a range, he figured. Maybe his best plan was simply to keep mov-

ing and outrun it. Assuming it had been making its
best speed, Ryan knew he could go faster. And it
looked as though it would be clumsy on anything other
than a smooth, flat surface. Get it outside, and it
would quickly lose interest in him.

Ryan stood, which turned out to be a serious error
of judgment.

The android made a peculiar whining sound. In his
imagination, Ryan thought it was like an inward cry of
triumph. Its head came up, and its eyes bored through
the semidarkness straight toward the waiting man. It
crossed Ryan's mind that the creature was probably
fitted with some sort of night sight.

The appearance of the hunter droid was so menac-
ing that the man instinctively ducked down again. The
steel frame seemed to quiver with a tense anticipation
as it stared fixedly toward him.

There was a long silence.

"Malfunction?" Ryan whispered. After all, the
thing was a hundred years old.

There was the faint noise of tiny gears meshing, and
then steal on stone as it began to move forward again.

Ryan risked another glance. His greatest worry was
that the droid could be equipped with some sort of laser weapon. The moment it centered properly on him
there would be a narrow beam of lethal red light that
would cut him in half.

But the carapace of steel across its chest didn't seem
to contain any kind of opening for a weapon.

It was moving slowly, with an odd, clumsy grace, picking its way around the fallen chunks of stone from the walls and the ceiling.

The distance between them was less than twenty paces and diminishing.

The idea of simply running away was still attractive, and Ryan glanced behind him to the mouth of the long tunnel.

He smiled to himself, remembering the Trader again. "Man who runs away, lives to run away another day," he used to say.

"Dead enemy won't trouble you again," Ryan said. "Logical advice sure gets you in a spin."

He stood and fired four carefully aimed shots at the advancing droid.

Two hit the middle of the chest armor, one at the narrow conduit of the throat and the fourth between the eyes.

The 9 mm full-metal-jacket rounds punched the android back in its tracks. The two to the chest region ricocheted in a starburst of sparks, screaming into the blackness of the tunnel. The one to the narrow throat clipped the side, ripping the metal, exposing a tangle of colored cables. The one to the chromed skull impacted solidly, leaving a neat circular hole in the forehead, an inch from the glowing eyes.

"Got you, you tin-can bastard," Ryan said, straightening up.

The droid leaned forward at an odd angle, then resumed its careful walk, picking its way among the rocks, clawed feet lifted high.

"Fireblast."

The gap between them had now shrunk to barely ten paces.

The SIG-Sauer carried fifteen rounds in a full mag. Ryan fired six more, concentrating on the droid's head.

At that range it was utterly impossible for him to miss.

All six struck home in an area no larger than a thumbnail, rocking the android. Ryan heard a grinding and grating sound. One of the crimson eyes blinked out. The mouth opened and closed a dozen times at lightning speed, giving him a glimpse of a triple row of serrated teeth, slightly rusted.

The right arm lifted, the pincers clicking together. The right leg lifted, slowly, then lowered again. Dented and holed, the droid's head revolved clear around through three hundred and sixty degrees, the one eye gazing toward Ryan again.

He fired two more shots, taking out the last eye, but still not knocking the creature over.

Ryan backed away, as silently as he could, toward the opening, the freezing air brushing against him. His boots scuffed at the loose sand, making only a whisper of sound.

That was enough for the hypersensitive aural receivers in the android's skull.

It began to stumble toward Ryan, both arms up, the knives whirring at the end of the elongated left arm.

He turned and ran toward the fresh evening air, taking care not to trip and fall. Behind him he could hear the robot coming after him.

In the entrance Ryan paused and looked back, seeing that the great hole in the misshapen head was leaking a thick, clear oil.

As soon as he stopped moving, the droid also stopped. Its blinded skull turning from side to side. Ryan noticed that one of the arms now hung motionless, and it was rocking unsteadily.

There was the hope that the bullets might have done sufficient damage to eventually render the machine totally harmless.

That might only take a few seconds. Possibly minutes?

Hours? Ryan thought.

Close to the open air he was conscious once more of the extreme cold. Standing motionless, he could already feel numbness at his finger ends.

There was a loud click, as though a contact had been thrown. The head of the sec hunter tilted to one side, as if it were listening to a particularly intriguing story.

The turgid oil was dripping over its splayed feet, pattering on the icy floor of the tunnel.

Ryan considered emptying the rest of the mag into the chest cavity, where he assumed the master controls lay. But if twelve rounds hadn't chilled it, another few bullets might just be wasted.

He made his decision. The one-eyed man raced to the very edge of the abyss and stopped there, calling to it. "Come on, you bastard! Here!"

Then he took four cautious steps to the side, near a pile of jumbled stones.

The crippled droid lurched toward the gap, out into the open, hesitating as if it sensed the sudden widening of the air around it.

It was less than six feet from Ryan, close enough for him to be able to hear its dying. Contacts were crackling and fuses blowing deep inside its armored heart. The blinded head turned very slowly, and he readied himself to avoid any attack. He could smell hot lubricating oil, taste the thin coil of brownish smoke that trailed from its gashed throat. Its head turned away again, with an uncomfortable grating sound. On the end of the dead arm, the knife blades were moving very gently, tinkling like tiny temple bells.

Ryan held his breath. He reached down and picked up a stone the size of his fist and lobbed it over the edge of the damaged roadway, hearing it rattle and clatter down the sheer cliff face.

The droid turned its head slowly, painfully, taking a hesitant step forward, its steel claws extended out into cold space.

Ryan braced himself. "Good night," he said, dropping a shoulder and hitting the droid in the middle of its back.

Its arm whipped round with ferocious speed, catching the man a glancing blow on the elbow with the steel hammer. Ryan yelped and staggered away, clutching at himself.

Knocked off balance, the droid couldn't do anything to save itself. Its feet raised and lowered, stamping on the crumbling stone.

As Ryan watched through a watering eye, it toppled over and vanished.

He sat and rubbed his bruised arm.

It was becoming even colder.

WHEN RYAN WENT to peer into the stygian depths of the valley half an hour after the sec hunter had disappeared, he thought he could still hear faint scrabbling sounds. A quarter of an hour later, the noises had stopped.

The moon had come out and he could now see the glittering remains of the killer droid, lying in fragments near the edge of the sulfurous river.

His elbow was still painful and swollen from the blow, and Ryan kept trying to massage it into movement.

Before going down into the valley, he needed to get some rest. The fight with the sec hunter hadn't been physically demanding, but the surge of adrenaline into the blood always left a person having to pay the price later.

Now he felt exhausted, conscious of the toll he was meeting for the tiring jump and its aftermath.

If he wasn't to risk freezing to death, it was vital that he found some kind of shelter, which meant plunging back inside the redoubt.

There was no point in trudging all the way to the section where he'd inadvertently triggered the security android.

The temperature rose slowly, the deeper he walked. It didn't get anywhere near above freezing, but warm enough for him to sit huddled inside his coat, legs tucked under him.

Sleep came easily to him.

Despite the rigors of the past twenty-four hours, Ryan slipped into a comfortable, dreamless rest, head slumped on his chin.

He woke only moments before the second of the killer androids attacked him.

Chapter Eleven

It had come sidling along the shadowy passage, dragging one useless leg behind it, the razored knives on its left hand constantly moving. It was like some dreadful monster from an age-old horror vid, the red glow of its eyes burning toward its prey.

Water had seeped through faults in the rock above the complex, turning to a sheet of ice on walls and floor for more than a hundred yards. This glistening surface enabled the sec hunter to move along in almost total, whispering silence.

Only Ryan's extra survival sense saved his life.

Though he wasn't consciously aware of it, he was actually moving even before his eye clicked open and the retina registered the chromed nemesis looming above him.

The knives sparked on the wall immediately behind where he'd been sitting, one of the blades snapping in half. At the same time the droid's clubbing right arm brushed against his shoulder.

Ryan had, of course, reloaded the SIG-Sauer right after his encounter with the first of the programmed robots. But he knew that there was little point in pumping a dozen precious rounds into the creature.

He always had two spare mags in his pockets, but that still meant that he had less than forty bullets for the rest of his venture to rescue Dean.

He rolled in a side-on somersault, the heavy coat making him clumsy.

If the droid hadn't lost power to its right leg, Ryan could well have forfeited his life in that dark, bleak place.

As it was, the attack was a clumsy, crabbed shuffle, both arms flailing toward the man. But Ryan was quicker, managing to get to his feet, running a few paces away from the android.

Though he'd automatically gone for the blaster, Ryan holstered it, weighing up his metal opponent, trying to see where its weakness lay.

From his experience with the first of the killer droids, Ryan knew that it was frighteningly well-armored against bullets, and that it had a speed that more than matched his own. His only edge seemed to be in maneuverability. So far he'd been able to dodge its lunges and thrusts. But the first android had been handicapped by the fallen rocks and this one by its damaged leg.

It wouldn't be fun meeting one out on dry, smooth ground.

The droid's head kept turning, gears buzzing noisily, both arms windmilling. But it seemed to be having difficulty in locating its target.

Ryan drew his panga from its soft leather sheath, balancing himself on the balls of his feet.

As the sec hunter moved, it revealed how thin its legs and knee joints were. The cables that activated the lower limbs, feet and claws were contained in an armored conduit no thicker than a man's forefinger, which in turn was covered by a polished tube of chromed steel. But where the joint articulated, there was a small gap, less than a half inch in width.

Ryan had seen pictures in old books of pre-Dark sec men, who were called knights and wore full body armor. Stories said that they'd been vulnerable to a thin knife slipped behind the knee or into the groin or the armpit.

He must have breathed more loudly than he'd intended. The droid's eyes burned toward him, and the thing took a dragging half step closer. Its right arm circled toward him, taking him by surprise as it extended to twice its normal length.

The cleaver parried the steel hammer, though the jolt ran up Ryan's arm to the shoulder, and the echo rang into the darkness.

"Shit bastard!"

Once again he had to roll away, boots sliding on the patches of slick ice.

The sec hunter came staggering after him, the dead leg skittering sideways, making it topple into the wall. While it was still off balance, Ryan went for it, swinging his eighteen-inch steel blade at the droid's undamaged knee.

His aim was true.

The whetted edge of the panga drove into the robot's leg, at the heart of the barely protected knee joint.

As the controls shorted out, Ryan felt a brief, sharp shock, numbing his gloved fingers, nearly making him drop the heavy weapon. But he wrenched it free as the droid fell sideways, both its jointed hands scraping down the curved wall of the passage.

The head faced away from the kneeling man, and a thin, keening sound erupted from its polished chest. Ryan took another swing at the robot, this time cutting clean through the thin leg, so that the android crashed full-length.

Ryan wiped a light yellow oil off the blade, checking that it hadn't been chipped by the impact. He was still examining it when the droid launched itself toward him, propelled by the pincers on its right hand, the remaining knives of its left hand cutting toward his ankle.

The blade sliced a curling sliver of black leather from the top of Ryan's combat boot.

Now the head was revolving on its narrow neck, the trunk vibrating metallically. The droid's arms pounded at the rocky floor, like a demented swimmer stranded on a beach.

Ryan moved a dozen cautious steps away from the thrashing droid, watching to see what other bizarre tricks it might have in its armory.

"Swift and evil son of a bitch, aren't you?" Ryan said.

He sighed, wondering what to do. The thing was clearly capable of heaving itself along by its arms, and he didn't want to risk getting any closer to try to incapacitate it further. Nor did he want to squander any precious bullets on finishing it off.

There was no way the droid could move at anything better than a crawling speed, and it certainly wouldn't be able to open sec doors. So, the safest way to go was back into the research section of the complex, where the other three sec hunters remained. It was also the warmest place he could think of.

He dodged around the disabled droid, sheathing his panga, and walked briskly into the bowels of the abandoned redoubt.

For several minutes he could hear the tortured scraping, grating noises as the crippled chill machine tried to track him. Following its programmed instructions to search and destroy, even though it was almost terminated itself.

After a while the silence came easing back into the deep tunnel.

WHEN RYAN FINALLY REACHED the doors, he had a momentary pang of something close to fear. Suppose he opened the sec door and found the other three droids all poised, waiting quietly for him to join them?

He uncoiled the white scarf from around his neck and dangled it on the end of the panga, pushing it very slowly through the gap.

Nothing.

When he finally squinted into the room, he saw the other three sec hunters were still on their pedestal, quite motionless.

With an effort Ryan managed to heave the massive doors shut, taking care not to lock himself in. Apart from the sophisticated electronic devices, there was also a simple manual override, high enough on the door to make it impossible for the crippled droid to reach it.

At last he was able to find peace and quiet to sleep safely.

RYAN GROANED. The sounds had jerked him back into wakefulness, dimly heard through the closed sec door.

First he heard scratching, as though a mutie rat was trying to burrow through the vanadium steel. This subsided as he got up and cat-footed across the floor to stand by the door.

He could sense the animatronic creature, lying on its side, useless legs trailed behind it. Its crimson eyes would be staring blankly at the cold steel, the relays and contacts puzzling at the problem. It had trailed him through the redoubt, hunting him down to this place, this dead-end room with nowhere to go but out.

Experimentally Ryan tapped on the door with the haft of the panga, mincing at the instant retaliation, hammering, metal on metal, loud and unbelievably fast.

Ryan sat again, sighing at the noise. After a couple of minutes the pounding seemed to come from inside his skull.

"Shut the fuck up," he said quietly.

On impulse he started to count the frequency of the blows, using his chron to check them.

The droid was pounding so fast that it wasn't possible to keep anything like an accurate count. But the number in a single minute was certainly over five hundred.

Ryan sat and tried to use one of the relaxation techniques that Krysty had taught him, skills she'd inherited from Mother Sonja back in Harmony ville. It involved sitting cross-legged, hands laid palms upward on the thighs. Ryan did that, then lowered his head and closed his eye, taking very slow, deep breaths, holding them for a comfortable time, then releasing them equally slowly.

He was supposed to be chanting some hypnotic, repetitive phrase as well, but he'd always found that part difficult. And it made him feel like a stupe.

Several minutes passed, but Ryan found the clattering so intrusive that he couldn't concentrate on properly relaxing.

He counted again.

Just below five hundred.

Next time it was around four-fifty, audibly slower than before.

The droids had to be powered by some kind of battery, and he guessed that they were too small to carry self-sufficient nuke packs. There were small panels on its chest that could be linked to a solar pack, but in the dark passages of the redoubt it wasn't likely to be much recharged.

"Running down," he said, nodding. He looked again at his small chron, waiting for it to reach the end of a minute.

He started to count.

"Three hundred and ninety," Ryan nodded.

In minutes the rate dropped away until it was below two hundred, around three hammer blows per second.

Ryan had moved away from the door, looking at the three surviving androids, taking care not to step inside the warning line.

It crossed his mind to try to incapacitate them where they stood, hack out the wiring controls inside the knee and elbow joints.

But to do that he'd have to get in real close, over the danger mark, risking triggering all of them at once. It was a risk that he didn't feel much like taking.

Not yet.

"SIXTY-FIVE."

An hour had drifted by. Now the noise was definitely weaker, as well as much less frequent.

Ryan got up and strode briskly around the room, singing quietly to himself. It was something that Doc Tanner had taught him, claiming it was one of his own personal favorites, about how you didn't need to put a wall around a graveyard, since nobody wanted to get in and nobody was able to get out. It had a mournful humor that Ryan liked.

By the time he returned again to stand by the door, the metallic thumping had slowed right down.

"Seventeen," he counted. The impact was now so feeble that the droid's hammer fist seemed to be barely making contact with the sec door.

"Only twelve." The interval was now five seconds between each blow.

Finally it stopped.

Ryan stood by the door for several minutes, straining to hear. He opened it an inch, ready to throw all his weight against it at any sign of robotic life. But the droid was dead.

It lay with its head near the sec steel, one arm resting against it. The hammer was pounded flat, the end of the arm bent and warped. Its eyes were dead and insensate, with not even the barest glimmer of a red light within.

The door shut again and Ryan walked slowly toward the remaining trio of sec hunters. His hand rested on the butt of the blaster, ready in case one of them suddenly became activated.

But all stood motionless, lifeless.

Ryan smiled as he stood just on the safe side of the red line on the floor. He reached up and snapped his fingers at the nearest droid.

''Fuck you all,'' he said.

As though he'd triggered a switch, tiny rubies glowed in the staring eyes.

Chapter Twelve

Dean was awakened by a hand on his leg, touching him just below the knee, very lightly. Then it became harder, moving up the outside of his thigh.

For a moment the boy kept still.

The warning from Zimyanin hadn't surprised him. Ever since he could remember there'd been men around who liked to take their pleasure with those of their own sex. Every now and again the boy had been approached, but he'd always made it clear what would happen to anyone who tried.

He could hear breathing, harsh and urgent, close by him, and smell sweat, rank and feral.

Still faking sleep, the boy breathed deeply, moving slightly, his right hand reaching behind him toward the small of his back. The fingers on his thigh stopped, frozen, then moved again.

Dean's finger touched the hilt, then realized that there were two men preparing to assault him—one who knelt between his legs, and another who was squatting near his head. A second pair of hands was reaching for him.

"He's waked."

"Keep still, son."

Dean opened his eyes, finally getting the knife into his fingers. The room around him was almost pitch-dark, lighted only by the faint glow of four central fires. He could see the bulk of the two men, though he didn't recognize either.

"Fresh meat."

"Tender."

"Fuck him good."

"Me."

"No, me."

"In his mouth?"

"No. Get his pants down."

"Hear that, son? Get your pants down, and you won't be much hurt. Quick, then, on your belly."

"I'll hold his wrists."

"No," Dean said. "I'll do whatever you want. Anything at all."

There was a quiet chuckle. "Then you and us'll be good friends, Will. Tonight and every night. Real good friends."

The dormitory was quiet. About half the stacks of bunk beds were occupied, the rest still waiting for more "recruits" for Zimyanin's mines. The main door was locked, with two armed men sitting in front of it, dozing.

Dean wriggled around, trying to judge better precisely where the two men were sitting. Now he could see, his eyes quickly becoming accustomed to the smoky gloom.

"Slippery, young lad. I'll be bursting before I get well-seated. You want to stop his mouth, Owen, do you?"

"Could, John, couldn't I?"

Dean fumbled with his belt buckle, pretending it was difficult. He rose to a kneeling position, the knife still hidden in his right hand.

The one called John was also on his knees, inches away, the front of his canvas trousers unbuttoned. His mouth sagged, and his eyes glistened wide and expectant in the firelight.

Owen had his own pants around his ankles, stroking himself with both hands, tumescent and erect. He was concentrating on his own rampant excitement, ignoring the young boy for the moment.

It was as good a time as any.

The blade of the knife was no more than three-quarters of an inch wide near the turquoise hilt, and less than six inches in length. But its point would have matched the finest embroidery needle. And J. B. Dix had praised its sharpness by using it to shave himself.

From beginning to end, it took less than six seconds.

The knife lunged toward John, giving Dean a perfect ace on the line, right into the center of the leering man's left eye. It arrowed through, colorless ichor squirting onto the boy's hand. He used all his strength to thrust it deep, past the back of the eye, grating for a moment in the bony hollow of the socket. Then it found the canal of the optic nerve and cut into the brain.

John began to die.

Before withdrawing the knife, Dean wriggled his wrist, twisted the steel point from side to side, making sure that the damage was terminal.

The man gasped in shock, stark terror freezing his breath in his chest.

Owen heard the sigh and began to giggle. "Can't wait, eh? You—"

In a savage downward blow, Dean completely severed the man's thrusting penis.

Under pressure, Owen's body began to pump itself empty of blood.

Dean had been already moving away, keeping clear of the torrent of steaming crimson liquid that gushed from the dying man's groin.

John had fallen backward, both hands pressed to his ruined eye, the beginnings of a shriek fighting free from his chest.

Owen was doubled up, clamping his fingers over the neatly amputated stump of his penis, the hot, slick blood making it impossible for him to get a grip and save himself.

"Turnaket," he gritted painfully. "Tie somethin' and—"

But he couldn't concentrate on what he wanted to say and do. Part of him knew that the skinny little new kid had done for him, but he felt much too tired to do anything about it.

The whole incident had taken mere seconds.

By the time that Owen was dead, and John's dying scream finally burst into the dormitory, Dean was twenty yards away, in a different aisle of bunks, lying under a moth-eaten blanket.

On the way he'd wiped his knife on the coat of a sleeping man, sheathing it once more in the small of his back.

Fights and killings weren't that uncommon, and the guards dragged the corpses out into the night. They didn't even bother to report the deaths to Gregori Zimyanin.

Chapter Thirteen

The red light in the blank eyes of the android flickered, then went out. There was a terrible stench of burning rubber and melting plastic, and thick black smoke began to pour from somewhere deep in the chest controls. A trickle of dark green liquid started to ooze stickily across where the sec hunter's genitals would have been. If it had any.

Ryan allowed his hand to relax off the butt of the SIG-Sauer.

The droid's metal lips parted, and its teeth began to grind down, sparks flying and shards of silver metal pattering on the floor.

The head nodded furiously backward and forward, so violently that Ryan could hear case-hardened gears disintegrating.

First one leg lifted, the sharp claws extending, then it came down again on the same spot. An action was repeated by the other leg.

The arms remained still, hanging uselessly at the droid's sides, the knives and pincers motionless. A throbbing vibration made the sec hunter quiver. When it became stronger, Ryan stepped well away.

The droid rocked from side to side, then fell to the floor, its feet moving as if it were walking uphill. A joint opened at the side of the chest armor, and tiny fiber-optic wires began to spew out, flailing like glittering, rabid worms.

Ryan watched the droid's autodestruction, fascinated by the awesome power and malice of the creature.

Both hands had come to life, seeking their partner with a scuttling frenzy, climbing all over the torso, the knife blades hissing against each other, the pincers clicking with a malevolent speed. Eventually the right discovered the left and attacked it. The left hand reacted to the assault by grappling against it.

The battle was brief.

Something very terminal shorted out in the chest of the droid, and there was a great flash of white flame. Thicker smoke billowed, and the sec hunter lay still, finally dead.

Ryan had already reached the conclusion that the five androids were somehow linked together. They only acted against him one at a time, the next one coming onto power only after the demise of its predecessor. But he had no idea how that worked, nor what kind of time interval was involved.

"Three aces on the line," he said. "Two to come."

AFTER A WATCHFUL HOUR, Ryan had decided that the finite malfunction of the third sec hunter had broken the chain of death.

There wasn't any sign of activity from the remaining pair of droids, though he'd gone and snapped his fingers at them, shouted and waved his hands, being careful not to cross that ancient red line. There was no point in pushing his luck too far.

Ryan was feeling desperately tired, and this was as good a place to sleep as any. He took the extra precaution of unlooping some of the cable from the dead droid, casting it carefully around the legs of the other pair of sec hunters and knotting it loosely, so that if either of them moved, they'd inevitably shift the charred metal corpse of their fellow.

Having done that, Ryan went to a far corner of the room.

And fell asleep.

WHEN HE brought himself awake, it was ten minutes to four in the morning. He pissed against the wall, seeing how it steamed in the cold, floodlit air.

Neither of the androids had moved, and their eyes remained as blank as ice.

The journey toward fresh air was endless and wearisome. Ryan trudged along, wishing that he had someone for company. As a younger man he'd spent most of his time alone. He'd chosen that and lived contentedly with it. But he'd then ridden with the Trader for many years, enjoying the friendship of good, trusted companions. And for many months there'd been Krysty, J.B. and Doc.

Most recent of all, he'd begun to relish his lost son, Dean.

"Lost and found and fucking lost again," he muttered bitterly.

THE EARLY MORNING was so cold it came like a slap across the face. Ryan wrapped the white silk scarf more tightly over his mouth and nose, pushing the gloves as far up his wrists as they'd go.

The wind had veered during the night, and Ryan could now catch the smell of the sulfur, bitter at the back of his throat.

It looked like the mine was working a multiple-shift system. He could see lights down there and small trucks rattling along narrow-gauge rails. There was a line of figures marching together, tools glinting on their shoulders. Ryan wondered whether one of them might be Dean.

There was enough light from the moon, half hidden behind ragged clouds, for him to understand the general shape of the canyon. Now he could make out a number of spidery-thin trails that cut across the flanks of the cliffs, with dozens of dark holes that he guessed must be old diggings.

There was so much activity by the meandering river that Ryan began to have doubts about getting in that way.

His eye followed the roadway down from the ruins of the redoubt, locating a narrow path that dived off it to the right. It seemed to circle completely around above the main workings, joining the maze of other tracks on the far side of the valley.

From there it might be possible to infiltrate one of the work parties, not far below.

The old tarmac was slick with patches of ice, and there was a faint mist of powdery snow falling around Ryan, dusting the shoulders of his coat.

There'd been the momentary concern that Zimyanin might have guards out, ranging them into the mountains around the mine, but common sense said that he'd have some sentries close in, to keep the workers from escaping. In such an isolated position it wasn't likely that there would be anyone wanting to get *into* the sulfur workings.

AS HE PICKED his way lower, Ryan was able, for the first time, to hear the sounds of the mines—the regular metallic wheezing of a large and powerful jackhammer, pounding away near the entrance to one of the shafts, the squeaking of iron wheels on rusting rails; pulleys and hoists whining; men calling out commands.

Once Ryan thought that he heard a shot, but he couldn't be sure.

The trail forked about three hundred feet above the river at the valley's bottom. The main blacktop carried on down, but a faint track led off to the right, just where Ryan had spotted it from above.

Here the going was harder and more treacherous, the footing unreliable.

Twice he found pockets of deeper snow, crumbling and dangerous. He tried to work his way across the first and ended throwing himself flat, arms and legs spread, clinging desperately for purchase to a spur of jagged rock. Below him the snow fell in a tumbled avalanche of ice and stones.

The second time he picked a more indirect route, going up and around the patch of snow, returning again to the path when he was safely beyond it.

Walking slowly along an exposed flank of the mountain, it occurred to Ryan that this wouldn't be a good place to meet any kind of animal coming in the opposite direction. There was also the danger that Zimyanin might have planted guards after all. In the moonlight, against the dusted white of the hillside, Ryan was aware that he'd stand out like a dog turd in a bowl of buttermilk.

From everything he could see, it seemed like the narrow track was probably used only by wild goats.

The encounters with the murderous sec droids had thrown his plans out of kilter. The need for sleep had been paramount, but now he was a little later than he'd intended to be.

Dawn would break in less than an hour, and by then he'd need to be safely under cover. Preferably close to the mines. Already he could detect the first pale glow in the eastern sky, and he was barely halfway around the perimeter of the bowl of rock.

Taking greater risks, Ryan started to move faster.

The snow was beginning to fall with more purpose, the flakes larger, the wind whipping them around with greater venom, making progress harder and even more dangerous.

The only slight consolation was that the drop in visibility would also make it more difficult for any guards to spot him.

Ryan wished he'd borrowed J.B.'s beloved old fedora. The melting snow was soaking his hair, running down his neck, trickling under his shirt.

The weather was deteriorating into blizzard conditions with the serious risk of becoming a total whiteout.

But Ryan Cawdor had no choice.

To turn back would mean that dawn would expose him on the winding trail, and it had been dangerous enough in fair weather. To stop would be to die.

He put his head down, set each foot carefully in front of the last and pressed forward.

THE TRACK HAD long vanished, and Ryan had to fumble onward. He leaned to his right to try to counter the fear of being sucked away into the abyss that beckoned on the other side. For the first time, the one-eyed warrior began to entertain the thought that he might die in this bleak, freezing wilderness.

He concentrated all his senses on remembering what the trail had looked like, how far he might have gone, where the first of the dark openings had been. Normally his spatial awareness was as good as anyone's, but the wind and the swirling blizzard were bewildering.

For some time he'd felt that the track had been moving slightly upward. From what he could remember, that could show that he was around the head of the box canyon and might be close to the first of the workings.

The cliff to his right had been becoming more sheer, almost vertical in places. This meant the wind had nowhere to go, bouncing off, tugging at him, dashing the icy flakes into his face. Away to his left, the drop vanished into the whiteness.

His ears caught a sudden slight change in the sounds around him. His right hand, feeling for support, found nothing.

Ryan cupped his face, peering into a shapeless darkness. Cautiously he took a step toward it, finding instant relief from the storm.

From the blackness ahead of him he heard a woman's voice, taut with fear.

"Get out, or I'll blast your head off."

Chapter Fourteen

The large dormitory, hewn from the living rock, was empty. All the slaves were out laboring deep in the sulfur mines, and the rows of bunk beds were deserted.

The trio of guards shuffled nervously, until Zimyanin turned and stared at them.

"Your feet are uncomfortable as a result of the seasonal chill?" he said.

They all stared at the ground, knowing that silence was often the best and safest reply to their unpredictable leader.

Zimyanin looked at the two stiff corpses.

One lay flat on its back, milky eyes fixed beyond the moist stone of the rough ceiling. The blackened gash at his groin was clotted with blood, showing how he'd met his ending.

The other was hunched up, hands frozen in death, pressed against the face. Dark blood had seeped between his fingers from his ruined eye.

"A good chilling, my brothers," Zimyanin said thoughtfully.

"We wouldn't have bothered you, Major-Commissar, seein' as how there's often dead meat in here in the mornings."

"You exercised your duty with a commendable skill," the Russian replied. "Whosoever performed these chillings did them with unusual capability."

"You mean we done good?" the shorter guard asked worriedly.

"You done very good. And you say there was no clue as to the identity of the slayer?"

The sec men glanced at each other. Again it was the shorter one who replied. "No, Major-Commissar. No clue. No trail of blood. No weapon."

Zimyanin leaned over the second corpse, moving the frozen hand from the face. "A knife with a slender blade, would you not say? Unusual, the delicacy with which the knife was used."

Something bothered him.

He took off his cap and rubbed his gloved hand over his bald pate. There was some lost half memory plaguing him. Not lost. Just mislaid. It would come back to him.

"Could it have been one of the new intake of laboring serfs?" he asked.

"Mebbe."

"I think I should perhaps parade them and then see if any— What is it?"

One of his mine foremen had come into the dormitory, coughing to attract Zimyanin's attention.

"Trouble in Number Six shaft, Major-Commissar."

It crossed Zimyanin's mind that it hadn't been such a great idea to bring his lengthy official title with him into Deathlands. Perhaps he should shorten it to just "Major."

"Trouble?"

"Ladder broke and took part the hoist with it. Knocked a barrel of nails down the side. Other end fastened to a windlass. Barrel of nails was heavier than the windlass, so it went down and the windlass went up."

Zimyanin turned away from the bodies and the sec men. The nagging worry about the identity of the killer disappeared under the torrent of words from the bearded foreman.

"Barrel hit bottom and broke, spilling the nails out. Now the windlass is heavier than the barrel, so it goes down and the empty barrel comes up. Man grabs it and swings off. Makes the barrel heavier again. So the windlass is going up, but on the way it hits the man hanging on the barrel and knocks him clean off it. The barrel's lighter now and—"

The burly Russian had reached the man, whose story seemed as though it might be never-ending.

Without breaking stride he punched the man full in the middle of his face, breaking his nose and sending fresh blood dribbling into his beard and over his coat, knocking him on his back and shutting him up.

"Enough," Zimyanin said. "I have got the picture." He swung out of the door toward the mine, shouting over his shoulder, "Yes, I see."

Chapter Fifteen

Ryan stood his ground. "You want me to go out into that storm?" he called.

The woman replied, sounding nervous, but still determined. "Unless you want to be cut in half, mister."

"If I go out there I get to die in the snow. Might as well stay here. Won't harm you."

He heard a new voice, old, tired and frail, barely audible by the cave's entrance. "Don't let him in, Kate. Please don't."

"Two of us, mister."

"One sick and the other scared."

He took a couple more steps inside the cavern, straining his eyes to try to see who else was in there. But it was so dark he couldn't make anyone. There was the smoldering remains of a fire much farther in, but that was all.

"I'll chill you."

"What with?"

"What?"

Ryan repeated the question. "Tell me what kind of blaster you got there?"

"You'll find out, you shit-eating sec bastard!"

"Think I'm a sec man, lady?"

Again, the old man's voice. "Don't tell nothin' to him."

Ryan laughed. "I'm freezing my ass off here. And you reckon... I've been called some stupe names in my time, but never a sec man."

"Don't try to talk your way in here. Just get out, will you?"

"No."

"No?" Desperation rode over the word.

Ryan was now convinced that the woman didn't have a blaster at all. If she'd been carrying one, then she'd have used it by now.

"I'm coming in now. I see a fire, and I'm colder than a grave-digger's cock. If you're going to pull the trigger on what you got, then you better do it right now."

"I got a knife."

"Sure."

"And I got a knife, mister."

Ryan sighed. "Look, the two of you. Standing where I am you can see me. See I got a blaster. You don't. I can just cut you both down where you are. Think about it. Fireblast!"

"How do I know you aren't one of the silver circle men?"

"The what?"

"You know."

Ryan nodded. "The bald man with the pocked face and mustache. He still got the mustache?"

"See, Kate! He knows Zim!" There was utter, abject terror in the trembling voice.

"Kate, I met a man called Gregori Zimyanin, way back. Now I think he's lifted my son to work for him in those mines. I come to get him back. If I can do it."

"And kill Zim?"

"Sure. Not an easy man to take out of living, but I can sure try. That is—" he took another couple of steps into the cave "—if I didn't freeze to death first."

RYAN LEANED BACK, his coat open, enjoying the feel of the flames on his cheeks. The fire was set far enough back into what he'd learned were ancient, pre-Dark mine workings to make it impossible for it to be seen by any watchers in the bottom of the valley.

He looked across at his two new companions.

Kate Webb was seventeen years old, as skinny as whipcord, with dark hair hacked off short. Her only weapon was a short knife made from poor, soft metal, barely able to keep an edge.

Her grandfather, Cody, was somewhere around the seventy mark. He wasn't sure about just where. He had no weapon at all.

Both of them wore a ragged assortment of patched and torn furs.

The girl had told Ryan their story, with occasional interruptions from Cody.

They'd been trawled in from New England about eight months ago—neither of them was sure about the precise passage of time—brought in through a gateway with a number of other people from their small rural ville.

It occurred to Ryan at that point that Zimyanin must also have stumbled upon the significance of the Last Destination control on the mat-trans unit to be able to go out and back with such facility.

The consequent thought was that if any of the Russkie's men used the nearby gateway before Ryan could spring Dean and get away, then the setting would probably be altered. Getting home again to New Mexico would be almost impossible.

Along with about two hundred slave workers, Kate and Cody had been put to labor in the depths of the sulfur mines.

"Many guards?" Ryan asked.

"Thicker'n jiggers on a dead dog," the old man replied.

The pair also seemed unsure about how many workers and sec men were around the mining complex. Kate explained that a lot of people died.

"The shafts are narrow, deep and triple dangerous. Folks fall. Rocks fall. Ladders fall."

"And the sickness," Cody said petulantly. "Don't forget the sickness."

Ryan had already noticed that both of them were showing signs of rad sickness, the old man much worse than the girl. She had a couple of small sores near her mouth, and he could see that she'd also lost her fingernails. Cody's lips were cracked, the skin on his face covered in nests of tiny, pustulent blisters. His hair was mostly gone, and all his nails had dropped off. He kept complaining about feeling sick.

"Used to be a big man, Ryan. That your name, Ryan? Hearing ain't what it was. Yeah, Ryan. Big man. Look at me now. Get your thumb and finger around my wrist. Not even half a man."

The small rad counter on the lapel of Ryan's long coat was showing crimson.

CODY'S MIND GOT CLUTTERED and he began to mumble to himself, eventually falling into a deep sleep. Once he called out. "Take the wagons to the sea."

Kate got up and peered out of the mouth of the cavern. "Morning shift's on," she announced.

Ryan was more interested in where the mine shaft went. It seemed to extend way back beyond the fire. He walked back for a short distance, tripping over the rusted remains of iron rails. As far as he could make out, the caverns went deep into the heart of the mountain. He asked the young woman about it.

"Don't know much," she replied.

"These workings join with the sulfur diggings in the valley?"

"Some said so. Zim got locals first when he came here. The mines was way small. But he brought in men with blasters. Took it over. Makes more jack than the world's seen. Got wags to take it all out and trade it."

"How did you escape? With that sick old man in tow?"

"Getting out the mines isn't hard." The girl's fingers touched the scabs around her mouth. "Isn't anywhere to go once you're out."

"Why bother?"

"Why?"

"Sure. If there's no hope of freedom, why bother to try?"

"Why not, Ryan?"

"Not an answer."

"Best I got." She hesitated. "Heard guards talk about trackies. Thought somehow they might help us."

"Trackies?"

Kate shook her head. "Don't know much. Kind of muties. Live in these caves. Reckon they run miles. Up and down and in and out."

Ryan put the last piece of broken wood onto the dying embers of the fire.

"You aim to die here?"

She looked at him with a mixture of confusion and muddled pride. "Better for Cody. We was all going to die anyway. Better here, out in the open."

Ryan shook his head. "Weak," he said, not bothering to hide his disgust.

Her dark eyes bored into him. "What kind of shit's that?"

"You get away and sneak here and hide up. Just so's you can both die. I say that's weak. The way a loser thinks. That what you are, Kate?"

"No."

He pointed a finger at her. "Yeah, a weak loser. Sure, Cody's heading out on the last train west. I can see that."

"So, what should I do?"

Her voice was raised, and the old man stirred again in his sleep. "Forgotten son...some yesterday," he mumbled.

"You want to die, then why not wait your chance and take Zimyanin with you? Do some good. Go out a winner."

The girl looked away from him. "Easy for you to say that."

"I'd have done it if I'd looked at all the ways and there was no better option. Sure. Go out on your feet, Kate. Not your knees."

She sighed, wiping at her eyes. "Don't matter now, anyways, does it?"

"Might not matter to you. Does to me. I'm going to find a way down to the sulfur mines, and track my son. Bring him out. Chill the Russkie if I get a good ace on the line at him."

"What about us?"

He stood, dusting off his pants. "You picked this for yourself. Nothing to do with me."

"Take us with you?"

"No."

"Why not, Ryan?"

"Cody's run his race."

"We can leave him and come back later. He'll be sheltered here."

"I don't have the time, Kate."

She stood up, shoulders hunched. "Don't give a rolling fuck about us, do you?"

"No."

"Bastard."

"No. Knew both my mother and my father."

Kate tried to slap him but his hand was faster, catching her wrist and making her moan.

The slight disturbance woke up Cody. He blinked his rheumy eyes, wiping a thread of white spittle from his unshaven chin. "Hey," he said vaguely.

"It's all right." Glaring at Ryan, Kate knelt by the old man.

"Need a piss."

Ryan moved away, looking out toward the cave entrance. "Thought I heard something."

"Goats. Only thing comes here. None of the sec men ever leave the compound. Too scared of the trackies up here."

Cody staggered to his feet, rubbing at his crotch. "Best go outside," he muttered.

"Don't go too far so's anyone could see you from the mines," the girl warned.

Silhouetted against the morning light, he tottered to the entrance of the derelict mine shaft, paused in the opening and looked suddenly to his left.

"Who the fuck're—" he began.

With a single sweeping blow the fourth of the sec-hunter droids opened his throat from ear to ear.

Chapter Sixteen

The apparition was so unexpected that Ryan nearly froze. For a couple of seconds all his fighting reflexes failed him, and he simply stood there by the girl, watching Cody's violent murder.

Both the droid's arms whirled in a blur of gleaming, chromed action. The blood sprayed out in a fine mist, splattering over the walls of the old mine shaft, puddling across the uneven stone floor.

Cody was being, quite literally, cut and pulped to pieces. Shreds of flesh were being sliced away, while the hammer and pincers on the other arm were pounding and ripping, tearing out hanks of hair and slivers of skin and cloth.

All the time while the droid was busy at its murderous work, its head was turned toward Ryan Cawdor, its red eyes like glowing coals in the half-light.

The only thing that was holding the old man's body erect was the ferocity of the sec hunter's attack.

"Cody!" the girl screamed, starting to move toward the struggle.

Ryan, on an impulse, reached out and grabbed her by the arm, the coat tearing, but enough remaining to keep Kate back.

"He's dead," he said, pushing as much urgency into his voice as he could.

"No, he's still..."

But even as she spoke, the robot, its techno-sensers aware of the lack of life in its victim, stopped the flailing attack and stood, just for a moment, quite motionless.

The flayed corpse, so cloaked in its own blood and mangled skin that it was unrecognizable, slumped to the ground with a sodden, finite sound.

"Oh, Cody," the girl said in a soft, whimpering voice, still tugging against Ryan's retaining fingers. "Oh, no."

The robot blocked off the entrance to the cavern, its strange metallic silhouette throwing a foreshortened shadow toward them. Its head was nodding gently up and down, as though it were mentally approving what it had done.

Ryan didn't move, whispering to Kate, his hand tight on her arm. "One way and that's back. You want to stay and die, fine. If not, come with me. Now!"

He turned and darted toward the blackness of the tunnel that opened up at their backs.

The one-eyed man didn't even bother to look behind him to see if the girl was following him. He could hear feet pattering close at his heels, and that was good enough.

From what Ryan had already seen of the ancient sec-hunter droids, he knew that they had impressive, terrifying strengths.

But they also had some major weaknesses.

Paramount among those was their inability to move fast over any kind of rough terrain and their lack of mobility in a close-combat situation.

What he didn't yet know was how good the robots were in conditions of almost total blackout.

Once he was away from the spilled daylight, the darkness shrouded him. Instinctively Ryan moved to the side of the passage, touching the rough-hewn stone with his right hand as he ran, moving slower as the floor sloped more steeply downward.

"Coming after us," Kate panted.

Ryan had already heard the familiar grating sound of the clawed feet scraping over raw stone. But in the tunnel all noises were magnified and distorted, and it was impossible to tell how far behind the droid was or how quickly it was moving.

The tunnel seemed clear of fallen rocks or debris, meaning that Ryan and Kate could move along reasonably quickly.

And so could the droid.

THE NEXT HALF HOUR was a nightmare. Even time itself became distorted.

All that Ryan knew was that he was traveling fast through pitch darkness. Not a glimmer of light showed anywhere, the only sound his combat boots pounding on the floor of the sloping, winding passage, Kate's feet close behind him.

On the couple of occasions when they stopped running for a moment, Ryan heard the remorseless noise of the droid tracking them through the shafts of the old mine.

Once they ran through water, as cold as death, splashing up over their ankles, deepening, slowing them down. It eventually came up over their knees before the passage wound its way upward again and the water receded and vanished.

Once the passage opened into a vast chamber.

Ryan felt the sudden change in the atmosphere around him, the sense of space surging above his head where there'd once been the low roof of the shaft. He could feel the wall meandering off to his right with a draft of cool air to the left.

He stopped, uncertain which way to go.

Kate bumped into him, gasping with the shock of the impact.

"What is it?"

"Passage is changed. We're in some kind of much bigger room. Higher."

"Yeah. I can feel it. What do we do?"

"Have to go around the wall. Risk going across and we get lost. Can't tell how big it is. Could be around fifty steps. Could be five hundred. Could be it has all kind of pits or traps in it."

"Sure. Droid's closing on us."

"I hear it." By now Ryan had figured that the robot had some kind of infrascopic night sight built into its controls.

The danger was that they would fumble their way around the perimeter of the cavern, while the sec hunter would simply stride clear across it.

As they picked a cautious route around the perimeter of the open area, they crossed three side passages. All were lower and more narrow than the main one they'd been following, and there was a feeling of dead air in them, as though they might finish in a dead end.

The idea of being trapped in the bowels of the mine, with the sec hunter closing steadily and inexorably, was something Ryan didn't much care to think about.

"Can't we hide? Never find us."

"No, Kate. Pick us up by body heat or our breathing. Even the heartbeat in this silence. Got to keep on going."

The draft was stronger from the far side, and Ryan finally felt a fourth side passage. This time it was much wider, and he could almost see a glimmer of light in the darkness.

"It's closer!"

The tone of the droid's feet had changed as it reached the large chambered cavern. There'd been a moment's hesitation as the creature considered its options, methodically balancing and weighing each one until it reached a thoroughly logical conclusion.

It picked the straight and direct route across, moving fast toward its preprogrammed target.

Ryan Cawdor.

"FRESH AIR," Kate said. "We must've gone clean through and out the other side of the mountain."

"No. Don't think so. More likely we've circled. Lower, I reckon. These are still old workings. No smell of mining going on."

They'd stopped about two hundred yards along the passage. From the sound behind them, the droid had only just left the large chamber, but it was undoubtedly closer.

"Come on," Ryan urged.

"Exhausted."

"Stay here and die. I won't save you. Can't save you. I stay and I get chilled as well. You got to keep moving."

"Please."

There was a break in the girl's voice, but Ryan ignored it. The Trader used to say that if you tried to be kind to someone you often ended up being downright cruel.

"So long," he said.

"Wait for me."

He turned around carefully, knowing how easy it would be to totally lose his bearings. "This isn't a fucking game, Kate. I won't wait now or anytime. You understand me?"

"Yeah."

The killer robot sounded much closer.

AHEAD OF THEM, Ryan could see a very faint gleam of light, a shimmering, silvery phosphorescence, like the moon under water.

He turned, pausing, and detected a flicker of metallic movement.

"Fireblast!"

"It's closer."

"If it had any sort of laser blaster, we'd have been dead meat an hour ago. Got to get in near to do its work."

"What're the lights?"

"Got to be good news, whatever they are. Must mean people and ways out."

"MUSHROOMS," Ryan spit with disgust. "Bastard mushrooms."

The fungi covered a patch of the mine shaft at least a hundred yards long. They ran up from some stagnant pools of dark water, a few inches deep, spread over the slightly curved walls and up over the tunnel roof.

Each individual mushroom was less than a half inch across, pot bellied, all glowing with a cold, unearthly light.

Kate glanced back, seeing the strange mechanical stride of the robot, now extremely visible.

"Can you shoot it?"

"Can try if worse comes to worst. Bit like attacking a war wag with a spitball."

The gap was less than eighty paces.

Over the past few minutes the floor of the passage seemed to have become smoother, making it easier for the droid to narrow the distance between them.

Ahead was a sharp corner.

Ryan set off, Kate close behind, running at a steady jog that he hoped might open up a lead for them again.

Around the corner, the distilled light from the fungi was weaker, but still bright enough for them to see that the shaft grew wider again, running straight as far as they could make out.

"Big pool in the middle," the girl panted, "right across. Hope it's not deep."

The surface of the water was totally flat, like oil, but mat. It didn't reflect anything at all, as though it had sucked all the light into itself.

It was about a hundred and fifty yards ahead of them.

Veins of colored minerals streaked the walls, silver, speckled pink and ultramarine. And a deep, rich yellow.

The strange pool was only fifty yards ahead.

When Ryan realized what it was he slowed down, holding his arm out to warn the young woman.

"Stop," he said.

"Why? Can't be deep water."

"Not water at all. It's a fireblasted hole!"

Chapter Seventeen

"A hole?"

Now that they were almost on top of it, the young woman could see that Ryan's guess was correct.

There'd been some sort of subsidence, perhaps into a lower level of the old workings, or perhaps an earth shift at the time of the saturation nukings a hundred years before. It was surprisingly smooth-sided, as though cut with a keen-edged blade.

On either side of the passage a small section of the lower wall had also crumbled away, making it impossible to get by.

There were no convenient pebbles to lob into the hole to find out how deep it was, and no light to penetrate more than a couple of inches into the blackness. It might have been only six inches deep.

Then again, it might have dropped vertically for a gut-churning thousand feet.

Ryan's guess was that the chasm might be nearer the thousand feet than the six inches.

The more important statistic was the distance from one side of the hole to the other. Eight feet wasn't very much, about three good strides for a man of average height.

Less than one hundred inches.

At the time that the world blew apart, the long jump record was held by Andy Burne of the United States, and it stood at thirty-two feet and one inch.

Four times as wide as the hole in the tunnel.

Right at that moment, eight feet seemed awfully long.

"No," Kate said.

"Up to you." Ryan looked behind them, hearing the steady, rhythmic pounding of the droid's feet on the stone.

"Too far."

"Sure." He ignored her, taking a half dozen steps back up the passage, toward the sec hunter.

"What're you doing, Ryan?"

"Stay here you get chilled. You saw what the techno-mutie did to Cody. Ripped him into a bloody pulp. Not me."

Kate glanced into the pale light that silhouetted Ryan, saw the remorseless stride of the robot toward them.

"Can't," she whimpered.

"So long."

He powered himself into a short sprint, digging in, knowing that the coat and everything he carried would hinder his jump. But there just wasn't the time to strip off and throw his gear across before risking the leap.

For one dreadful splinter of frozen time, Ryan thought that the young woman was going to try to grab at him as he made the jump.

But she didn't.

He didn't risk taking off on the brink, in case the rock there was loose or undercut. Nor did he look down, keeping his eyes fixed on the far side, looking for a good landing.

He cleared the chasm by five or six feet, dropping as his feet hit, going into a tucked shoulder roll. He landed upright and turned to watch Kate.

Face paper-white, fists clenched, she was standing rooted to the spot. Her head kept moving, peering over her shoulder at the droid, then back to the hole and then up to Ryan's face.

The sec hunter was less than fifty yards from her, its pincers opening and closing, the knife blades rubbing against each other with the soft whisper of death.

"What's wrong?" Ryan yelled, making Kate jump. "Got a chill wish, you cowardly fucking bitch!"

It did the trick, rousing her from the catatonic terror that kept her paralyzed.

"Catch me, you bastard!" she shouted back.

The robot was thirty yards from the young woman, arms stretching out to welcome her into its embrace.

To make the jump, Kate had to actually move toward the advancing nemesis, and her nerve nearly deserted her.

Ryan had stepped to the edge of the hole, glancing down into it, feeling the bone-cold chill of the damp air that seeped up from the depths below him. He braced himself, ready.

It was going to be a close call.

Kate gasped at how near the droid was.

Twenty yards.

She took three strides toward it, then her nerve failed her and she spun around, made a stuttering start and flung herself into space.

Eight feet wasn't so long. When you had the chromed angel of death at your heels, it was an infinity.

Ryan's brain told him Kate was going to fall short of safety. Survival meant letting her go down, rather than risk his own life.

At the same time his reflexes pushed him into a crouch, arms out, fingers reaching for her.

Kate's mouth was gaping in a soundless scream of utter terror. She reached for him with both hands, stretching, desperate.

Once before Ryan had been in a similar situation, when he'd been much younger, and he'd tried for both hands then.

And a good friend had slipped from his grasp and died. In Deathlands, living often depended on lessons learned.

Ryan ignored Kate's right hand. He reached with his own right hand and grabbed at her left sleeve, fingers tightening like steel bands into the material. His left hand clamped on Kate's left forearm, giving him a double hold.

There was the sound of cloth ripping, but the coat sleeve held and he was able to take her weight. Kate's legs dangled into the void, her feet kicking against the stone walls, scrabbling to find a purchase. And failing.

"Don't struggle," he hissed. "Just keep still and limp. I'll get you up."

Ryan was half kneeling, his own weight thrown backward. He gritted his teeth and heaved, straightening his back, using the strength of his thighs to pull her up. The young woman came out of the hole like a cork from a bottle, knocking him over, falling on top of him.

"Thank . . ." she began.

But Ryan wasn't interested in her gratitude. His eye was filled by the looming figure of the killer droid, now only a couple of robotic steps from the brink of the drop.

Maybe it would just keep on walking, its attention so fixed on its prey that it never noticed the shadowed hole.

But its makers were too clever for such an obvious mistake.

It paused, marching on the spot, its red eyes turned downward.

Ryan watched as it slowly extended a foot over the drop, like a nervous bather testing the warmth of the water. There was a whining sound, as though extra gears were being engaged, and the leg began to protrude, telescoping across the hole. The claws also lengthened, becoming at least nine inches from base to needle tip.

Kate was breathing fast, gasping with shock. "Can it..." she began.

"Hope not. Too far."

The droid's leg reached out, balanced delicately, moving a little from side to side. Its head was also turning, as the creature examined the options available to it. It finally decided that it was beyond its capabilities to get across the hole.

The leg retracted and the sec hunter stood motionless, ruby eyes fixed on Ryan.

Its programmer, probably dead for a hundred years, must have had a macabre sense of humor. Thwarted of its prey, unable to get at Ryan, the android slowly lifted its right arm, raised the center of its knife blades and gave him the finger. It then turned and slowly strode off in the opposite direction, vanishing into the silvery glow of the phosphorescent mushrooms.

"And fuck you, too," Ryan said, holstering the SIG-Sauer.

Chapter Eighteen

It took several minutes for Kate Webb to recover sufficiently for them to carry on through the old mine shaft.

After the robot had stomped off into the blackness, the sound of its feet echoing for more than a minute, Kate sat and wept, her shoulders shaking.

Ryan watched her for a moment. "It's gone," he said. "Can't get at us."

"What if it finds a way around?" she sobbed.

"We'll be long gone. Come on."

She stood, wiping her eyes on her torn sleeve. "Yeah. And thanks for..."

But Ryan was already moving down the passage into the darkness.

TIME WAS DIFFICULT to calculate, groping through the endless corridors. The tiny battery on the chron derived its power from the sun, and Ryan was hesitant to use its light facility in case it ran out. But he checked every now and again.

"Been down here about five hours," he said.

"Seems longer." Kate sniffed. "Colder."

"Feel fresh air. Noticed it some time back, when we went off down that side shaft and had to come back again. Could be getting closer to the outside. You feel it?"

He rested with his hand just touching the rough cold wall. Now, standing still, he listened to try to hear... anything. But there was just the tidal swell of blood coursing through the secret canals of his inner ear.

"Can't feel anything, Ryan. Just double cold and triple tired."

"Want to take five?"

"Yes."

They sat side by side, backs against the wall, knees tucked up for warmth. Ryan felt Kate's hand move onto his arm, down to his wrist, touching his gloved fingers.

"Ryan?"

"What?"

"You got a woman?"

"Yeah."

"Where?"

"Back where I come from."

"Where's that?"

"South."

"Never been south. Heard it's hot. You know any barons down south?"

"Met some. Why?"

"Cody used to say he could've been a baron once. If he'd had the luck."

Ryan laughed quietly. "Friend of mine called Trader used to say that if he'd had big enough wings he could have flown to the sun."

But Kate didn't laugh. She wasn't even listening to what he'd said.

"You hear water?"

"No."

"I got good ears. Used to hear them bringing the soup around in the sulfur mine, way before anyone else did."

"No. Still can't hear it. What kind of water? Louder or nearer?"

Kate let go of his hand and Ryan could almost feel her concentration.

"Running water. Like…like a stream, but real far. Not getting any louder."

Despite the biting cold, Ryan's first thought had been that there might be a flash flood racing through the twisting caverns.

"You sure about the noise not being louder?"

"Sure, Ryan. Can't you hear it? Guess I got young ears. Cody used to tell me that. Young ears."

Ryan had a strange momentary flash of realization that he knew hardly anyone as old as he was. Virtually every friend he'd ever had was dead. There were so many kids in Deathlands.

"Mebbe we should go take a look at this water," he said.

IT WAS an embarrassment to him that they'd walked another ten minutes before he was certain that he, too, could hear the sound.

It was a dull pounding, like a river going through a deep gorge. Ten more minutes on their blind trudge along the tunnel, and he could feel vibration coming through the wall to his fingers.

Despite the difficulties of keeping any sense of direction in the pitch blackness, Ryan had thought for some time that they'd been moving generally downward.

"Air smells damp." Kate was still close at his heels.

"Yeah. There's ice forming on the floor again. Watch your step."

The round walls of the shaft were also carrying a thin coating of frozen water, slick against his gloved fingers.

THE NOISE SWELLED, until normal conversation became impossible.

From a murmur it became a sullen roar, filling the ears. Now they could both taste the dampness of spray on their lips, the water filming their faces and clothes, freezing almost immediately.

Kate was excited at the thrill of something to break the grinding monotony of the endless, featureless passageways. Ryan was apprehensive.

By the deafening thunder, it was obvious they were near to a massive underground river, maybe one that drove the power turbines of Zimyanin's sulfur mines.

To encounter it in the swamping blackness of the shafts was a terrifying prospect.

But the reality was worse. The noise made the senses reel. The air shook with it, taking away all awareness of time and place.

The footing had become treacherous. The floor had generally been very smooth, but now there were small pebbles and larger stones. The walls were rougher, with slabs fallen away and patches of something that felt like a coarse lichen.

Ryan stopped and pressed his mouth to Kate's ear, bellowing at the top of his voice. "This must flood some times. Triple care."

He felt her head nod understanding.

KATE FELL FIRST. She grabbed at Ryan as she went down, but her fingers slipped off his wet coat and she crashed to the stone floor.

He stopped and knelt, fumbling to try to find her. But the girl had completely vanished.

Ryan shouted her name, though he realized that shouting was utterly useless. She could be only six inches away from him and she wouldn't hear a word.

The ice at this point was thick, swirling under his hand in ribbons of frozen velvet. The passage was sloping downhill, and he had to struggle to keep himself from sliding.

Something brushed against the side of his head and he turned toward it, feeling Kate's boot on his cheek.

Ryan grabbed at it, reaching his way up her leg, pulling the young woman closer to him.

She was wriggling, her hands beating at him in a feeble, protesting way, as if she were trying to push him off.

Ryan rolled on top of her, pinning her down, feeling both of them slipping on the slick floor. He managed to get his face somewhere close to hers, calling out as loudly as he could.

"You all right?"

He lay his stubbled face against her mouth, feeling her lips moving, her breath warm in his ear.

"Yeah. Bit bruised. Get..."

He couldn't hear the last part so he yelled for her to repeat it.

"Said get off me!" she screamed.

With an effort, they both managed to regain their footing, clinging to each other like a pair of drunken dancers.

Ryan's worry was deepening every moment. The idea of having to go back was depressing and potentially life-threatening. He hadn't found a side passage they could have tried for what seemed like hours, and there was always the serious hazard of the sec hunter, mindlessly wandering the dark passages, hunting him down.

To try to make sure they stayed together, he linked hands with the young woman, picking his way over the solid floor of ice past tumbled boulders, their progress slowed to a crawl.

He was soaked and frozen, the spray that filled the chambers penetrating through the layers of his clothes. Every movement brought a stiff crackling from the delicate tracery of ice that covered every inch of his body and head.

A few yards farther on, disaster finally struck.

A huge fallen rock had tumbled from the roof of the passage and lay smack in the middle. It was eight feet high, shaped like a pyramid and sheeted in pebbled ice.

Ryan was leading the way over it, fingers locked with Kate's, when he lost his footing on the farther side. He gave a soundless cry, swamped by the rumbling of the water, and began to slide, out of control.

When his boots struck the passage floor, Ryan knew that they were in serious trouble. It sloped steeply away from him, toward the sound of the river. He tried to let go, but the young woman was also slipping, her hand tightly gripping his.

In desperation, Ryan kicked out with his steel-tipped combat boots, chips of ice flying around them. But he couldn't get a purchase, sliding faster and faster, feet first.

For a moment he was aware that they were both falling through space, then Kate was whirled away from him as they both plunged into the racing, icy river.

Chapter Nineteen

The shock was so terrible that it nearly stopped Ryan's heart. Though he'd been cold and wet before sliding helplessly into the black waters of the underground river, it was immeasurably, unimaginably so much more ghastly.

It was as though his entire body had been dumped into a whirlpool of razored ice crystals, while making a particularly bad mat-trans jump.

He lost contact with Kate immediately, their hands torn apart by the astounding pressure of the water's flow.

Ryan was rolled head over heels, trying to bring up his knees to make himself as small as possible. But control was out of the question. There wasn't the tiniest glimmer of light as he spun along, nothing that would give him the slightest clue which way was up.

Even holding his breath was difficult with the pressure of the river squeezing and pushing him. For a moment he felt something brush up against him, which he guessed must be Kate. But the current wrenched them apart again.

He knew that death was grinning close by, ready to take him into its own endless darkness. A river like this

might run for miles beneath the mountains, sometimes dropping hundreds of feet over a jagged abyss,
or squeezing itself into a narrow tunnel, filling it from
floor to roof.

He grabbed another breath.

The water turned him, so that he was going feet
first, carried at what seemed a dizzy speed, the icy
flood surging into mouth and nostrils, nearly choking
him.

THREE TIMES Ryan had bobbed to the surface, the
blackness and the bitter cold of the air seeming little
different to the darkness below the freezing river.

Each time he was able to take in less air before being dragged under again.

Despite his desperate efforts to survive, he could feel
that he was losing control.

J. B. Dix had once told him that a man falling
through ice on a winter lake, in the farthest north,
could measure his life in seconds. Even if he was
hauled out immediately, the chill would have gone
bone-deep and death was almost certain.

The immense weight and power of the water was
drowning his mind as well as his body. Despite his efforts to fight for air, the weight of his clothes and the
cold were dragging him down.

Deeper.

But he became dimly aware that the movement of
the river had changed. The crushing force that had

toyed with him was slowing and becoming more gentle.

Ryan kicked hard, hoping he was moving in the right direction, feeling his lungs close to bursting. His long-held breath whooshed out as his head again broke the surface.

After the torrent, it was more like floating in a gentle lake. He was conscious of space above and around him, like in the huge chamber that he'd encountered earlier in his explorations of the old mine.

By swimming out, he was able to move even farther from the center of the current, eventually bumping into a wall of smooth, wet rock. Though the turbulence and pace had all eased, he was still being carried along at a brisk walking pace, unable to find any purchase at all on the sides of the tunnel.

Ryan shook his head, clearing his ears. The brain-numbing sound of the torrent had faded away behind him. Or was it in front of him?

"Kate!" In the vast midnight space, his voice sounded feeble and strained.

He tried to drift on his back, but the weight of his water-filled boots and sodden clothes kept pulling at him.

"Kate! You hear me? Kate!" This time his voice seemed louder, but he was also uncomfortably aware that the rushing noise of the river was swelling again. The water was flowing faster, sweeping him into its center once more.

The echo of his shout was shorter, warning him that the roof of the cavern was becoming lower, closing in on him.

A vicious undertow heaved at his legs, like the clinging hands of drowned mariners, trying to draw him down.

Just before Ryan's head dipped once more below the freezing river, he thought he heard a woman's voice, calling his name.

But he couldn't be certain.

RYAN CAWDOR was unconscious. The channel had become smaller, shrinking to a narrow flume. Now the underground river was racing twice as fast as it had before, dropping almost vertically at times, hurling its helpless victim around and around until he blacked out.

When he came to, he was tangled in a net, his head above the surface of the water.

"What's..." he mumbled, realizing at the same moment that there was some sort of light gleaming around him, a pallid and watery light, coming from burning torches stuck around the walls.

Ryan rested for a few moments, trying to register some of his lost strength. Over to his right there was a sort of quay, carved from the bare rock. It was obviously man-made, with rusting iron rings set into it at intervals. He figured its length around two hundred feet, and its width close to fifty feet. Beyond it he could just make out the gaping mouths of two more tunnels.

With an effort he managed to ease his right hand out of the strong plastic folds of the net, slipping the panga from its scabbard and taking the greatest of care not to drop it into the black water. The honed edges sliced the coils apart, freeing his left arm completely.

The net was stretched clear across the river and was, by the feel of it, weighted down at the bottom. At this point the water was much wider again, running more slowly and steadily. As Ryan jerked at the mesh, he saw that he wasn't the only prisoner. There were a number of slim, white fish, with protruding eyes, much too large for their narrow skulls.

"Ryan."

"Yeah."

"You all right?"

"Cold and wet and— Where are you?" He strained his head to look around.

"Here."

The girl's voice came from the deepest shadows.

"Can't see you."

"Caught in this bastard trap."

"Can you pull clear?"

The girl actually managed to laugh, the sound rising above the noise of the underground river.

"Got fishes stuck all around me. You on the right?"

"Yeah, close to a kind of a jetty. Come to me."

Kate was only a few feet away when he finally spotted her. There was a bruise on her forehead, and a trickle of watery blood seeped from her nose. She reached out a hand and he grabbed it, pulling her close to him. Her body was trembling as though she had the quaking sickness, and her eyes were very wide.

"Life's packed with thrills, ain't it?" she said. "Could do with a quiet few minutes now and again. Make a sort of change, you know."

She laughed again, her voice ragged and loud. Ryan put an arm around her thin body, hugging her close.

"It's all right, Kate," he said. "Let's get out of the water."

Ryan had to use his panga once more, cutting away a thick tangle of netting. Then he was close enough to the rough stone of the quay to reach out and grab one of the rusting rings.

"Hang on," he said, letting go of the young woman while he heaved and kicked his way out of the freezing grip of the river.

Once he was on dry land, he knelt, panting, and reached down for Kate. The weight of water in her clothes made it a struggle to lift her out.

"Going to die if we don't start moving," he panted. "Least we could get a fire going from one of those torches. If we can get some wood to burn."

"Who laid the net?" she asked.

A part of Ryan's mind had been working on that one since he first broke the surface. Over his years of traveling through Deathlands, he'd sometimes come across small groups of people who lived in caves. And in a desolate wilderness like this, fish were likely to be one of the few things you could depend on for survival.

The unanswered part of the question was whether the fishers would turn out to be friendly or not.

Less than two minutes later they found the answer to that question.

Friendly or not?

Not.

Chapter Twenty

Once they started to move along the quay, Ryan and Kate saw a number of passages leading back into the depths of the mountain.

All of them had torches smoldering at intervals along the walls, but Ryan was puzzled at the poverty of the lighting. The flames were feeble and smoky, casting so weak a glow that they were hardly better than no lights at all.

Behind them, the ceaseless rumbling of the great river was drowning out any other noises.

His infallible sense of direction had finally failed him.

The tumbling ride through the midnight maelstrom had totally disoriented Ryan. He'd been spun around like an egg through a whisk and had lost all idea of their whereabouts. The only thing that he knew for certain was that they were a whole lot lower than they'd been when they started their journey.

They had to be close to the bottom of the steep-sided valley, near to the sulfur mines, near to Gregori Zimyanin.

And near to Dean Cawdor.

"This one," he said a moment later, leading the way toward the nearest of the narrow, vaulted corridors.

"Why that one?"

"Why not?"

The passage bent in a sharp dogleg, only fifty paces long.

"Fireblast!"

He snatched at Kate's wrist as he turned, tugging her with him, around the corner.

"What?"

"Shut up!"

He was pulling the young woman behind him, back toward the river, glancing over his shoulder as they moved clumsily together.

Behind them, soaring over the hissing roar of the water, Kate suddenly heard a sickening sound, a rising, ululating howl, like a pack of hunting wolves suddenly striking a trail.

"What are they?" she managed to ask as they reached the jetty.

"Not sure. Mebbe it's some of those trickies you spoke about."

"Trackies."

"Yeah." He looked around, desperate to try to find a hiding place. But the expanse of cold gray stone was bare, featureless. Apart from the other tunnel openings, there was nowhere to conceal themselves from the shrieking horde.

Except the river again.

"Here."

Ryan slid into the last of the ill-lit cavern entrances, beyond the trapping net, so that they could at least hurl themselves back into the torrent as a final resort.

The screaming had reached a crescendo, then died away just a suddenly, as if someone had given a signal that had brought a total hush.

Kate was quivering, pressed against Ryan, but he couldn't tell if it was terror or simply the biting effects of the freezing water. He drew his SIG-Sauer from its holster and held it in his right hand.

He risked a quick glance from cover, immediately pulling back into hiding. The one look had told him all he wanted to know.

And more.

Instinctively Ryan guessed that these people *were* the "trackies" that the young woman had mentioned earlier. But they surely weren't going to be any help against Zimyanin and his sec guards.

There were about a dozen of them, and most of them seemed to have mainly male characteristics. But even that wasn't very certain.

What was certain was that they were among the most bizarre muties that Ryan had ever seen.

Not one of them stood taller than five feet, with a couple barely making four feet. All of them were stockily built, wearing dripping layers of what looked like sacking. Most had long spears, some with multiple points, like tridents, and every one seemed to have a knife, sheathed or drawn.

But it was their heads that had caught Ryan's attention in that one snatched look.

Most were uncovered, showing bald skulls, with only a few strands of stringy hair stretched across them. The ears were peculiarly large, farther back on the head than usual. Their noses were simply gaping slits in the front of their faces, with threads of slimy mucus dripping from them. Mouths hung open, lipless, revealing pallid gums and uneven rows of ragged, broken teeth.

At a glimpse, it seemed to Ryan that their eyes were lidless. They protruded from their sockets, goggling around the quay for their prey. Their skin was deathly white, with an iridescent tone of green, like rotting meat.

Ryan sensed that the young woman was about to speak, and quickly laid his hand across her mouth, turning to stare intently at her, shaking his head. He put the barrel of the SIG-Sauer to his own lips to accentuate the need for silence.

Against the background of the river's pounding, it was difficult to hear anything else. Flattened against the rock wall, Ryan was all too aware that the trackies could be creeping up on them. They could be only inches away.

Finger on the trigger, he peeked around the corner of the tunnel again.

The group was motionless, gathered near the net, staring out into the foaming water. One of them pointed with its spear, its mouth moving as it gabbled

a few words. Ryan's uneasy guess was that they'd
spotted the damage to the coils and were able to see
that it had been done with a knife. He also began to
suspect that the unusual eyes and ears might well in-
dicate peculiarly exaggerated hunting skills, essential
in the cold stone arteries below the mountains.

Kate stared up at him, seeking some clue as to what
was going on. But she had enough sense not to try to
look for herself.

Ryan lowered his mouth and whispered into her ear.
"Think they got double-hearing and dark-seeing.
Can't spot no blasters. Got be real quiet."

She nodded.

He risked a third look.

They were about twenty yards away, and the light
was extremely poor. But the fractional movement of
his head around the rock was enough to catch the eyes
of one of the muties.

The damage to their nets had already made them
suspicious, and they were all peering about. There was
a cry of anger and triumph from the trackie that had
spotted Ryan, and the horde began to move toward the
hiding couple.

They ran with a curious, flat-footed shuffling
movement, rocking at the hips like plump women.
They waved their spears threateningly.

"Back in the tunnel," Ryan said.

He led Kate into the deeper darkness, finding a
passage that seemed to parallel the river. Less than

fifty paces along there was a cutoff to the left, which he took.

"Fireblast!"

They stood together on the quay, now deserted.

"Where are they?"

Ryan looked behind, teeth bared in anger, frustrated by the surging roar of the tumbling river. He didn't expect any fight to be fair, but he didn't like the way the trackies were holding almost all of the cards.

"Might be a mess more of them," Kate said.

"Probably are. Don't much like the idea of picking around in these tunnels with those goggle-eyed sons of bitches waiting around every corner. Rather trust us to the river again."

The brief surge of adrenaline had fought away the bitter cold that was seeping through his body with a fatal ease. Now, standing still, Ryan realized that time was running out for them.

He looked both ways, but the jetty was completely empty and bare, except for a low wall of fallen rock, no more than two feet high, right at the very downstream end of the quay.

THE FIRST OF THE TRACKIES padded out onto the leveled strip of wet stone, its bubble eyes looking both ways.

"Gone!" it wailed.

It banged the haft of its triple-tined spear on the rock, making it ring and echo. The rest of the muties did the same, snarling in frustration.

"In water," one of them said, its pendulous breasts swinging beneath the filthy sacking.

"In water," the leader repeated, shaking its head from side to side.

"Water, water, water..." they chorused.

"Black water takes and black water gives!" the leading trackie shrieked.

They began a rhythmic stamping, feet slapping on the rock, back and forth.

Behind the tumbled boulders, Ryan and Kate pressed together low, backs against the stones. The SIG-Sauer was drawn and ready while the young woman gripped Ryan's honed panga.

"Take and give. Take and give!" The chanting went on, louder and louder, finally beginning to fade away, the noise of the feet also quietening.

Still Ryan and Kate kept motionless, not daring to risk a glance along the quay.

At last there was silence.

He felt the girl stirring and laid a warning hand on her arm.

The river, racing by only a yard away from them, was making enough sound to cover any approach by the muties. Ryan waited, counting his own pulse, reaching four hundred before he decided to chance a move.

He shifted sideways, managing to keep under cover, and cautiously lifted his head above the barrier.

To see a crude iron spear thrusting straight at his face.

Chapter Twenty-One

There wasn't even time to squeeze the trigger on the blaster. All Ryan's reflexes allowed him to do was to push the automatic pistol at the jabbing spear, getting the barrel between two of the prongs, deflecting the thrust away from his face.

His brief look at the trackies had led Ryan to figure them for physical weaklings, which made the demonic power behind the attack even more disconcerting.

The trackie pushed with such force that Ryan was barely able to hold him off, the spear lunging in, knocking him backward. Kate yelped as Ryan and the mutie toppled into her, squeezing her into the narrow space at the extreme end of the jetty, inches from the river.

The pistol was stuck between the points of the trident, twisting Ryan's wrist sideways, making him gasp with pain.

"Bastard norm!" the trackie shrieked, its goggling face pressed close to Ryan's. Its breath was foul, stinking of ancient, rank fish. Its free hand, slightly webbed, clawed toward the man's eye.

"Bastard mutie," Ryan retorted, kicking out and upward, feeling the satisfying thud of the steel-toed combat boots grinding into the creature's groin.

The next few seconds held the familiar insanity of a lethal fight.

Ryan grabbed at the trackie's left hand, ripping the coarse cloth of the sleeve, feeling the sinewy strength of the corded muscles. It spit at him, slimy saliva running down his cheek.

There was a flash of bright metal, and he felt the whisper of sliced air against his skin. The mutie jerked in his grasp, and he saw its face open like a peeled orange. The white skin and flesh parted under the hacking blow from the cleaver. Its right eye was cut clean in half, bursting into a pinkish jelly.

"Got him!" Kate gasped, heaving the eighteen-inch steel blade clear of the splintered cheekbone.

"Watch out for others," Ryan panted.

The trackie had rolled sideways, letting go of its long spear, both its hands reaching toward its ruined face.

Not wanting to waste bullets, Ryan drew his own thin-bladed skinning knife. The wounded mutie was turned away from him, crouched over, showing the back of its neck.

It was the easiest of instant kills for an experienced knife man.

Ryan picked his spot, precisely where the skull joined the spine, and thrust the narrow blade in as hard as he could. Sliding the delicate point perfectly

into the narrow gap, severing the spinal cord and killing the trackie instantly. To make sure, Ryan jerked his
wrist from side to side as he withdrew the knife, but
the albino creature was already down and done for.

In its last dying spasm, it kicked the spear toward
the edge of the jetty and the dark water.

Ryan dived for it, managing to free the blaster,
hefting the trident as he turned and straightened.

Kate was battling two more of the trackies, weaving a pattern of whirling steel in front of herself,
hacking at the spears as they came lunging toward her.

Though the balance of the weapon was less than
perfect, Ryan hurled his trident at the nearest of the
trackies. It caught the creature through the wrinkled
throat, sending it staggering back, where it finally
slipped sideways and vanished into the foaming water. The haft of the spear rose for a moment, then disappeared.

Out of the corner of his eye Ryan saw the young
woman open a great gash across the chest of the
trackie that was attacking her. Blood gushed out,
pouring onto the jetty. For a moment he had the illu-
sion that the steaming liquid was glowing in the semidarkness.

The remaining nine muties backed off, chattering to
one another in an incomprehensible gibberish. Ryan
had sheathed his flensing knife and now leveled the
blaster at the group. Half a dozen rounds would chill
most of them and scatter the rest, but it might also

bring the rest of the subterranean tribe flooding from the tunnels. He didn't have that much ammo to spare.

"Do it," Kate panted.

"Too late."

"Why?"

"Look." He pointed at the trackies with the 9 mm automatic.

One of them had broken from the huddle and scampered off in its flat-footed waddle, down one of the side tunnels.

"Fetching reinforcements?"

"Got to be."

"What do we do, Ryan?"

"Looks like we go swimming again. We're on the right side of the netting. Downstream of it."

"No," she said with a firm shake of her head.

"You got a better idea?"

"No."

SOMEHOW THE WATER didn't seem quite as cold as before. Ryan had a suspicion that this was because they were both sinking fast into the welcoming arms of hypothermia.

He took the panga from Kate and sheathed it safely, holstering the SIG-Sauer. Then, keeping a watchful eye on the trackies, Ryan slid into the river, hanging for a moment on to one of the ancient iron rings. Kate joined him, and they let the current bear them away from the torch-lit quay.

One of the muties shrilled out a cry and hurled its spear at them, but it missed by several feet.

By then the freezing water was carrying them out of range, into the mouth of another dark overhang and into a tunnel of pitch blackness.

To try to keep them together Ryan had hastily ripped a length of sacking off the clothes of one of the trackie corpses and they each clung to one end of it.

Now the flow was slower, the walls and roof of the tunnel feeling wider and higher. But his body was growing stiff with cold, the muscles reluctant to work to keep him afloat. There was a temptation to close his eyes and slide painlessly beneath the surface.

His legs were kicking more slowly; his arm pulled at the water with less and less strength.

Ryan was suddenly walking along a high trail, with a towering escarpment of orange rock, sunlit, to his right. A heather-covered hillside sloping gently toward an amethyst lake far off on his left, and ahead of him walked a young boy with black, curly hair, hand in hand with a tall, attractive woman whose hair blazed like living fire.

Krysty and Dean, Ryan thought.

His mouth and nose filled with the freezing river, and he coughed and spluttered back to a kind of consciousness.

Kate was close by him, pummeling his back with her free hand, screaming at him.

"Don't you fucking dare die, you selfish bastard! Not without me."

HE SAW THE LIGHT FIRST.

They seemed to have been moving in slow, massive loops for an eternity. Ryan's failing brain had already wondered whether they were miles below the valley, driving ever downward toward the core of the earth itself.

Kate had passed out and he was hanging on to her as best he could, struggling to keep her face above the water. That was how he'd realized there was light—he looked down and was able to see the white blur of her face.

"Light," he croaked.

Now they were accelerating, gathering speed, the glistening walls of smooth rock racing by them, faster and faster.

The light grew brighter, gaining from the prick of a pin in a black sheet to a semicircle that seemed dazzling after the long immersion in the netherworld.

The noise was there again, a distant roar, like thunder.

Ryan wondered, rather distantly, whether he should try to do something to check their progress.

But the idea was . . .

"Farfetched," he muttered through a mouthful of spray. He remembered that Doc used to say that something farfetched was "like a bucket of shit from China."

It made him grin.

Ryan was still grinning as he and Kate shot from the opening in the mountainside and plunged out into the afternoon sunshine, riding a plume of rainbowed spray that plummeted nearly a hundred feet into a shining pool.

It lay near the head of the main valley, off a side canyon, surrounded by spruce and piñon pines. A thin covering of snow topped the cropped turf all around.

Circling on a frail thermal, way above the water, a falcon looked down from hooded eyes, considering whether there might be good eating below. The two bodies both floated facedown, motionless in the small lake, as the ripples gradually subsided back into stillness.

DEEP, DEEP within the heart of the mountains around the pool, the shredded corpse of a young male trackie lay on the deserted jetty. One of its protruding eyes had been torn from the socket and the other stared blankly at the cave roof. Its left arm had been ripped away, and its intestines tumbled in yellow loops around the blood-speckled feet.

The fourth of the killer sec droids stood over the body, at the edge of the underground river. Its ruby eyes glowed in the dim light as it stared intently at the rushing water, watching it vanish into the distant tunnel.

After nearly a minute it turned around and moved slowly away into one of the maze of adjoining passages.

Chapter Twenty-Two

Major-Commissar Gregori Zimyanin was carrying out the morning examination of his demesne. The weather was warmer than it had been for several days, the thermometer outside the main office of the sulfur mines rising very close to the freezing point. There had been a chem storm during the small hours, with jagged streaks of purple lightning followed by a brief, torrential downpour, which had raised the level of the main river by several inches.

One of the lowest levels of the mine had become flooded, meaning that several of the working shifts had to form a chain, bailing out the stinking, yellow water by hand.

A senior overseer had suggested that excavation could resume once the level dropped below a man's knees. Zimyanin had smiled gently and suggested that perhaps it could begin again once the water was less than waist deep.

A ''suggestion'' from the bald Russian was something like a message from the Almighty, hewn from granite. Three of the older workers had drowned in the first hour, but the sodden corpses had been quickly removed before Zimyanin came around on his tour of inspection.

Since he'd taken over the mining complex, the Russian had managed to improve production, mainly by bringing in ruthless sec guards to drive the slave laborers on.

But the linked chambers, tunnels and shafts were still chaotically undermechanized. A few gas engines powered hoists and elevators, but virtually everything in the mines was still man- and woman-powered.

If a worker in a medieval sulfur mine had been miraculously transported to Zimyanin's complex, he'd have found very little changed: a bird's nest of rickety wooden ladders held together by frayed lengths of rope; smoking oil lamps that gave a frail yellow light, leaving great lakes of black shadow; narrow passages where a man could hardly stand upright that linked up with other equally stooped tunnels.

To reach the main working areas from the entrances in the valley floor could take more than half an hour, involving as many as twenty ladders. Descending into foul air and a slippery ocher ooze.

Each work period lasted twelve hours. Food was dragged down in iron pots, so that it was as cold as stone by the time most workers received it. Two ladles of cornmeal mush and a hunk of bread were served up halfway through the shift. Rusting oil drums were filled with water and placed at the end of each main gallery in the mine. But within a few minutes a scum of yellow sulfur powder would form on its top, thickening during the twelve hours.

Permission to drink was needed from the armed sec men who patrolled the mine, each of them only working below ground for three hours at a spell.

Bodily functions were exercised in the darker corners of the mine.

Dean Cawdor had been in worse places in his young life.

The survival skills that he'd learned in ducking and dodging were invaluable in the depths of Zimyanin's mine.

Even in the short time that he'd been a prisoner in the freezing north, the boy had learned what could and couldn't be done.

Being small and slight, he could weave his way through the midnight crevices, slipping away from the attention of the guards and shepherding his energy by digging and carrying as little as possible.

Dean also contrived to get to the food first, stuffing himself with the tasteless gruel. He watched other slave workers, not used to the hardship, turning their noses up at the food. By the time hunger drove them to accept the gray sludge, they'd already become weakened.

And they'd soon be dead.

"I HOPE the inclement weather has not meant hardship for the workers," Zimyanin said, pausing to wipe the yellow muck from his high leather boots.

His overseers were used now to the odd way that the pockmarked baron spoke to them.

"Sure. Yeah, Major-Commissar. No problem with them at all." His fingers crossed behind his back that the Russkie didn't learn about the drowned corpses.

Zimyanin didn't have much of a reputation for liking men who lied to him. The last sec man he'd caught in an untruth had been crucified upside down over a slow fire.

The Russian stood, legs slightly apart, hands locked behind his back, surveying the main galleries. The workers scurried over the scaffolding and ladders like golden ants.

A group of laborers trudged by, a guard at their heels, a carbine slung over his shoulder. They all paused at one of the water butts, immediately in front of the Russian and his sides.

"Been a slide in Tunnel Three, Major-Commissar," one of the foremen said.

"Slow work?"

"No."

"You are certain?"

"Yeah, Major-Commissar."

"I shall peruse the control invoices for Tunnel Three on the morrow. I trust that you will be correct in your judgment."

Despite the bitter chill of the afternoon, the man's forehead was suddenly beaded with sweat. "Sure thing, Major-Commissar. No problems."

Zimyanin patted him on the shoulder, lips parting in the thinnest and bleakest of smiles. "I am sure of that."

The workers were filing past, all gulping down a ladle of the filthy water. They were of all shapes and sizes. Last in line was the smallest of the shift, a skinny youth whose face and head were covered in a mask of sulfur.

"There's someone who's been working hard, Major-Commissar," the overseer said, hoping to slide back into the Russkie's good books.

"Someone who hopes to make us believe that he has been working hard," Zimyanin corrected.

The boy seemed oblivious to them, swilling down a beaker of water and then stooping and leaning over the drum. He dipped his entire head below the surface and brought it out again, shaking himself like a dog after a swim.

"Wipe his face," the Russian said very quietly. "Show him to me."

"What?"

Zimyanin swung his right fist around and drove it into the overseer's lower stomach, all of his considerable strength behind it.

The man, stout and wearing multilayered furs, doubled over as though he'd been shot, his soured dinner gushing over his boots from his gaping mouth. Zimyanin grabbed him by the back of the head and brought his knee up sharply into the foreman's face.

The crack of the nose splitting was clearly audible throughout the mine.

The Russian ignored his victim as he slumped to the wet stone, rolling on his side, unconscious.

"Wipe his face," he repeated.

"Yes, Major-Commissar," one of the guards replied. "At once."

"Show him to me."

The boy glanced up at Zimyanin, shrugging off the hand of the sec man. "I can wash my own face," he said quietly.

He dashed more water over his head, streaks of crusted sulfur running over the chiseled planes of his high cheekbones. Dean rubbed his sleeve across his mouth and eyes, spitting on the floor.

"Look at me, boy," the Russian ordered.

"Yes, Major-Commissar." It was said with enough insolence to be recognized, but not *quite* enough to be worth punishment.

Gregori Zimyanin stared intently at Dean Cawdor. The light was very poor in the gallery of the mine, but he still had the nagging suspicion that he should recognize the boy.

"Name?"

"Will Goode."

The Russian smiled. "Of course. I saw you when you arrived here. I warned you about—"

A tiny alarm bell began to ring in a distant, dusty room at the back of Zimyanin's mind. He hadn't been a senior officer in the Internal Security Section for the whole of the massive ville of Mockba for nothing. He had great cunning and deductive powers, linked with a ferocious intuition.

There had been a corpse found in . . . no, there had been two corpses, both slaughtered with great skill by someone who had a delicate touch with a knife.

The boy stood still, not shifting his feet or showing any discomfort. There was something about the mat of black, curly hair and the determined jaw that tugged at the Russian's memory.

"Very well," he said, waving his hand at the young man. "You may leave us for the present, but I might require your attendance at some later time. Go, now, Master Goode."

Dean Cawdor nodded and turned away to follow the rest of his working party, leaving Gregori Zimyanin looking after him with a thoughtful expression on his face.

Chapter Twenty-Three

Ryan had been winded by the fall, landing belly-down in the shallow lake. But he recovered consciousness in a few moments, kicking out, coughing to clear his throat. His feet flailed against the rounded boulders that lined the bottom of the icy pool, and he quickly looked around to get his bearings.

The drop had torn the ragged cloth from his hands and he saw Kate, floating a dozen yards away from him, arms and legs spread wide.

His body felt swollen and stiff, as though someone had injected all his arteries and muscles with a mix of frozen concrete. It took an enormous effort of will for Ryan to force himself toward the young woman, stumbling chest-deep.

When he reached her, Ryan slid a hand under her chest and turned her, managing to support her head. She lolled in his arms, eyes closed, a thread of blood oozing from her blue, parted lips.

"Kate." Ryan's voice was barely audible, even to himself.

There was no movement. His fingers were too numb to try to locate a pulse, so he simply dragged her out of the pool onto a shingled beach. He rolled her onto her stomach, pumping at her, kneeling astride her hips.

"Come on, you stupid bitch, or we'll both freeze to death," he panted, thumping her between the shoulders with clenched fists.

There was a groan, and the girl puked up a few mouthfuls of pale yellow water, moving her hands feebly to try to push the small stones away from her face.

"Better?" He stopped pounding on her.

"Terrible."

"Got to keep moving. Find someplace to try and get warm."

"Oh, Judas on the tree!" She was sick again, her body racked with the effort.

"Get up." He stood himself, rocking a little with a nauseous vertigo, and reached down and grabbed Kate by the wrist.

"You don't ever give up, do you, Ryan?" she said weakly.

"Never."

He'd managed to work out where they were, marveling at the weaving extent of their perilous journey far within the heart of the surrounding mountains.

Allowing for the doubling and snaking of the river, Ryan's guess was that they'd traveled ten or fifteen miles. But, as the crow flew, they were less than four miles away from the part of the canyon where the mines were situated.

From the position of the clouded sun it seemed to be late afternoon.

Not far from the lake, Ryan and Kate found shelter in caves, less than five feet high, and only a dozen feet deep, that looked like they went back a thousand years or more.

"Valley must flood," Ryan said through chattering teeth. "Lots of driftwood caught on this corner."

Kate was close to coma, lying just within the cave opening, eyes shut, hands folded across her breast. She hadn't spoken another word to him and had passively let him heave her into the shelter.

Ryan dragged a couple of armfuls of the brush-wood, trying to dust some of the powdery snow off the dry branches. With the panga he managed to whittle a few slivers of bark, laying them in a circle, piling on some larger chips. His fingers wouldn't cooperate in the struggle, and he kept dislodging the base for his fire.

He was certain there was a single, old pyrotab in one of the pockets of his coat.

Doc Tanner had once kept them enthralled around a campfire with his retelling of an old story. Ryan could vaguely remember that the writer had been called "Jack" but the second name had gone. But he did recall the name of the story—*To Light a Fire*.

A man in a freezing wilderness had fallen into water and knew that his life was done if he failed to get a fire going to warm himself. But in his haste he had tried to light it beneath a tree, branches loaded with snow. The snow had melted and put out his precious flickering flames.

And he'd died.

Kate sighed and he glanced across at her. The young woman's face was as pale as the bleached granite where her head rested, and her breathing was becoming more and more rapid and shallow.

Ryan rummaged through his pockets with wooden fingers that didn't belong to him.

Like J. B. Dix, Ryan used his long coat as a receptacle for all manner of useful—and useless—things. Various bits and pieces tumbled onto the floor of the cave: a spent round of 9 mm ammunition; the torn top off a can of self-heat soup; a green pebble with a streak of silver quartz running through it. Ryan was puzzled by that and was about to throw it away when he remembered that he'd picked it up, many months ago, because it reminded him of the emerald eyes of Krysty Wroth.

There was an assortment of crumbs and unidentifiable shreds of paper and fluff. A small side pocket produced a plastic key with the number Six stamped on it, and a picture of an old penny-farthing bicycle. The handle of a tiny screwdriver was in the same pocket and a length of neatly coiled fishing line.

No pyrotab.

"Fireblast!"

The last pocket, deep and narrow, produced an iridescent bird's feather, a splinter of broken mirror and . . . a pyrotab.

Ryan muttered a prayer to Krysty's Gaia that it wouldn't malfunction.

The metal was slippery and difficult to hold at the best of times. Ryan made three abortive efforts to grip it and start the ignition process, but three times it fell to the floor.

Feeling sick and dizzy, Ryan managed to shove his right hand into the waist of his trousers, pressing the numb flesh against the faint warmth of his stomach, down into his groin.

He leaned back against the wall of the cave, breathing slowly, eye closed. The past few hours had been among the most bleak and exhausting of his entire life. Now all he wanted was to get a fire going and fight off the icy lethargy that was creeping through his body.

Creeping through his body.

His body.

The afternoon thunderstorm had been soaring high above the circle of snow-topped peaks, lightning flashing vividly against the pewter sky.

A bolt lanced to break against the hillside across the river, the noise bursting into the valley with a thunderous roar.

"Not my brother... What?" Ryan jerked awake, looking out of the cave to where a heavy rain had begun to cascade from the north.

The realization that he'd slipped into what might have been a final sleep startled Ryan, and he deliberately found a less comfortable way to sit, resting his cheek against a sharp spur of the rock.

Now his right hand was feeling a little warmer. He experimentally wriggled his fingers, finding a degree of response.

"Go for it," he urged himself.

The pyrotab clicked into action and he laid it carefully, hand trembling, onto the chips of wood. The ends of the white splinters darkened and began to smolder, glowing crimson. With the utmost caution, Ryan put a few more tiny shards of pine on top of the pyrotab.

The flames gathered strength, working its way along the kindling, biting at the dry twigs that Ryan placed on the fire.

Now there was the sound of crackling as larger pieces of wood were fitted into the heap. The dark red flames were turning yellow, then white as the heat raced through, consuming the driftwood. Ryan rose and went outside, looking cautiously around, bringing back several bigger branches, some pine and some from an old sycamore. There was a little pale smoke coming from the mouth of the cave, but the rain was dispelling it.

And they should be far enough from the main complex of the sulfur mines to be safe from any roving sec guards.

The storm seemed to have settled directly overhead, and Ryan could smell the bitterness of ozone in the air.

A couple of feet away from the edge of the fire, Ryan's coat was already beginning to steam, and the dusting of blown snow on some of the rocks was beginning to melt.

"Kate," he said, moving to kneel beside the unconscious young woman and to place a hand on her forehead, which was cold as any stone.

IT TOOK RYAN several minutes to get Kate completely stripped from her sodden, clinging clothes. He placed them by the fire to dry, taking off more of his own wet clothing.

The SIG-Sauer and the panga were near at hand, and he kept going to the entrance to glance into the torrential downpour. Before the huge pile of driftwood became soaked through he dragged several more big branches into the cave.

The young woman moaned once as he rolled her onto her back. She looked absurdly young, lying there naked and helpless. Her bare feet were puckered and white from the long immersion in the river, and the skin on her palms was also wrinkled, with a corpselike pallor to it.

Her eyes were closed, and a fringe of black hair clung to her temple. The roaring flames glowed off her body, making parts of it seem ruddy and healthy, flickering shadows dancing across her small breasts, the nipples erect with the cold.

"Come on, lady, come on," Ryan urged, chafing her wrists and ankles, trying to get the blood flowing through her frozen veins.

In the confined space of the low-roofed cavern, the heat built up very quickly. Ryan had to stop and move their clothes farther away, as her shirt was beginning to char at the edges. He was already sweating, stripping off to his underpants and a sleeveless T-shirt.

Kate groaned again as he rubbed hard at the insides of her arms and her calves, massaging her knees. He noticed a slight change in the color of her skin.

"Hot," she said, eyes still squeezed tight shut, fingers clenching into her palms, her toes curling as she arched her feet.

"Yeah. Better than cold," Ryan muttered, breathing hard with the labor of trying to restore the young woman to life.

A burning branch off a lodgepole pine collapsed in a shower of bright sparks, some of which settled on Kate's body. Ryan leaned forward and brushed them away from her breasts, extinguishing a few that had landed and hissed in her damp tendrils of pubic hair.

Feeling his hand touching her, lower, Kate opened her eyes. Her lips were now restored to their normal color, and they parted in a half smile.

"Good job Cody isn't around, Ryan. Might take what you're doing a tad different."

"You feeling better?" He sat back on his heels, his T-shirt sticking to his chest and shoulders with perspiration.

"Feel like a living woman again. First time for... Hours I guess. But it seems like days in that blackness."

She reclined and extended her back, not making any effort to cover her naked body. Stretching her arms above her head she stared into the writhing dragons of the fire.

"Wish we had some food," Ryan said.

"Can't have everything. I'll settle for this warmth and shelter from the storm. Listen to that old idiot wind raging outside."

The rain poured down in a ceaseless curtain, and the afternoon seemed as dark as dusk. Ryan moved to arrange his clothes again, finding that they were drying well. The butt of the automatic was hot to the touch, and he moved it farther from the fire.

"Need some more wood at this rate," he said. "Get some in when the rain eases. Let it dry off in here for a while."

As he sat again the dizziness returned, making him bite his lip, putting his hand to his forehead.

"You okay?"

"Sure."

"I'm real tired, Ryan. Could we mebbe sleep awhile?"

"Should move on." The truth was that he was bone-weary, on the ragged edge of exhaustion. Nobody functioned well at that pitch of fatigue.

"Can't we..." she began.

"Yeah. Good a place as any. Recce at first light. Catch up on some sleep."

She knelt on her clothes, close by him, reaching out to touch him gently on the bare arm.

"Ryan?" she whispered.

"Yeah?"

"You know?"

"What?"

She drew closer, and he could almost taste her.

"You know, Ryan. Please." He didn't say anything, and Kate moved against his body, her arms around him, hands reaching. "Please."

Chapter Twenty-Four

When Ryan woke it was full dark outside the entrance to the cave. He could hear that the rain had stopped falling and the night was still. The fire had died away to a pile of glowing ashes that would need further nourishment if it was to see them through the night.

The sound of the river was louder than he remembered, and he guessed that the downpour would have raised its level.

Kate was still fast asleep, flat on her back, mouth open as she snored slightly. One arm was stretched above her head, the other lay under the pile of clothes that had provided them both with a covering. In the warm half-light from the dying fire, Ryan noticed for the first time that the young woman's nails were bitten down clear to the quick.

He sighed. His body felt drained, and as he glanced down at himself he saw that he was a mass of patched bruises, mostly fresh and purple, where the river had pounded him.

His wrist chron told him that it was still an hour shy of midnight. The pile of wood had diminished, and Ryan glanced again into the blackness beyond. Lying warm and naked by the side of Kate was a good feeling and wasn't one that he wanted to disturb.

But that had been the last pyrotab.

Ryan was as good a backwoods survival expert as any ever born, but not even he could conjure fire from nothing. J.B. had once demonstrated, back on War wag One, that it was possible to start a fire from *almost* nothing.

But it had involved a small bow and a pile of carefully tended tinder and sawdust and the right kinds of wood. The Armorer had labored for a good quarter hour, scraping away until sweat burst from his forehead, drilling until the small hole began to show a tiny thread of dark smoke. Then it had been an inelegant struggle on hands and knees, blowing to make the scorched wood glow, dropping a few pinches of the sawdust until it finally caught.

Ryan grinned to himself at the memory of the ironic cheer that had greeted J.B.'s achievement. The Trader had remarked dryly that it reminded him of watching a frog trying to shit a bowling ball.

In the cold and damp Ryan recognized the utter impossibility of trying to repeat the Armorer's laborious achievement.

Very slowly he eased himself sideways, not disturbing the sleeping woman. He hauled on his pants and the crumpled T-shirt, picked up the SIG-Sauer and moved to the mouth of the cave.

It was a fine night, the stars pin sharp and diamond bright. The moon was almost hidden behind the peaks

opposite, filling half the valley with a clear, cold light.
The river had risen but was running steadily, not
showing any signs of coming higher up and threatening their hiding place.

It was freezing hard, and Ryan's bare feet began to
feel cold as he moved slowly over the bank of icy
shingle.

He reached the mountain of driftwood and paused
again, taking a long slow look around him. Down toward the sulfur mines he could see reflected lights and
a narrow plume of smoke rising steadily into the
windless sky.

His eye was caught by a flicker of movement, way
across the far side of the valley, high up on the slope
of the hill. Ryan stared intently into the shadowed
blackness, using the old hunter's trick of looking
slightly to one side. But the movement wasn't repeated and he decided that it must have been an animal on an isolated track.

Maybe a goat.

Maybe not a goat.

THE FIRE RESPONDED eagerly to fresh wood, blazing
up brightly, the flames throwing capering shadows
across the hewn walls and the low roof. Kate stirred at
the brightness, rolling on her side, muttering inaudi-
bly, not waking.

Ryan slipped under the covers, his own body cold
from the night air. But the woman was hot, her
shoulders and back moist with perspiration.

He pressed against her, one arm going across her shoulders. His knees fitted comfortably behind hers, her buttocks warm against his groin, snug as two spoons in a drawer.

Eventually Ryan slept again.

"FIRST LIGHT," Kate announced.

Ryan blinked his eye open, feeling infinitely better and stronger than when he'd fallen asleep the previous evening. He stretched and looked around the cave. The fire had crumbled again into glowing embers, a pale haze of gray smoke hanging above it.

"Could do with something to eat," he said, unable to restrain a yawn.

"What?"

"Some quick-fried back bacon, with a mess of hash browns and four eggs."

"How do you like your eggs, Ryan?" she asked.

"Anyway they come."

"Anything else?"

He considered the question. "Mebbe a couple of slices of fresh-baked bread with salted butter. Some strawberry preserve."

"Coffee?"

"Sure. Hot, and strong enough to float a steel wrench."

"Coming right up, sir." Kate was wearing only a skimpy shirt and she curtsied to him, mimicking the gaudy sluts in frontier villes. "And is there anything else you want?"

Ryan didn't answer, standing up and starting to get dressed with his usual quiet, unhurried efficiency. The morning looked bright and clear, though all the rocks he could see outside were white with frost.

Kate tried again. "What do we do today, Ryan?"

"I try and get inside the mines. Try and find my son. Try and get out alive and then get the dark night out of this place."

"How about me?"

He knelt to lace the steel-toed combat boots, not even looking up at the young woman. "You?"

"Sure. What about me? You just going to leave me here?"

Ryan tested the knot before straightening and finally facing Kate. "You walk your road and I'll walk mine. You understand?"

"Yeah. You leave me to die."

"I never asked you to come. You and Cody both. But you'd have been chilled for sure anyway."

"So you gave me a day!" She put her hands on her hips and laughed bitterly. "Thanks a lot, Ryan. Big friend."

"That's the way it is."

"Take me."

"I don't have the time."

"Please."

"Time's wasting. Early morning's good to get in. Everyone's tired. Probably a shift change. Got to move, now."

Kate took a half step toward him, and Ryan wondered for a moment whether she'd try to threaten him.
Or make him some kind of an offer that she hoped
he'd find difficult to refuse.

She did neither. She simply let her arms drop to her
sides, head hanging, eyes down at her feet. Ryan
watched her, still wary in case she went for her knife.

"You got no choice, Ryan," she said flatly, not
looking up.

"How's that?"

"I'm coming anyway. You can't stop me. And if
you try, then I'll betray you to the Russkie." He was
moving toward her, but she hadn't noticed. "You let
me die, and not even spit to save me, I'll let you—"

She was cut off by a roundhouse slap along the side
of the jaw that sent her flying across the cave, feet
dancing for balance, finally falling just short of the
warm ashes of the fire.

"I'm sorry," Ryan said quietly.

"Bastard."

"You made a real mistake, Kate. Closed off all the
doors for yourself." His hand went for the hilt of his
panga.

She sat up, rubbing her fingers over swollen lips,
bringing them away and staring at the smear of crimson. "Didn't mean it," she muttered. "Wouldn't turn
my coat for you."

"Too late." His eye was like flint and his lips were
a chiseled line of anger.

"No," she said disbelievingly.

"You have to understand this, Kate," Ryan explained patiently, as though she were a fractious five-year-old child. "There are lines you don't cross. My son is probably in those mines, and you're my main threat at this moment."

The cleaver was out, gripped firmly, and he was close to her. One foot was in front of the other, like an antique print of a samurai swordsman, poised to strike the lethal blow.

"I wouldn't..."

He shook his head. "It doesn't matter anymore. Don't you see that, Kate? Words are spilled. Can't put them back."

"Oh, Judas..." Kate began to cry, head lowered onto the thin arms, her cropped hair as black as jet. Her nape was exposed, giving him the perfect killing opportunity.

He raised the blade, muscles tightening in his forearm.

"I know my way all around the inside of the yellow mines."

Ryan eased his breath out, whistling softly between his teeth. "You do?"

Kate didn't move, remaining in a frozen, huddled ball. "Yeah."

The eighteen-inch blade slithered into the soft leather of its scabbard. Ryan touched her on the back of the neck, feeling her flinch.

"Get up and dress. We got places to go."

"You believe me?"

"If I didn't believe you, then . . ." He allowed the sentence to fade away into the stillness.

JUST ABOVE THE FLOOD MARK of the river, there was a straggling line of stunted pines, their tops weighted down with snow. Ryan led the way through them, pausing every few yards to look around, making sure there were no sec guards patrolling this far from the main entrance to the mines.

The slopes above them were deserted, though he spotted a fall of jagged rock that looked fresh, the hillside showing a bright scar.

Ryan moved fast, only glancing over his shoulder every now and again to make sure that the young woman was still keeping up with him. It was bitterly cold, but in dry clothes, well protected, it was little hardship.

He called a halt as the gorge doglegged to the right. "Wait here while I recce." His breath billowed out around his mouth and nose in a white plume.

"Sure. You'll come back, Ryan?"

"Do fishes shit in the sea? Yeah, I'll be back. No more than ten minutes."

He was as good as his word.

The belt of trees thickened, spreading to a hundred feet wide, over a shallow bank of rocks and dirt. Keeping well within the shadowed depths, Ryan picked his way forward until he could see the scene of busy activity that was Gregori Zimyanin's sulfur mines.

He collected Kate, and the two of them crouched among the brush, as close as they could safely get to the river without being spotted.

There was a narrow-gauge railway line, with a small locomotive chugging busily up and down, towing a row of rusted iron trucks behind it. Beyond that were a number of huts of various sizes, with people milling about outside them.

At that distance it wasn't possible to make out any details, but Ryan could clearly see the guards, each with the distinctive silver circle on his cap.

There were at least fifty of them, all carrying blasters.

"We'll never get in there," Kate whispered, even though the river lay between them and the mine, and the nearest guard was at least two hundred yards away.

Ryan didn't answer, his fighting brain working in high gear, weighing options and opportunities.

There was one enormous factor in their favor.

"All the workers look about the same," he said. "No kind of uniform. Just a collection of ragged-ass people."

"Like you and me," she said, smiling for the first time since they left the cave.

"Right. Just like you and me."

The river was about fifteen feet wide at that point, but it ran fast and deep.

Ryan looked around again, judging the profile of the land, seeking dead ground. "You realize that nobody's looking this way," he said. "No reason for them to bother. Be risky, but we can do it."

Chapter Twenty-Five

The line of trees grew thinner as Ryan picked the way between the stunted, twisted trunks. He'd seen enough plant malformation near hot spots throughout Deathlands to recognize the effects of pollution on the pines. Branches had withered and died, and many of the needles were a sickly yellow color and brushed off against their clothes as he and Kate moved deeper into the heart of the valley.

But there was still enough cover to pass the main workings without being observed.

Once Kate tripped and rolled toward the foaming water, only stopping herself by a desperate grab at a tangle of dead roots. Some snapped under her weight, some held.

"Keep moving," Ryan urged. "Got to get across as quick as we can."

The river was narrowing, but it was also moving more quietly, showing ominously deep swirls of green over some of the bigger boulders.

Not far ahead, Ryan finally saw clearly what he'd only glimpsed from their earlier vantage point. At some time, probably a century or so ago, the railway had stretched farther up the canyon. Then, during the dark years after the long winters, the river had carried on its process of erosion and had undercut the iron rails. There'd been a bridge, a narrow, wooden pontoon that crossed the rapids, but that had fallen, leaving a solid tangle of rusted metal and rotting, mangled timbers.

"There," Ryan said.

Kate sighed. "I won't bother saying no, Ryan. You sure this is the best way?"

"It's the only way."

IT WAS A TIME of maximum danger. They moved along under the shelter of the trees, aware of the cliffs closing in on their right. By the time they reached the ruined bridge, the line of pines had diminished. But from there it was possible to see farther along the canyon.

The river was no wider, but it was moving faster, whirling around jagged rocks that stuck their fangs above the white foam. And the valley narrowed until either side glistened with black ice.

"Here or nowhere," Ryan said, having to raise his voice above the noise of the torrent.

"But they can still see us from back there. What if someone looks around when we're halfway across? What then, Ryan?"

"Then it'll be swimming time again."

He went first.

The Trader had always warned that to move too fast was to draw attention to yourself.

Ryan eased out of the trees, keeping himself hunched and small, walking straight to the end of the bridge, picking his way over the nest of warped rails. He quickly reached a point where he was out of sight of the sec guards.

"Now," he called, beckoning for Kate to come and join him.

She obeyed his instructions, keeping low, making sure she didn't stumble on the icy rocks, not turning her face toward the mine.

When the young woman was concealed among the jumble of splintered timber, Ryan saw how pale she was.

"You making it?"

"Sure."

He stared at her. "You don't look it. Fall off and someone'll likely spot it. That way we both get chilled. Ask you again. You making it?"

"Starving hungry, Ryan. Murder for a bowl of pork stew."

"Hell, I know that. But can you make it over to there?" He pointed to the fragile spiderweb of corrosion and rust that dipped low over the river.

"You going to cut my throat if I can't?"

Ryan didn't answer, biting his lip in barely suppressed anger.

Kate sniffed and wiped her nose on her sleeve. "Let me go first. If I fall in then they won't see you and you can still get out. Find another way into the mines to save your little boy. I'll go first."

Ryan considered that. What the young woman said was true, and it took away any worries about having to chill her.

"Yeah." He nodded.

TWICE HE THOUGHT she'd lost it. Once in the middle her weight brought the old rails dropping within inches of the water. Her legs were crossed over the top of the reddened iron, thick-coated in ice, and she was finding it difficult to make any progress toward the far side.

It crossed Ryan's mind to put a 9 mm round through her skull. The corpse would float away from the sec men, and all of the noise would be effectively muffled by the SIG-Sauer's built-in baffle silencer.

But Kate kept control, waited a few moments, shepherding her strength. Then she kicked and wriggled toward the farther shore.

She was within easy spitting distance when she lost her grip with her fingers, dropping head-down, only her feet keeping her from the river and from death.

"Fireblast!" Ryan exclaimed.

Her dark hair was splashed with the spray of the raging water, her face away from Ryan. He could see her breathing hard, then almost feel the pain in the muscles as she swung herself up and forward, fingers groping for a tenuous hold.

Moments later she was off the makeshift bridge, lying flat on her stomach among the heaped stones on the far side of the river.

"Real ace on the line, lady," Ryan said quietly.

HE WAS ACROSS FAST and easy, with only a single moment of danger.

Ryan was heavier than the girl, and the rails dipped far more under his weight.

He could feel the iron straining and hear some of the main timbers creaking. Ryan had chosen the same way of getting over, hanging froglike, sliding with crossed feet and gloved hands.

Despite his strength, there was nothing he could do as he felt himself slipping lower.

The roar of the river filled his ears, and his skull seemed to swell with the pressure and the strain. He relaxed his head backward and immediately gulped in a mouthful of freezing green water. It ran into his nose and down into his lungs, nearly choking him, but he fought it and lifted his head again, clear of the torrent.

Kate was frantically beckoning to him from her hiding place, and he nearly managed a smile at the irony of it—an irony that the young woman would never know. She was encouraging him, while he'd been prepared to put a bullet into her brain when their positions had been reversed.

"So it goes," he muttered.

He snaked over the last few feet and dropped down to safety.

"They see us?"

Ryan shook his head, showering her with drops of icy water. "No. Reckon we'd have heard it by now if they had."

THE TIMING WAS RIGHT. The changing over of the night and day shifts was taking place and it was, inevitably, a period of near chaos.

One lot of workers, split into a dozen or more sections, was gut-weary, covered in stinking yellow mud, and frozen. The replacement shift had only just been roused, grudgingly, from their bunks in the packed, lousy dormitories. They were still half asleep, stumbling into one another, snapping like line-camp curs.

Both groups were hungry.

Zimyanin had altered the arrangements to try to improve efficiency, calculating that the same heating of gruel could suffice for both the finishing and the starting sections of slave workers. Now great metal vats were bubbling over smoky fires, near long tables. Dishes and spoons were heaped on the cold, snow-layered dirt. Filthy baskets contained hunks of bread.

The turnover in laborers was so great that the Russian had never bothered to try to instigate any system of name checks or rotas. There was a count at the beginning and end of each shift, but he wasn't all that concerned if the numbers didn't match.

Some died every day, their bodies tipped into worked-out shafts or heaved into the river, depending on where they were when life released its frail hold on them.

Zimyanin also was aware that every now and again one or two of his captives would slip away from him. There was no wire fence, no electric arc lights and no armed men scouring the country around. He knew the land for miles around his canyon.

"They may run, but they will not be able to eat" was his catchphrase.

"MUST TAKE CARE not to get in the same working group as the one you ran from," Ryan warned.

"Nobody knows anyone else," she said, her teeth chattering with cold.

"How many in a gang?"

Kate shook her head. "Can't say. Varies a lot. Mebbe fifteen or twenty. Mebbe more. One or two were lifted from the same place, and they stick together. Some triple crazies, Ryan."

"What way?"

"You'll see."

They were within less than forty paces of the nearest group of workers. All were dressed in a mix of furs and rags, and Ryan's only worry was that he might stand out as being dressed too well. The guards all stood with their own sections, watchful, holding their rifles at the port, ready for any trouble.

There was no sign of Dean, though Ryan kept looking for him. He saw mainly adults, with hardly anyone under top teens.

The sky had darkened and a few flakes of snow were beginning to drift down into the sheltered valley, carried on a leaden northerly wind.

"You got ice all over your face and hair," Kate said, gently touching his stubbled skin with a gloved finger.

Ryan was aware of the way the river water had begun to freeze in his long black hair, tangling into tiny balls of ice. He'd cleared his nostrils, but there was a patina of ice around his cheeks and down over his prominent chin.

"What do we do now?" she asked.

"Food serving's going on. Lot nearest us hasn't eaten yet. Everyone's looking the other way."

"Just walk up and join in?" she asked disbelieving. "What if the sec men see us?"

"They won't."

"Sure?"

"Yeah, sure."

Kate glanced around, then reached up and quickly kissed him on the lips. "I believe you, Ryan. Don't know why, but I do."

"That's good. Then let's do it."

His hand was gripping the holstered blaster, now hidden under the long coat.

"Now?"

"Why not?"

Chapter Twenty-Six

Krysty Wroth finished off the last of the smoked-ham-and-potato pie, wiping her mouth with the linen napkin. She placed knife and fork neatly together on the plate, pushing it to the middle of the table.

"Your turn to wash up this morning, Jak."

He grinned at her. "Want coffee? Put on stove ready. Doc?"

"Please. A steaming brew of finest java would bring tears to the eyes of a plaster saint and make an old man very happy."

"Where's Christina?" Krysty asked.

Jak was clearing the table, the morning sun lancing through the thin blue curtains on the eastern wall of the cabin, turning his white hair to the star flare of magnesium brightness.

"Stayed bed. Sick."

"Nothing serious? I'll go take a look if you like."

He shook his head, glancing away from her, betraying an unusual nervousness. "Thanks. No. Christina's all right. Been sick some mornings."

"Does this nausea only set its teeth to her intestines in the morning?" Doc reached out for another spoonful of the homemade peach preserve.

"Yeah. Morning."

"Really." Doc looked across, catching Krysty's green eyes, dropping a slow wink to her. "Really?"

Jak paused in the doorway, carrying a loaded tray of dirty crockery and cutlery.

"Got something to say, grinning old fart?"

Doc cackled. "Damned fine peach preserve, this." He held it under his hooked nose, inhaling, eyes closed. "Wonderful. Nectar. Did I ever tell you I met a man who rode with Kit Carson when the red-eyed son of a bitch burned out the Navaho peach orchards in Canyon de Chelly?"

Jak nodded. "Yeah. Told me. Get coffee."

He walked through into the cool, airy kitchen, pushing the door behind him with his heel.

Krysty stood and walked to the window, the heels of her dark blue boots clicking on the floor. "Sick in the mornings. You're a doctor. What do you think, huh?"

"My dear Miss Wroth..." He placed his hand over his heart and bowed, nearly spilling preserve on the cloth. "I am a Doctor of Science from the great and sadly missed University of Oxford in England. Oh, my dear... The sun on the quadrangle at Balliol. The bells at midsummer from the golden towers. The warm, green-muffled Cumnor Hills."

"Doc!"

"Sorry, Krysty. Yes, I'm sure that the lady in question is with child. I'm delighted for both of them, of course."

"Little Jak, going to be a father. Gaia, how I wish..." She shook her head. "Wonder how J.B. and Mildred are doing on their morning jackrabbit hunt?"

"I heard them leave around dawn. Good that they've found each other, isn't it?"

Krysty turned, and her face was carved from marble. "Sure is. Seems like everyone's finding someone. Me, I just keep on losing someone, Doc."

"How about sitting a spell on the porch and enjoying this fine morning?"

She nodded slowly. "It's not like me, is it, Doc? Getting all antsy about Ryan?"

He joined her by the window, looking out across the rolling New Mexico countryside. "The saddest news I have ever learned, my dear, is that time can heal *some* of the pain. But it can never heal it all. Let's go outside."

JAK HAD GONE IN to join Christina, taking her a cup of fresh coffee. Doc and Krysty sat together on the swing seat, rocking very gently, back and forth.

In the corral, a couple of foals were running together, kicking up their heels, butting each other on the flanks.

A quarter mile away, on the edge of a draw, some wild turkeys wandered up and down, pecking idly at the dust.

"I miss Emily still," Doc said suddenly.

"I know that."

"If Ryan was never to return—though I am certain sure he will—then you have had the chance to bid him a fond farewell and tell him how you care for him and what he means to you. I never had that chance."

Krysty nodded, glancing across, not surprised to see a single crystal tear coursing down the old man's wrinkled cheek. "I know, Doc."

"I wish... By the three Kennedys, how I wish it! That I could have that last morning over again. Just to tell her how I loved her. But I was torn away from her and from my age, untimely plucked. I would have told her to live her life well without me, had I known all."

"What happened to your wife and the children, Doc? You never said. Did you find out?"

The silence stretched on. The wind blew straight and true from the northwest, making the vanes of the wind pump spin. Krysty didn't look to her side, staring straight ahead to the farthest edge of the distant horizon, where she detected a tiny pillar of dust. It gave her a passing moment of unease, but her mind was locked onto Doc and she brushed the fragmentary worry away.

"I was able to find out." His voice was as grim as ice upon a blurred tombstone.

"And?"

"They died, Krysty. All died."

"When?"

Doc slurped at his coffee, noisily blowing his nose on the familiar swallow's-eye kerchief. "I do believe that I would greatly appreciate a change of subject, my dear.''

"Sure.''

"Perhaps we might consider this place.''

Krysty was surprised. "How's that, Doc?''

"Good land. Clean water. Plenty of space to grow and spread.''

"I don't get it. You saying you're thinking of staying here?''

"Not just me.''

"J.B. and Mildred?'' Krysty finished her coffee and placed the mug on the white scrubbed planks of the porch.

"All of us, my dear.''

"Oh.''

"I know that you and Ryan have been seeking a promised land, a Shangri-la, a place without fear or darkness where a man and woman could wed and bring up their children. A place—'' he waved his gnarled hand at the horizon ''—that is not unlike this place here.''

Krysty sighed. "Sure we want to settle. One day. But this... Oh, Gaia!'' She looked away from the old man. "I'd greatly appreciate a change of subject, if you don't mind, Doc.''

"Of course.''

But neither of them could come up with anything particular to talk about.

In the far distance a rising wind blew away the column of dust that had briefly attracted the attention of Krysty Wroth.

Chapter Twenty-Seven

Some of the most dangerous adventures that Ryan had ever been involved in had turned out to be surprisingly easy and safe.

The moments between leaving the cover of the snow-roofed buildings and actually joining one of the working parties were among the most hazardous of his entire life.

Feet crunching on the muddy ice, faces down, shoulders hunched, they stepped out as if they had the right to be there. Ryan had the deep concern that he might suddenly bump into Major-Commissar Gregori Zimyanin, who would immediately recognize him from the eye patch.

He'd taken off his long white scarf and knotted the soft silk three times over the top of his head, covering as much of his upper face as possible. His turned-up collar concealed his mouth.

Ryan knew that it was ridiculous to expect every one of the throng of sec men to keep staring stonily away from them.

Several glanced around, peripheral vision caught by the movement. But all they saw was a couple of the slave workers joining their shift. None of them was close enough to give them a kick or a curse.

There were about eighteen huddled figures in the group they'd tailed onto. At a first hasty look, Ryan noted that about four of them appeared to be female, a slightly higher proportion than in some of the other work gangs he'd watched.

Only one of them took any notice.

An older man, so stooped he was almost a hunchback, turned his head toward the strangers, eyes glowing malevolently in the parchment face.

"You're not with us," he hissed.

"Guards beat anyone talking," Kate warned angrily.

"I'll tell them you aren't in our unit. Then they'll shoot you."

"No, they won't." The conversation was in a suppressed, angry whisper.

"Will."

"Won't. We got sent to work with your gang."

"Who sent you?"

Ryan pushed his face close to the man. "We got sent by the Russkie. You want to argue, then go argue with Zimyanin."

"No."

"I'll come with you."

"No, no."

Ryan smiled, talking without moving his lips. "Then keep your mouth shut. If the Russkie doesn't chill you, then I will."

There was a flurry of movement near the front and their shift started to shuffle forward. Ryan looked queryingly at Kate, who lifted her fingers to her mouth, miming eating. He nodded. Ryan was ravenous hungry, regardless of what was on offer.

They were only allowed one helping of food each. Risking drawing attention to himself, Ryan snatched a second piece of bread. The man who was ladling out the gruel caught the movement and opened his mouth to complain. He closed it again when Ryan bared his teeth in a threatening smile and offered him a clenched fist.

The old man with the stooped back also saw what happened. "Get us all flogged," he snarled at Ryan.

A whistle blew, interrupting the argument. Ryan had already decided that he might have to draw his flensing knife and stab the man through the heart to silence him.

A guard had a clipboard, and he was shouting out where each group had to go. That was how Ryan and Kate found that they were in Work Unit Twenty-five.

"Shaft Four. Level Six!"

There was a groan, quickly stifled. Kate had joined in and Ryan looked across at her.

"Bad news?" he whispered.

"Shaft Four's one where they get a lot of slides and falls. Level Six is down the bottom, deep as you can go."

RYAN WAS RELIEVED to find that there didn't seem to be any sec men specifically attached to any of the units, so nobody would recognize them as illegal newcomers.

And once they were under cover, in one of the shafts, the guards had fixed posts, keeping an eye on activity in their own narrow area.

All they had to do was follow their leader, which, for Work Unit Twenty-five wasn't too difficult as their leader was six and a half feet tall, with a mane of white hair and a flowing beard like fresh-fallen snow. Ryan wondered how the man, who was referred to by the others as Elder Bluffield, managed to keep himself so clean when everyone else was filthy dirty.

Part of the answer was that he took special care of himself and his clothes, while the others helped him at every climb and turn, showing him such unusual respect that Ryan was even more puzzled.

As they reached the main opening down to the next level, Ryan noticed a second working party trudging toward them from a side passage. The light was far from good, but he thought he'd caught a glimpse of a small figure that looked familiar.

A blow in the kidneys from the butt of an M-16 sent him to his knees, gasping for breath, a fiery pain ripping through his body.

''Be pissing blood for a week if you stop and stare again, shithead,'' the unnoticed sec man said.

By the time Ryan had gotten up and was able to breathe again, the other group had vanished deeper into the mine.

"YOU ALL RIGHT?"

Ryan nodded, waiting at the top of the slippery wooden ladder to climb down into the yellow depths toward Level Six.

"Might piss blood, like he said."

"You okay to work?"

From behind and above them one of the guards shouted at her. "Shut your fucking mouth, slag! Or come here and I'll give you something to shut it."

Kate ignored him.

By now everyone on the working gang knew that they had two new members. Ryan had seen the beckoning fingers of the elder, calling the venomous hunchback to his side, watched the whispered conversation and heard the name of Zimyanin mentioned twice.

But nothing more had been said or done by anyone in Unit Twenty-five.

THEY WERE ALLOWED only minimal breaks during the long working shift. During one of them Ryan sat slumped against a wall of black rock, streaming with icy water. He was soaked through, covered in stinking yellow mud, so tired he felt ready to drop.

"This is the nearest I ever want to get to hell," he said quietly to Kate.

The only good thing about laboring on Level Six was that there weren't many guards around. Why should there be? When you were right at the bottom of the world, there was nowhere else for anyone to go.

The rest of the group sat together in a tight, huddled circle, centered on the imposing figure of Elder Bluffield. Ryan was relieved to see that his pristine perfection was marred by patches of wet and smears of sulfur.

Nobody had spoken to them, and they'd only learned what work was expected by watching the others. There were eighteen, including the elder, and six were women, four of them relatively young.

Most wore gloves, but a couple dug without. Ryan nudged Kate. "Seen the hands of the women?"

"No."

"Look at them when you get a chance."

"Why?"

"They've all lost three fingers from the left hand."

"What?"

"Kept the first finger and thumb. Every single woman here."

"Why?"

Ryan shrugged. "Go ask Bluffield."

"Maybe I will."

He held her arm. "Not now. Now we work, wait and watch. I don't want anything to happen that'll bring guards down on us."

"Sure. How's your back from the bastard with the blaster?"

"I've pissed and I didn't see no blood." Ryan hesitated, automatically correcting himself as though Krysty had been standing at his shoulder. "I mean I didn't see *any* blood."

THE REST OF THE DAY crept by. Gradually Ryan slipped into the repetitive pattern of grinding labor, trying to get by doing as little as possible, without bringing trouble down on himself or Kate.

He'd lost track of just how deep under the mountain they were working. To reach Level Six had meant a number of steep ladders, each of them at least twenty feet long, some nearer fifty feet. And there were steep, twisting tunnels between each level. Ryan's guess was that they were at least five hundred feet deep.

They'd been issued shovels, picks and buckets. There was a manual hoist, with ropes and pulleys, bearing a large iron caldron. It took eighteen heaped buckets of earth and ore to fill it.

From the moment they climbed down the first ladder, Ryan and Kate were never dry. The sides of the shafts ran with yellow-brown water, as cold as charity. And at the bottom, on Level Six, it lay in a sullen pool, nearly two feet deep in places.

The shift was nearly ended before any of the others spoke to them. One of the younger women stumbled and splashed toward them. She had on black rubber boots, but the mud slopped ceaselessly over their tops.

"You two strangers."

"What?" Ryan held his shovel defensively across his chest.

"Elder Bluffield wants to talk with you."

"We don't want to talk to him."

"How's that?" A note of surprise was evident in her voice. She looked back over her mud-caked shoulder, toward the rest of the group.

"Tell him we'll think about it. Mebbe we'll talk to him. Mebbe not."

Chapter Twenty-Eight

At the end of the day there was still no sort of security check on them. As long as a reasonable amount of sulfur was produced and not too many people died, then everyone seemed to be happy.

"We get a chance to wash?" Ryan asked as they walked slowly toward the huts that provided them with their sleeping accommodation.

"Sure. You get a couple of minutes with a kind of trough of cold water. That's it."

He wiped his hand over his forehead, looking at the golden scum that came away.

"Better than nothing."

The huts contained bunks, one above the other, partitioned off to accommodate a number of disparate groups. For Work Unit Twenty-five there was an area of about one hundred and fifty square feet, with a small anteroom for washing and for other bodily functions. The latter was a round hole in the floor that opened onto a narrow stream.

Ryan and Kate took a pair of empty bunks nearest the door.

The rest of the group was huddled together at the opposite end of the room, gathered around Elder

Bluffield. As soon as they'd been locked into the rusting hut, two of the women had helped the older man to undress, taking his soiled clothing to wash, dressing him in clean trousers and shirt.

Ryan and the young woman sat together on the top bunk, legs swinging, watching their breath as it steamed out into the freezing air.

"Russkie doesn't look after his workers, does he?" Kate said.

"Why should he? Plenty more out there where this lot came from. What's the longest you heard of anyone surviving in the mines?"

She considered for a few moments. "One skinny kid on—think it was Seventeen—reckoned he'd been here a full year. Could've been lying, though."

Ryan looked up. "Here we go," he muttered.

The same young woman who'd spoken briefly to them earlier was approaching.

"Elder'll see you now." Her voice was a cracked, thin little whine.

"I can see him from here," Ryan replied.

"Come talk to him."

He leaned down, making her take a stumbling step backward. "If that old prick wants to speak to us, then he can come all the way over here. Go tell him that, will you?"

"Sure. Sure, mister, but he won't." She turned on her heel and walked the few short feet to where the rest of the group was waiting.

"You have to be so shit angry?" Kate whispered.

"I've seen these 'elders' before. Know them. Think the sun shines out of their asses and they piss pure silver."

"Could betray us."

"More likely to leave us alone if they're frightened of us. A little terror buys a lot of friendship."

The discussion was ended.

Elder Bluffield swept across the room, his flock of acolytes behind him. Ryan thought that all he needed was a shepherd's crook and the old man would have looked like one of the paintings of the prophets in old Bible pix.

"You are not of our group." The voice was booming, rich and deep.

"You spotted it, huh?"

The elder's hair and beard were washed, glistening damply. His eyes were narrow, close together, and Ryan guessed he was shortsighted. He was peering at the two on the upper bunk with a strained expression that made him resemble a constipated goat.

"Why have you joined our closed group? Where have you come from?"

"Come from out there."

"I believe that you have escaped."

Ryan grinned. "Sure. We've escaped and we're eccentric, wealthy barons from the sunshine west. We just love twelve hours digging in yellow crap while we starve and freeze."

"Unless you obey our rules, then we shall report you."

This was obviously the biggest ace on the line. Elder Bluffield clearly expected Ryan and Kate to fall to
the floor in shock and dismay.

"Who to?" Ryan said quietly.

"To the Russkie."

Ryan nodded and slipped from the bunk to the
floor, where he stared at the old man. "You got
something right, Elder. We don't belong here. We've
been put here. So, think about reporting us. Who to?
To the...what did you call him? The 'Russkie,' wasn't
it?"

"Yes, it was," he replied, trying to gather his fading dignity around him like a torn bathrobe.

"The Russkie. That wouldn't be Major-Commissar
Gregori Zimyanin, would it? Don't think he'd take to
the name of 'Russkie,' do you, Kate?"

"Think he could get angered. We know what angered means, don't we, Elder? We've seen it. Haven't
we, Elder Bluffield?"

"Yes, yes we have. You mean that . . . Zimyanin has
placed you here?"

Kate wasn't finished. Joining Ryan on the floor, she
poked out a finger at the old man, the ragged, gnawed
nail snagging on the cloth of his jacket. "Seen them
chained up to die, Elder? Just for talking out of line a
little. Cuffed up under the rubbish chutes so everyone
in the mine pisses and shits all over them. For stealing
a blanket, wasn't it?"

"It was, it was."

Ryan took over again. "So, you and your followers think triple hard about going to report us being here, won't you?"

Bluffield nodded, the corner of his mouth working in a nervous tic. "Silent as a grave, my friend. Sorry to have troubled you."

Ryan knew men, saw that he'd slightly misjudged this one. The elder was cowed for now, but there was a streak of resentment in his face and hatred in the narrow eyes. It would be wise to watch their backs while around Elder Bluffield.

"What do you call your group?" Ryan asked him.

"We are a small religious order."

"Yeah?"

The old man stretched a couple of inches in height, feeling on safer ground. "I was once a deacon in the Brothers of Perpetual Waiting. But there was a rift, and I became a warden with the Warriors of the Bright Lamp. After a quarrel over dogma I left and took my own apostles with me and formed the Greeters of the Third Coming."

There was a muttered chorus of "Amens" and "Hallelujahs" from his followers.

"How come you all finished up in here?" Ryan asked, genuinely interested in the scope and scale of the Russian's operation.

"We were at prayer," the oldest of the women told him, holding her mutilated hand above her head in what looked like a practiced gesture.

"I still recount it, Sister Ruth," Bluffield said sternly.

"Keep it short," Ryan warned.

"We were at one of our meetings, locked together in our mission house near to what was once Kansas City, Kansas. Naked in the eyes of our Savior, cleaving together, one to another."

Kate nudged Ryan, face puzzled. He leaned down and put his mouth to her ear, whispering softly, "Means they were fucking like rabbits."

Bluffield half heard him, but carried on. "Next thing there's dead-eyed sons of bastards with carbines taking off to some infernal kind of sleep wag, and when we woke up we were in this frozen Hades."

"How long ago?"

"Twenty-two days. One of our sisters and one of our brothers have been enfolded into the bosom of our blessed Savior."

"You mean they got chilled?"

Bluffield nodded.

"How about those missing fingers?" He pointed at the nearest of the young women, who tried to hide her left hand behind her back.

"Our way."

Ryan's eyes flashed with a sudden, flaring anger, something that he generally managed to keep buried and safe, but which occasionally would slide out and reveal itself.

"Your way, Elder?"

"They sacrifice their fingers to me…to us, as a way of showing their love, loyalty and readiness."

"Why?"

"It was ever so."

Almost like a separate living organism, Ryan's right hand was creeping around toward the small of his back where the long cleaver was sheathed. Kate saw the movement and touched him on the arm, warning him. He looked at her and for a moment the girl shuddered at the cold blankness she saw in his face. Then he took in a deep breath and nodded to her.

"Right," he said very quietly.

Bluffield was moving away, his flock opening like the Red Sea to let him through.

"Just as long as we understand each other, brother," he said, gluing on a smile that showed his broken front teeth and never got within a mile of his cold eyes.

"Not your brother. And *you* understand *me*. You better."

RYAN WAS BUSHED from the heavy labor, his shoulders and back feeling like they were filled with hot sand.

He had taken the top bunk, leaving Kate to quickly fall asleep on the bed beneath him, the two thin blankets tucked around her.

Before dropping into a dreamless darkness, Ryan squinted across the hut at the elder and his followers. There was a low-wattage bulb burning in the middle of the stained ceiling, and it gave enough light for him to see that they were having what looked like a prayer meeting.

Ryan was worried about Elder Bluffield. He wasn't the usual blowhard religious crazy, like so many others running their own splinter groups throughout Deathlands. This one had a backbone, and Ryan had pulled him down in front of his loyal followers.

Perhaps it might be possible to take the old man out during the shift tomorrow. There weren't many better places than the deep sulfur mines to arrange a terminal accident.

RYAN AWAKENED in the middle of the night. Pressure on his bladder sent him into the cramped alcove that served as toilet facilities. The iron door was half closed, and he pushed it behind him to bring a little privacy.

Outside, a hailstorm was blowing up, the granules of ice rattling noisily on the roof of the hut. Ryan figured that it had probably been the sound of the blizzard that had jerked him from sleep.

He finished urinating and buttoned up his pants, checking that the blaster and the panga were still secure. It wasn't until he turned around to go back to the sleeping quarters that he realized the door had swung shut.

He pulled at it, but it didn't move at all.

Through it, muffled and faint, he heard Kate suddenly begin to scream.

Chapter Twenty-Nine

There were only three screams, the last cut off short, as though someone had gagged the young woman, or knocked her unconscious.

Or chilled her.

The only illumination in the small room came through a tiny slit window high up, allowing the weakest of filtered light from outside.

Ryan drew the SIG-Sauer and looked quickly around him, seeing what options there were.

"Not many," he said grimly.

The door was iron, hanging on rusting hinges, with a simple bar lock. Someone on the other side must have slipped it, intending to keep him in there while they did what they wanted to Kate.

"Don't worry," a voice called through the door. "Stay quiet, brother, and it'll be quickly over and then she'll have paid the elder the due price of respect."

Ryan didn't waste breath on replying.

The red killing mist had swept down over his eye, filling his brain, and he fought against it, looking carefully at the door as he recovered something of his combat composure.

The room was so small that he could lean against the wall opposite the closed door. He'd taken the usual precaution of sleeping fully clothed, including the steel-tipped boots.

Ryan braced himself against the wall, powering both feet into a devastating kick at the door. The hinges crumbled into shards of orange rust, and the door crashed open.

It gave way so easily that Ryan slipped and fell, nearly dropping the blaster into the gaping shithole. By the time he recovered, the elder's flock had a few moments to try to recover their composure.

But as he stepped into the sleeping quarters, Ryan realized that they could have had most of eternity and still not managed to recover. They stood in a frozen tableau, with Kate at their center.

She was spread-eagled on one of the top bunks, tied by wrists and ankles. Elder Bluffield stood by her left hand, holding a small open razor, its blade winking in the glow of the overhead lamp.

He was gripping the young woman's left hand, forcing her to open her fingers.

Ryan waved the gaping muzzle of the 9 mm automatic at them, seeing nobody else seemed to be armed at all.

"This has a silencer, so nobody beyond these four walls'll hear a sound. But you'll all be dying. Starting with you, Elder. Cut her free with that blade, and be real careful. If I see any blood, I start blowing holes in stomachs."

"If the guards come they'll chill us all," squeaked a tiny man with a weathered face.

"Make the wrong move and *I'll* fucking chill you all," Ryan said, calm and quiet.

"Let this happen, brother, and we can all live and work as one." Bluffield nodded like a child's puppet.

Ryan shook his head in disbelief. "You are about the sickest triple stupe I ever did see. Just use that knife slow and cut the girl free."

Bluffield looked around at his followers. "Will nobody rid me of this troublesome man?" he asked. "None of you?"

"Living beats dying, Elder. Do it now."

Only the reality of having to conceal corpses or do a runner from the mines checked Ryan's finger on the trigger of the powerful blaster. To put a couple of rounds through the bearded old man's belly would have been a rich and genuine pleasure.

The razor moved toward Kate's neck, past the balled gag of cotton waste that forced her jaws apart, on to the cords around her wrists. The sharp steel breathed through the thin ropes and cut her free.

"And her ankles."

The young woman sat up, fingers frantically unknotting the gag. Her eyes were wide with shock, and there was a dark bruise on her right cheek.

"You know what these . . ." she began, but Ryan hushed her with a movement of the SIG-Sauer.

"I know."

Bluffield finished cutting her free and stood there, still holding the gleaming blade, not sure what to do with it.

"Off the bed and over here," Ryan ordered. "You're all right?"

It was a statement with only the barest hint of a question. Kate simply nodded and moved across the narrow room to join him.

"Now what?" the elder asked, struggling to retain a tattered vestige of authority and dignity.

And failing.

Ryan stepped closer to him, the muzzle of the automatic drilling in toward the center of the elegant white beard.

The slitted eyes became even more narrow, and a thread of spittle dangled from the parted lips.

"Put the razor down on the blanket. Then place your hands together in front, like you're praying. That's good."

"What are you going to do?"

Ryan beckoned to the youngest of the women who stood fearfully watching. "Here."

Elder Bluffield turned his head like a cornered rat. "We'll leave you alone. Won't do anything. Help you. Carry your shift for you."

"Shut the mouth. No, on second thought, you can open your mouth a little wider and lay your left hand on the blanket there."

"Why? What are..." The penny dropped and he moaned. "No."

"Pick up the razor, lady," Ryan ordered, "and do like the elder tells you. Come on, Reverend, you tell her what to do."

"No, no. I beg you to—"

He gagged as Ryan rammed the muzzle of the automatic between his lips. Blood coursed from his upper lip where the silencer tore the flesh, and two of his front teeth were snapped off at gum level.

There was a collective cry of distress from the watching group at their leader's suffering, which was only just beginning.

"Pick up the razor. Two of you men come across and hold the elder's hand real still. Don't want any mistakes here."

Nobody moved. Ryan moved his wrist slightly, making Bluffield's head wobble up and down, his eyes wider than silver dollars.

"I pull this trigger, and it'll take an hour just to scrape his brains off of the ceiling."

Kate cleared her throat, and Ryan glanced over his shoulder at her. She simply shrugged and said nothing.

Two of the older men came and reluctantly held the trembling hand, pinning it down to the bunk. Elder Bluffield tried to speak, but only a choking gargle came past the muzzle of the blaster, accompanied by a wider streak of blood that stained the immaculate white of the beard.

The girl picked up the razor and stared at it with a hypnotized fascination.

Ryan smiled at her, making her even more terrified. In the total stillness they all heard the pattering of liquid on the floor of the hut, and she glanced down at the spreading damp patch between her bare feet.

"Don't worry, sister. Soon be done. Show this sick-hearted bastard just what it feels like to make a small sacrifice. Cut deep and firm, just along the line of the knuckle there." He pointed with his left hand. "Make sure you get in close to the joint, or you'll have a real hard job trying to hack through bone with that razor."

"I can't do that."

"Sure you can. Elder Bluffield truly *wants* you to cut off three of the fingers from his left hand, don't you, Reverend? Just nod, or I'll blow the whole top of your head away."

The white head nodded slowly.

Ryan smiled again. "There you go, sister."

Bluffield passed out before she was even halfway through the second finger.

RYAN LAY BACK on his bunk and watched the clucking women as they gathered around their stricken leader, tearing up blankets and their own clothes to try to staunch the flow of blood and bandage his mutilated hand.

Kate was sleeping on the bunk below him, one arm thrown across her face as though she were trying to blank out the memory of what she'd seen.

Bluffield had recovered consciousness, biting on a wad of cloth to stifle his own moans. He ignored the efforts of his apostles to help him, keeping his narrow, amber eyes fixed on the man who had caused him the suffering.

Ryan stared back, expressionless, the blaster still drawn and ready in his right hand.

The elder suddenly snatched at the arm of one of his women and pulled her head down so that he could whisper something to her.

She listened, then nodded, tiptoeing across to Ryan's bunk.

"I have a message from the elder," she said, spitting out the words, keeping her eyes on the concrete floor.

"Yeah?"

"He says to tell you to look for the morrow, for no man knoweth what it will bring."

"Tell Elder Bluffield that I couldn't agree more."

Chapter Thirty

The yellowish eyes were open wide, protruding from their sockets as though someone had pushed at them from inside the skull. The whites were suffused with blood. The mouth was wide open, the lips purplish and swollen, the tongue thrust far out, blackened and engorged. The front of the white trousers still showed the thrusting erection, the area around the groin moist and stained.

The arms hung limply at the sides, though the palms were encrusted with dried blood, scarred with deep, raw gouges from the fingernails. More dark crimson had seeped through the makeshift bandages around the severed fingers, dripping down to form a sticky congealing pool.

The feet just reached the floor, the bare toes scraping on the damp stone.

The rope, made from plaited strips of torn blanket, was knotted so tightly around the neck that it had almost disappeared into the dark, swollen skin. Its other end was tied securely around one of the water pipes near the ceiling.

One of the women found Bluffield's corpse when she went into the toilet room in the dark hours before the dawning.

Surprisingly she didn't scream. But her stifled gasp of horror and shock were sufficient to wake Ryan.

He pushed the blanket from his chest and swung his legs over the side of the bunk. One of his boots clunked against the metal frame, pulling Kate from sleep.

"What is it?" she whispered. "Not more trouble, Ryan?"

"Could be the end of one of the troubles."

The member of Elder Bluffield's group was standing in the narrow doorway, looking around at the rows of sleepers.

"Gone," she said loudly.

"Has he escaped?" Kate whispered.

"In a way," Ryan replied.

"The Lord has taken the elder to dine with him in the fields of Elysium," the woman called, her voice shrilling out.

Ryan walked quickly and glanced into the anteroom, shaking his head, rejoining Kate by her bunk before any of the others were out of their beds.

"Hanged himself," he said.

"What?"

By now there was a babble of shouting and crying, everyone wanting to go and view the body, but nobody eager to go in and move it.

"Oh, why did you leave us, Master?" shrieked one of the men, banging his head against the wall of the hut until the iron frame rang like a gong.

"Better shut him up or the sec men'll come in blasting!" Ryan shouted, bringing a kind of a hush to the hut.

But things were going from bad to worse, with the women tearing at their hair, down on their knees, eyes streaming with tears, the men staring in horror at the sagging body.

Ryan had an inspiration.

"He left a message with me," he said.

Kate looked at him, puzzled. One or two of the followers stopped and turned to face him, but the others carried on with their weeping and lamentation.

"Elder Bluffield spoke to me and left a message for you all."

This time more of them heard, and they hushed and quieted the rest.

"Why would the elder speak to you, an outlander and an unbeliever?" asked the oldest of the women, eyes screwed up with suspicion.

"Because I *am* an outlander and an unbeliever. That was why."

"What?"

Ryan held his hands up over his head in what he profoundly hoped looked vaguely religious. "Last night, as he slept, the elder had a wonderful dream. A true vision."

There was a collective drawing in of breath all around him.

"He told me that meeting us and the small trouble between us had convinced God that—"

"Not Jesus Christ, the blessed savior whose coming we wait?"

"What? No, though…just a minute. Yeah, he said that Jesus was in the vision as well. And that he'd been told we were a sort of a…" He struggled for the word.

"A sign," said the man who'd been banging his head against the wall.

Ryan nodded. "Right, brother, a sign. A sign that his labor here on earth was done, his race run. God has called him to heaven to work for…" Again he hesitated, looking at the expectant faces all around him.

"To work for the blessed second coming of Jesus the savior."

Ryan pointed at the speaker. "You got it. The biggest and best ace on the line, sister. That's what he's been called for. He told me all this himself. In the middle of the night."

"And hanged himself without a farewell to any of us?"

"No, he told me to pass on this message, as his unworthy…messenger."

The oldest woman was on her knees again, hands clasped. "And he has brought, as need arise, no soiled or tainted sacrifice."

"Right," Ryan agreed.

"What should we do, brother?" asked a younger man with a dreadful nervous tic that made his head tremble on his narrow shoulders.

"Elder Bluffield told me that you shouldn't mourn for him. That he has gone..." A phrase he'd heard from Doc Tanner came to him. "Gone to a far, far better place than he has ever known and done a far, far better thing than he'd ever done before."

"Oh, bless him and keep him safe in the bosom of Abraham."

Ryan looked at the man who'd spoken, wondering who this "Abraham" was, who'd suddenly appeared in their prayers.

"Should we seek a sign, outlander?" called the oldest of the women, looking up from the floor at him.

"A sign?"

"A raven with an ear of corn in its beak?" someone suggested.

"A flood of fire that passes by but scorcheth us not," another offered.

"The mighty rushing wind that brings honey and locusts to feed us in the wilderness?" said the youngest woman nervously.

Ryan closed his eye for a moment. "No, he didn't say anything about that sort of a sign. Just to remember him and keep your mouths closed when the sec men come in here."

"Oh, we will, we will," they chorused enthusiastically.

"Shouldn't we take him down?" Kate whispered to Ryan as the followers of the dead leader began to return to their own bunks.

"No. Hard enough getting the old bastard strung up there in the first place."

Chapter Thirty-One

It passed off without any trouble at all. When they were called out into the bitter grayness of the dawn, one of the older men in the shift reported to the sentry that one of their number had topped himself during the night.

"Drag it out" was the sec guard's response, not even bothered enough to go into the hut and investigate the corpse.

The rest of them lined up for their bowl of gruel and hunk of bread, all shivering in the icy wind that came howling down the canyon.

"Be a relief to get into the mines out of this cold," said Ryan.

ZIMYANIN STOOD on the balcony of his main control hut, looking through the smeared glass at the straggling lines of workers as they filed off toward their respective areas of the mine.

He held the reports in his hand of the deaths during the night. There had been only three, one of which could have been natural causes. One was stabbed with a concealed knife and the third was a suicide.

"Work Unit Twenty-five," he said to the charge sec man who stood uneasily by the door. "That is the one that came together from the Middle West?"

"Believe so, Major-Commissar."

"A religious community, was it not? And you think the man dead was their leader?"

"Believe so, Major-Commissar."

The Russian turned from the window, his deep-set eyes boring into the guard. "There is something happening here and you don't know what it is, do you?"

"Happening, Major-Commissar?"

"I can feel it in my bones. There is some rat boring away behind the wainscoting and I need the services of a rodent control operative."

"Lot of rats in the mines, Major-Commissar."

Zimyanin took a slow, deep breath. "Rats everywhere. I think that we will have a thorough check on our workers after this shift. I will personally examine their testimonials tonight. Man by man, face by face. Make it known."

"Yes, Major-Commissar. At once."

Zimyanin watched him leave, then turned back to look out over the dull, wintery scene. His fingers stroked across his cheek, exploring the pitted pockmarks, brushing his luxuriant mustache.

"Rats," he said to himself, his hand dropping to the butt of the Makarov in his belt.

Ryan heard the two guards talking as the line of workers filed their stumbling way through the yellow slime toward the top of the first ladder.

"Russkie wants a big sec check tonight," one said.

"Fuck it."

"Doin' it himself."

"Fuck him."

"Seems he wants to see every worker, face-to-face sort of thing."

"Fuck them."

If there was any more to the conversation, Ryan didn't catch it, intent on taking his turn on the slippery rungs, down into another fetid layer of darkness.

On the next level, he pulled Kate toward him, glancing around to make sure none of the others on the shift were close enough to hear what he wanted to say to her.

"Trouble."

"What?"

"Heard sec men talking up there. Said that Zimyanin's going to take a double-special inspection. Sort of a parade."

"When?"

"Tonight. At shift change."

Kate bit her lip. "You reckon he'll recognize you, Ryan?"

"Yeah. Yeah, he'll recognize me."

"Could..." But the ideas ran out.

"Why's he doing this?" Ryan wondered.

"Coincidence."

"No such thing, Kate. If Zimyanin orders a special check, just a day or so after I get here, then he feels something. Man like that... No, it's surely not a coincidence."

THE SHIFT WAS STILL in the same place. Level Six, right at the bottom of Shaft Four.

Kate and Ryan were waiting their turn on the last ladder when she turned to him.

"Got a question."

"Sure. Go ahead."

"Your story about Bluffield coming to you before he got... before he hanged himself."

"What about it?"

"They believe you!"

"Course."

"Why?"

Ryan grinned. "Because they wanted to believe me."

IF HE LINED UP in front of Zimyanin, then he was dead. So, they had to get away from their working party and make for another section of the sulfur mines, and either tag onto a different shift or simply try to vanish into the labyrinthine tunnels.

Ryan and Kate dug and shoveled a little away from the rest of their group, giving them a chance to talk and plan. They were near one of the guttering lamps, so Kate tried to make out a plan of where she thought they were, and how they might get away.

"Here's the main entrance. Shaft Four is about a quarter mile this way."

"Where's the river we came down?"

"Here," she replied, using the point of the pick to scratch a snaking line.

"And the huts are there?"

The young woman nodded. "Right."

"Can we get from where we are now, up this direction, and then around the back, mebbe a ways higher up the mountain?"

She looked at where his fingers had traced a faint path through the mud. "Wasn't here long enough to be sure, but I think I could find a way. Might take us around where those boggle-eyed trackies live. Up here." She touched the rough plan with the muddied toe of her boot.

Ryan nodded and sniffed. "Rather face fifteen dozen of those trackies than just one Gregori Zimyanin."

"Best get on with work!" a woman called from behind them. "Sec men'll be down here soon to see what we been doing."

Ryan shuddered. "Fireblast! Felt like someone just walked across my grave."

TWO OF THE SEC GUARDS were patrolling near the highest point of the mine workings. It was an area of some danger, as the muties who scurried through the passages of the mountains sometimes came that way. One or two miners had been butchered by their crude spears.

It wasn't a popular region of the workings, and Zimyanin often used it as a punishment.

The men knew that they'd probably be safe just as long as they kept alert; their M-16s were more than enough firepower to keep the trackies away from them.

The only good thing was that they were also close to the fresh air. A small tunnel cut off to the right, leading to one of the maze of narrow trails that wound around the sides of the massive canyon.

Saul was just about the biggest of the Russian's men, standing six and a half feet tall and weighing over two-eighty. The other man on duty with him happened to be his brother, Ben, who was nearly as tall but only half the weight.

They'd been arguing since dawn about reports that there was some kind of weird mutie moving around the mountain. Three different patrols claimed to have seen something moving, but it had been at impossible heights and in appalling weather.

Neither Saul nor Ben believed it.

"Too high."

"Too cold."

"They'd been at the home brew," Saul suggested.

Ben leaned against the cold wall of rock and laughed. "Be so lucky, bro," he said.

"Reckon that— Hey, you hear something?"

"No."

Saul punched him on the shoulder. "Me neither."

They were both doubled over with laughter and didn't hear the faint sound outside of metal on stone.

Nor did either man notice a slight shadow pass across the tunnel, as if something had moved between the passage and the pale light of morning.

Saul nudged his older brother. "Hey, want to see something real scary?"

"What? Not that old one where you shove your fingers up your nose and peel your eyes wide open? Come on, bro."

Saul nodded. "Yeah. Look at..." His eyes wandered beyond his brother, just a few steps farther up the tunnel. "Oh, my..." he began.

"Pull the other one," Ben said. "The one with bells on it and..."

He half turned.

And opened his mouth to scream.

THE STANDARD OF SECURITY in the lower depths of the sulfur mine was absurdly lax. Nobody could escape from there, and the work quotas were easy to check. So the guards generally contented themselves with walking around in the less wet sections and occasionally clubbing a worker who wasn't showing sufficient enthusiasm for their task.

Kate and Ryan waited and picked their moment, simply climbing up the nearest ladder and then moving laterally through the twining passages and dark corners.

They saw sec men only on a couple of occasions and simply waited in the shadows until they'd moved past them.

"You want to try and get someplace we can keep a look out for your little boy?"

"Sure. Keep in touch. Like, on the fringes of the mine, where we can move in or out. That's all we need to try for.

Kate wiped a smear of mud off her forehead. "Then let's go."

ZIMYANIN SAT at his desk, his polished boots settled on its scarred top. His chin rested in his hands and his eyes were drilling into the senior sec man who'd come to report to him.

"I am having a difficulty in the credibility of all this misfortune," the Russian said.

"Sorry, Major-Commissar?"

"Do I believe you?"

"It's true. Both of them were just sort of ripped apart, like a gang of triple crazies got to them. I seen corpses after stickies finished their funning, and they wasn't no worse than these two."

Zimyanin picked up a metal ruler from the desk and gripped it between his muscular hands. "And not a single one of your men saw this battalion of maddened muties?"

"No, Major-Commissar."

"No." The syllable was flat and finite.

"There was just those one lot of tracks in the snow outside, and they didn't come into the open again."

There was a sharp crack as the ruler snapped in the middle, leaving bright jagged ends. Zimyanin pressed one of them against the ball of his thumb until he drew a tiny round ruby of blood.

"This battalion is then but a single creature who rips into slivers a pair of armed men."

"One lost the top half of his skull, but the rest of his face wasn't touched. The other had the bones in his arms just kind of splintered. Must've been a hundred fractures. And the eyes of both was—"

The Russian held up a hand. "I will peruse a written report on their injuries in one hour from now. See to it."

"Sure, Major-Commissar."

The door clicked shut and Zimyanin swung his feet onto the floor, walking to stare out of his window at the cold gray day.

"Like the Kamchatka peninsula," he muttered, "but more profitable." He coughed and spit on the floor, rubbing at it with his toe. "So why do I not feel more contented?"

Chapter Thirty-Two

Ryan realized early during their escape that they faced one serious problem.

"Fireblast! The lights are stopping."

Kate was leading the way and she had slowed down, halting at a junction of two tunnels. The one in the direction they wanted was in total darkness and was obviously not in use.

The other that remained lighted seemed to drive more toward the east, which would simply bring them back into the main workings.

"We going on into the blackness?"

"No." Ryan's voice was flat with disappointment. "I hoped that there'd be lamps, even in the farthest workings. Have to go the other way and keep a real good watch out."

"Sure."

"You know the way through from here?"

"Oh, yeah." Kate's reply was that fraction of a second too fast and infinitely unconvincing. She realized it at the same time as Ryan. "I kind of know the way. Really."

"It saved your life, telling me how you could find your way through this warren." His face was as blank as death as he looked at her. Tiny beads of ice glimmered in the stubble around his mouth, giving him a surreal appearance.

"You'd have done the same," she replied, failing utterly to keep the tremor from her voice.

He nodded very slowly. "But if I'd got myself caught out, I wouldn't ever have expected any more favors. You understand me, Kate?"

"Sure." Wisely she left it at that.

ONCE AGAIN they had to rely on Ryan's highly developed sense of direction. But it was like trying to teach him. You had to take account of every movement in two interlocking planes, each of three hundred and sixty degrees.

Once they found themselves moving fast toward a very busy area of the sulfur mines, with powered compressors wheezing and drills hammering. They could hear men shouting, and the occasional noise of leather on flesh.

Ryan pointed to a narrow cross tunnel and they both ran quickly for it, avoiding being spotted by any of the sec men.

A hundred yards farther on they were in a totally different atmosphere. The air was thick and still, filled with the stench of the yellow powder. The lamps in the walls were fewer and farther apart, leaving great pits of stinking darkness between them. It felt like nobody had been down there for days.

"Someone?"

The voice came from one of the areas of blackness immediately ahead of them. It was very quiet, almost ruminative, as though the speaker were having a private conversation with himself.

Ryan held up his left hand, drawing the SIG-Sauer with his right.

"You got the scythe, mister?"

There was the faint rattle of iron chains, giving them the clue.

"One of the prisoners," Kate whispered, "left here to rot."

Ryan nodded and led the way forward, straining his eyes until he could just make out the pale blur in the gloom.

"No scythe? Death and no scythe? Just my luck. Well, who then?"

The voice was gentle and resigned, though hoarse and muted.

"Any sec men around?" Ryan asked.

"None. Not for... What day is it? No, a stupe question. What is a day? What a night? What immortal hand or... Time has no meaning to me or to you."

Now they were near enough to see him more clearly, standing half stooped against the right-hand wall of the narrow passage. He was naked, and his head was on his chest. He had thick cuffs around both wrists as well as a rusting collar locked around his thin neck, all linked to a massive bolt that was hammered deep into the raw rock.

Ryan noticed the dark rings of blood that had trickled over his hands as well as down his chest. Despite the bitter cold, the man seemed amazingly well.

"How long you been here?" he asked.

"How long is a piece of string, you might as well ask me. The petty pace has crept by with an infinite slowness. If I were forced to guess, then I'd say five days. Or seven."

"With no food in this chill? And with nothing to drink?" Ryan's voice was frankly disbelieving. He knew that a man could live for an amazing time without food, but would die within hours if deprived of water.

"Small trickle behind me. I can turn my head and lap at it. Undignified, but there it is."

Kate spoke for the first time. "What did you do to for them to..."

"I fear that I made the mistake of trying to preserve my wife from the unwelcome attentions of the powerful Russkie."

"Zimyanin?"

"Yes." For the first time the calmness lost its hold on his voice. "Him."

"What did—" Ryan began.

The man interrupted him by lifting his right arm and pointing into the next pool of dark shadows. "There," he said. "She's just along the tunnel."

Kate moved first, Ryan at her heels. Both saw what hung there.

"Oh..." The young woman dropped to her knees and crossed herself in what he knew was the Catholic way. "Hail Mary, full of grace, the Lord is with thee. Blessed art thou..." Her voice faltered into tears.

The man behind them coughed once. "Bad, isn't it? Can't see too well as the lights are poor. But there were a dozen brought us here and they all took her. Used her in every way you can think of. Couple used me, too. Laughing and laughing and laughing and... I'm sorry. Then they did what you see. Sharp knives, weren't they? Opened her throat last of all. Wish they'd done it first. Or done it to me first."

"I'm sorry," Ryan said quietly. "Bastard useless word, isn't it?"

"Best I've heard in a while, friend. I may call you my friend, might I not?"

"Sure."

"Last word she said was my name. Even as the blood was drowning her, she called my name. Said she'd wait for me."

Kate had finished her prayer, rejoining Ryan. "Can't we break him free?"

"No. Not without ex-plas, and that'd chill him. Chains too thick. Wish I could."

The man was smiling in the dimness. "I knew that, friend. Just a matter of waiting."

Ryan stepped closer, the blaster holstered. "I've got a good blade. I can finish it for you. Put you out of—"

"Misery? I am not miserable, friend. And once I am dead, then everything that my wife and I did and meant and loved will end."

"There's the world beyond," Kate said fiercely. "You said she promised to wait for you."

"No, child, no. You get given a single ride on the carousel. The horses go up and down and around and around. Then the music ceases, the dust gathers in the manes of the painted ponies and the ride is over. I know that, friend. No, you leave me here. I don't think it'll be very long. Few hours and then I'll sleep, and it'll be done."

"You're sure? We won't likely come past this way again."

The chains rattled as he shook his head. "I thank you, friend. Go your way."

Kate stepped close and stretched up, kissing him on the cheek, turning away to hide her tears.

Ryan touched the man on the shoulder, feeling the flesh deathly cold to his hand. "Go well," he said.

"Put out the light. I loved reading, you know."

The voice faded behind them.

When they'd turned a corner, there was a sudden shout.

"You ever meet the Russkie again, friend?"

Ryan paused in midstride. "Yeah. Suppose I do?"

The voice echoed behind and in front of them. "Make it slow and hard for him, friend. For me and for her. Don't forget."

"You got it!" Ryan called.

They went on their way in silence.

KATE BROKE THE STILLNESS when they were walking up a steep sloping gallery ten minutes or so later.

"Miserable, rotten ending." Her voice was ragged, close to weeping.

Ryan stopped. "Let's take five."

They both squatted on their heels, Kate avoiding Ryan's eye.

He sighed. "Miserable? He's not in pain. Too cold and numb. Soon be over."

"But I don't believe that the soul—"

"Shit! Listen, I'll tell you something I once saw in some stinking pesthole frontier ville, not far from Juarez. Ten years ago. Mebbe more. Baron had died. Big occasion. Lot of jack. Prettiest death wag you ever saw. Glass sides and lots of polished brass, silver and ebony. Coffin inside was covered in a mess of flowers. Four horses. Hooves painted black. All four were colored like a dream of midnight. Silver harness jingled soft in the dusty stillness. Each horse had a big plume of black feathers on its head that tossed, rustled and whispered as they moved. Best damned send-off a man ever had."

"So what? I don't understand."

Ryan looked at her, his face white under the faint light of the lamps.

"On the way out of the ville that evening I saw a pair of fat gaudy sluts kicking the corpse of a naked man into a sewage ditch. Worst send-off a person could have.''

Kate stood up. "Yeah, I get the parable. They were both dead so it didn't matter to either of them.''

"You're right, Kate,'' he said, standing and leading the way deeper into the isolated sections of the mines.

Chapter Thirty-Three

There wasn't a single second of warning. The weight of the man dropping from a shaft in the ceiling knocked Ryan down to his knees. The coldness of the attacker's skin and the aura of fishiness told immediately that the trackies were onto them. He heard Kate yell out, then he was fighting for his life.

Despite their small stature, the muties were lithe and muscular. The one that had fallen from the roof had locked an arm around Ryan's neck, while it attempted to kick its heel into his groin. Instead of trying to get up off the floor, Ryan rolled himself over, pushing back hard, so that his full weight was on top of the creature.

Two more of them were on the edge of the fight, both holding tridents, darting around, waiting for a moment to thrust at him, unable to do so because of the closeness of their colleague.

Ryan tucked his chin down and loosened the arm around his neck, grabbing it and biting as hard as he was able. He gagged at the vile taste, his teeth barely penetrating the tough, scaly skin. But it was still enough to make the mutie yelp in pain and let go for a moment.

With an effort, Ryan managed to snatch hold of the trackie by its sacking, heaving it at the nearest of the waiting pair. With a defensive reflex, the creature tried to fend the flailing body off with its spear, succeeding in ramming the triple points deep into its fellow's guts.

Ryan didn't even watch, drawing his blaster and pumping five rounds into the trio of attackers. The spear in the belly had already killed the first of them, and the other pair went down, shot through chest and head respectively.

"Help me!" The voice, shrill and terrified, would have shattered crystal at a quarter mile.

Two of the trackies had seized Kate and were trying to hustle her off through the passage they'd just left. The young woman was taller than the muties and was kicking and struggling. But with one clinging to each wrist, she was almost helpless.

Ryan leveled the SIG-Sauer and shot both of them carefully through the head.

"Oh, Blessed Mary! Ryan they... Look out, behind you!"

He spun, seeing a bunch of trackies stalking toward them from an unseen side tunnel, all holding single-pointed spears.

There were so many of them, so close, that Ryan had no choice. All he could do was squeeze the trigger and hold on to the bucking automatic. The silencer kept the noise down, so that there was just the snuffling ripple of sound.

But the muties danced and screamed and fell and bled.

And died.

It was only when he went around with his cleaver, administering the finishing blow to any still living, that Ryan realized there had been seven trackies in the second wave of the attack.

He slid in the last magazine, looking back at Kate. "Fifteen rounds left. Won't last us that long. You okay?"

"Sure. Ever since I met you life's been a whole mess of laughs. I can't wait for the next excitin' adventure."

Within two hundred yards they were attacked by three more of the diminutive, murderous trackies, coming howling at them, all armed with strange, short-hafted hatchets.

Ryan expended seven more rounds to chill them, the P-226 blaster growing warm with its exercise.

"Eight bullets," he said.

"ANY IDEA WHERE WE ARE?" he asked as they walked along.

"No. I'm sorry, Ryan, but—"

"Forget it."

"What time is it?"

He angled the compact wrist chron toward the nearest light, peering to read the digital display. "Closing in on four in the afternoon."

"Hungry."

"Yeah." At least they'd had plenty of drink. The mine was riddled with innumerable streams, small rivers and spraying falls of water. Some were brackish and soured with chemicals, but most were fresh.

"Got to find a place to hole up for the night. Go for it in the morning."

"I can't make it, Ryan."

"Then you stay here and die, Kate. I'm not about to argue with you."

"Why can't we try to hide in one of the huts, just for one night?"

"Think about *last* night."

"But we—"

"Fireblast!" He kicked out in anger at some loose stones, sending them skittering along the passage. "Zimyanin's called a parade where he'll check out every man. He'll remember me from this." He touched his eye patch with his gloved right hand. "And it'll be goodbye time. Get it?"

"Sure, I know—"

She was interrupted by a cold voice from the shadows. "You fuckin' lovers best get back on the shift face or I'll turn you in to the Russkie."

Ryan looked around, taken completely by surprise, staring into the blackness and not seeing the speaker.

"I got an ace right on the shittin' line for you, so do like I say." The man laughed. "Might've gotten away with your bit of suck 'n' fuck if you hadn't disturbed them stones."

THE ONLY SMALL PORTION of good news was that
Ryan was able to conceal the SIG-Sauer in the small of
his back before they walked out with the sec guard.

There'd been the faint hope of jumping the sentry,
but as soon as Ryan saw him he forgot about the idea.
He wasn't one of the lazy timeservers you found in
most sec forces. This was someone who took a true
pleasure in his work. He was around six feet five
inches tall, skinny as a Kentucky musket, with narrow eyes that watched Ryan and the woman over the
top of the sights of his M-16.

"She worth the risk, One-Eye?" he asked, a thin
grin breaking through a dark beard.

"Good as they come," Ryan replied.

"Now get shoveling."

Ryan walked slowly away from the guard, picking
up a shovel and going to the rock face. Kate hefted a
pick and joined him.

"Work off some of that energy." The man laughed.
"Seein' how much you like it so much, lady, I'll mebbe
come a callin' on you after lights-out tonight. What
hut are you in?"

Kate turned and looked at him. "Mean you don't
know which hut?"

"Sure. Nineteen with all the rest of your shift. Look
out for me. Keep your eyes open and your legs shut.
Later I'll want things t'other ways around. You hear
me?"

"I hear you."

"Now get workin'."

RYAN KEPT LOOKING, with increasing desperation, for some way out of the section. But he gradually came to realize that they'd achieved part of their objective by fumbling their way through the deserted mine workings toward the main entrance again.

They'd succeeded all too well.

They were at Level One, within a scant three hundred yards of the openings that carried iron carts on their wavering rails. The small trucks rattled and bumped, wheels screeching as they came in empty, then labored and groaned as they were filled with the wet mixture of earth and ore.

Because of their proximity to the freezing open air, the guards were far more numerous and alert than in the deeper recesses of the tunnels.

The tall skinny sec man paid them particular attention, as though there were something about them that interested him. Kate's concern grew less when she realized that the sentry was fascinated with Ryan.

"I don't recall seein' you before his afternoon," he said.

"I been around."

"How long?"

"Long enough?"

The muzzle of the rifle caught him just over the kidneys, making him wince.

"Try a better answer."

"Four weeks, near as I can remember."

The man nodded. "Better. Where did they pick you up?"

"In the Darks."

He considered that answer. "I don't... But there's all kinds of comings and goings here. You come in on your feet and go out on your back, down the river. One-way ticket, thanks to Major-Commissar Gregori Zimyanin."

Ryan sniffed. "I know that."

"Sure you do." He half turned away from Ryan, then stared at him again. "Somethin' about you I can't get a handle on. You was never in Tucumcari, was you?"

Ryan had been down there several times with the Trader. "No. Never."

"Louis?"

"No."

"Around the Lakes?"

Ryan shook his head again. "Never."

The guard spit. "Shit! You ain't never been nowhere, have you? Get on digging. Not much longer before you can stop early tonight."

"Why?" Ryan knew the answer.

"Russkie got a special parade for himself. Don't know why. Sure as shit won't ask him why. Last man to question an order went into the river bit at a time. Took two days."

THE CHANCE OF MAKING a break for it never came. A whistle blew several long blasts, followed by a couple of shorter ones.

"Shovels and picks down! Move your asses! Come on, outside."

As they were the nearest to the entrance, their working party was first into the chill evening. It had been snowing once more, whiteness piled everywhere, stained yellow around the spoil heaps.

Ryan looked around for a sight of the Russian, but Zimyanin was keeping in the warmth until they were all ready and waiting.

"Kid just waved at you," Kate said out of the corner of her mouth.

"Where?"

"The coming shift. Two work units to the left. Second row."

"Can't see anyone."

"He was there. Short kid. Mebbe he's pulled back to hide."

"Mebbe."

Ryan scanned the rows of faces, trying to spot Dean. But it was a hopeless task. The shift going into the mines was at least reasonably free of the stinking mud. But all wore an array of rags and furs, including hoods, piled around themselves, so that it was impossible to tell man from woman, old from young.

"What now?" Kate whispered, terrified of drawing attention to them.

"Wait. Trader used to say that if there was a bullet coming your way, it was only a triple stupe that ran toward it."

"More mud."

Ryan looked at her. "What?"

"Smear mud on your face. Hide the patch."

"Zimyanin'll be looking for that."

"There he is."

The stocky figure was unmistakable, striding along a balcony at the front of one of the main admin buildings.

He was clearly visible through the dark green railings, pacing back and forth in gleaming black leather knee boots, with built-up heels to increase the five feet and six inches. His snug-fitting jacket of black leather sported two silver circles on the lapels, and was belted tightly around his barrel chest.

Despite the cold the Russian was bareheaded, the lights above gleaming off the shaved, polished skull. His black mustache seemed fuller and more luxuriant than when Ryan had last seen him. He wore a side arm that looked like a 9 mm Makarov. He clapped his gloved hands together as he walked, his breath hanging in front of his mouth like a cloud of steam.

As Ryan glanced up at him, the Russian leaned over the railing and called out an order to one of the senior sec men below.

The command was passed along the line and whistles began to blow. Voices were raised and the working shifts were organized into roughly straight lines, ready for the inspection.

"Here we go," Kate said.

Ryan grabbed her by the elbow. "Give me your knife."

"What?"

"Quick! Just give me your knife!"

Chapter Thirty-Four

The weather in the cold north of the American continent was harsh. It was a bleak land of raw rock and deep gorges where howling gales came screaming from the Arctic Circle. It snowed most days of the year, and when it wasn't snowing it was generally raining. For three hundred days of the year the temperature never rose above freezing.

For Gregori Zimyanin, it reminded him very much of the Kamchatka peninsula where he'd made his reputation as a tough military commander.

He'd hated the weather then, and he hated it now. Perhaps the weather at the sulfur mines was even worse than the wilderness of northeastern Russia.

But there was an important difference.

Back in Mother Russia, Gregori had been under orders—orders that had to be obeyed without fail, or the reward would be the muzzle of an automatic pressed to the nape and a muffled explosion.

Here, his own word was law.

There was nobody to cross him, no chain of command stretching across thousands of miles of open tundra to headquarters in Moscow.

"This land is my land," Zimyanin said proudly to himself.

DEAN CAWDOR COULDN'T BE certain. The light was poor in the gloom of the wintery evening, and everyone looked more or less the same in their collection of patched and torn rags.

But the man standing next to the crop-headed woman had looked, for a moment, like his father. Dean had risked waving, knowing the danger of drawing attention to himself. And to Ryan.

If it was Ryan.

The boy had heard the news about the Russian's demand for an extraspecial parade and wondered why. Now, if it was really his father standing across the trampled dirt of the mine entrance, then his heart leaped into his throat at the thought that Zimyanin might be suspicious.

But there wasn't a thing that he could do.

"As I GO BY I want each rank to take one step forward march, if you please," the Russian ordered.

"Yes, Major-Commissar."

There was a relay of orders and a ragged shuffle of feet in the frozen slush. Zimyanin stepped into the center of the spotlight's cold glare, his eyes scanning the long lines of slave workers.

"Red alert," he said quietly. "Every man will find himself in the state of highest readiness in the event of there being trouble."

Again, the word ran through the sec men, and all of them stood that bit taller and tried to look triple alert for the Russian's benefit.

Zimyanin began his patrol along the rows, starting with the shift that was waiting to go into the mines, so that less laboring time would be wasted by the interruption.

Face after sullen face, with an occasional worker attempting a scared, sycophantic smile. Most looked at the ground, until he issued a general order that everyone was to lift their heads and stare him in the eyes.

Every now and again the muscular Russian would stop and tell a man or a woman to remove a hood or a scarf, peering intently into their faces.

"Now the second row, if it is not too much trouble for you?"

Dean was in the second row, away toward the far end. But as the ranks opened up, it was easier to see.

"It's him," Ryan said quietly.

"The boy?"

"Sure."

His son seemed fit enough, standing among the other workers. Ryan noticed that Dean deliberately avoided looking in his direction. With someone as cunning and perceptive as Zimyanin, that might be dangerous.

To Ryan's dismay, the leather-coated Russian stopped directly in front of the boy and was obviously speaking to him. Whatever he was saying, Ryan felt that it wasn't likely to be good news.

"WILL GOODE." The voice was flat and gentle, eyes alert and interested. The pockmarks that scarred Zimyanin's face were harsh and shadowed in the bright sec lights. "Will...Goode."

"Yes, Major-Commissar."

"Why do I have the sense of something hidden about you?"

"I don't know."

The Russian cupped the boy's chin in his hand, gripping the sides of his face so hard that Dean thought he could hear his own teeth creaking in protest.

"I look at you and my memory shakes. Why is that, Will Goode?"

"Don't know," the boy mumbled, trying to pull clear of the iron grip.

"I think you do. Perhaps you should come to my quarters for a few hours, Will, and I could ask you some questions. I could show you my collection of knives, Will." Zimyanin finally let him go.

Dean licked his lips, tasting the salty bitterness of his own blood.

The Russian smiled, making the boy feel very alone and frightened. "We'll see, won't we, Will. Yes, we shall see."

"Yes, Major-Commissar."

Zimyanin moved on several places along the line, then suddenly walked back to Dean, making him jump.

"Why have you been looking so very carefully in every direction, Will? Every direction but one. You have been avoiding looking over there." He pointed behind himself, toward the general area of Ryan's working party.

"No. No, Major-Commissar."

"No, what, Will?" The voice was gentle as the hissing of a cobra—just before it rears up and strikes.

"No, I wasn't looking at anyone."

"But were you *not* looking at anyone, that is more the question?"

"No, I wasn't not looking at nobody."

"Good, Will Goode. Will Goode will be good, will he not, Will?"

Zimyanin threw back his head and roared with laughter at his own clumsy joke. Less than a hundred yards away, Ryan's fingers tensed, the nails biting into his own palms. His hands itched for the familiar butt of the blaster.

"It's good, young man, very good. Yes, you and I will certainly speak together again." He turned to the sec man who stood watchfully at his elbow. "Dismiss this shift."

"You haven't seen them all, Major-Commissar."

"Your perception does you credit. Perhaps you could go into the mine and perceive some trackers for me. Could you?"

"Sorry, Major-Commissar. You want to see the out shift, Major-Commissar?"

"Yes."

Again there was shouting and pushing and the occasional soft noise of rifle butts connecting with padded flesh. Eventually Ryan's work party was hustled into place, with him standing next to Kate in the front row.

Zimyanin walked toward them, hands behind his back, a distant smile on his face.

His eyes were roaming along the huddled, filthy, mud-slobbered figures, all seeming identical. Ten steps away from them he stopped dead, the dark stare focusing on Ryan.

The gauntlet lifted and a finger drilled directly toward him.

"You," Zimyanin said. "Yes, you."

Chapter Thirty-Five

Out of the corner of his eye, Ryan could pick out his son, an upright, sturdy little figure, marching away with his own work party toward the main entrance of the sulfur mine. He felt utterly certain now that he'd never ever see the boy again.

There might just be enough time to snatch out the SIG-Sauer P-226 and empty the last remaining eight rounds into the unmissable figure of the powerful Russian.

"You!"

"Yeah, Major-Commissar," Ryan replied, playing the futile game out to its last moments.

"Your eye."

"What about it?"

"What is wrong with it?"

Ryan lifted a hand to where his left eye had once been, bringing it away with a smudge of bright blood against the golden yellow of the sulfurous mud.

"Rock fall, Major-Commissar."

Zimyanin stepped closer, head pushing forward as he peered into Ryan's face. "It is a severe wound that merits treatment at the nearest practicioner of medicine."

He was proud of remembering that sentence from the age-old phrase book.

"Wash it and put a rag over it. Be fine then, Major-Commissar." Ryan was trying to put a nasal whine into his voice, like the speech of some of the people from the swamps.

"You are sure."

Zimyanin grimaced at the sight of the man in front of him.

He was tallish, though standing in a slumped, beaten kind of way. Since he'd just come off a twelve-hour laboring shift, the Russian didn't find it very surprising. His clothes were covered in the ubiquitous golden slime, crusted and cracking, making it incredibly difficult to tell what he looked like. There was a rag of white cloth knotted around his throat.

His feet were also completely caked with thick dollops of stinking mud, layered with the sheen of fresh ice.

It was faces that intrigued the Russian.

He looked at the man, trying to penetrate behind the mask of dirt. The wound to the left eye was obviously severe and he felt a momentary pang of respect for courage.

"Grace under pressure," he muttered to himself.

There appeared to be a ragged gash just above the eye, puckering the skin under all the dirt. Blood had flowed down, completely filling the socket and clogging the eye itself, covering it under an impenetrable mixture of dark earth and fresh, bright crimson.

Zimyanin shook his head. There was something still not right. His sec boss's intuition told him that. A tiny bell was ringing in an abandoned room at the farthest edge of his memory. He could hear it ringing, but still couldn't make any sense from it.

He moved even closer.

The man started to cough, struggling to muffle it with the palm of his hand. Failing, he doubled over, gobbing out a stream of yellow mucus and phlegm, missing the polished toes of the Russian's boots by a couple of inches.

"Fucking piece of shit! Bastard prickless son of a gaudy whore!"

Zimyanin swung his fist toward the man's stomach, feeling the impact, smiling as the worker went crashing down at his feet. He lifted his boot to stamp on the wretched dog's neck, then checked himself, remembering with some surprise that he'd just been admiring the man's courage with the severe wound to his left eye.

For a moment the small bell rang a little louder, but Zimyanin didn't listen to it.

"Take him to the doctor," he ordered.

Ryan had seen the punch coming and had hardened his muscles, riding the worst of the savage blow. Now he looked up at the Russian.

"I'll be fine, Major-Commissar. Thank you kindly, but let me have some food and a wash up and I'll be good as new by morning."

He wondered for a moment whether he'd overdone the part.

But Zimyanin had moved on, hardly looking back at him. He called over his shoulder, "Let him do what he wishes. It is not a matter of any conceivable concern to myself."

Ryan pulled himself erect, hanging on to Kate's arm.

"You all right?" she whispered.

"Been better," he said. "Been worse."

AFTER THE GRUEL AND BREAD, Ryan washed himself, taking great care not to do anything about the self-inflicted wound to the empty socket of his left eye.

Using the young woman's knife on himself had turned out to be one of the hardest things that Ryan had ever done.

If it had been his arm, or even his cheek, he'd have jabbed in the point without more than a moment's hesitation.

But his lost eye...

Ryan lived all his days with that memory. At times he felt he still had both eyes, so vivid was the image of the knife in his brother's hand, moving toward his face.

Striking.

He saw it, actually saw the tip of the blade as it grated into his left eye socket. There was liquid trickling down his face that mingled aqueous humor of the eye with a little blood. Surprisingly little blood.

In the icy bleakness of the sulfur mines, Ryan had had little time to think about his plan, knowing that the patch would trigger the Russian's memory, whereas a bloody wound might slip by. He'd had no choice. It was done, and it had worked.

THE REST of the working shift seemed totally indifferent to the presence of two strangers in their hut. Kate had a brief conversation with an older woman, who told her that they'd lost more than half their number three days earlier in a cave-in not far from the main entrance. As a consequence, most of them hardly knew any of the newcomers.

Ryan lay flat on his bunk, the damaged eye socket throbbing painfully. His mind was racing over the possibilities now left open to them. He couldn't keep the wound open and bloody. Zimyanin had already noticed it. In two days, at the most, it would begin to heal and reveal the fact that there was no eye in the socket at all.

"And then, we're in the deepest well of shit in Deathlands," he muttered to himself.

DURING THE NIGHT Ryan and Kate sat close together while he ran through a summary of his thoughts. Kate had her own blanket across her shoulders, knees crossed, hunched up for warmth.

Ryan, one eye on the sleepers around them, kept his voice quiet.

"First, we know that Dean's here and that he looked okay."

"Seemed it to me."

"Second, I can't stay hidden from the Russkie more than a day or so."

"Could break away and hide up in one of the abandoned tunnels."

He shook his head. "No. He's on the watch for something that's out of the ordinary. You've got to realize, Kate, that Zimyanin is one of the most triple-dangerous men in Deathlands."

"I know that. Remember I worked in this fucking mine, Ryan."

"Yeah, sure. The third thing is I'm nearly flatlined on ammo. Half a dozen rounds. Got to get into their armory and stock up. Once we do that, Zimyanin'll be even more on the edge."

"When are you going to try for the ammo?"

Ryan looked around the room. "Have to try it in the night, then go after the boy and spring him the next day."

"So, when do we move?"

"We don't move. *I* move."

"When?"

Ryan's teeth flashed white in the gloom. "Like Trader used to say, now's as good a time as any."

Chapter Thirty-Six

Xavier Hutson was dying. He'd spent most of his thirty years down near the Grandee, when a misunderstanding with the youngest son of a local baron had sent him off and running, as far north as he could get.

But he'd had three bouts of pneumonia, the last one leaving him with weakened lungs.

He'd heard about work at the sulfur mines, tending human cattle. It was the kind of job that he'd always been good at.

But the weather had been appalling. When it wasn't snowing it was freezing and raining. In the past couple of weeks Xavier had started to cough up blood. Only yesterday there'd been a spasm that had racked him, gouts of thick, clotted blood splattering on the stones of the cavern.

The major-commissar wasn't the sort of man to carry passengers. Xavier had seen enough bodies to be certain sure of that. He'd already decided that he'd swallow his own pistol when the time came.

The trouble was knowing just when that time was.

Right now he didn't feel so bad. One of the senior sec men had a birthday and there'd been some jugs of the colorless high-alk drink that sometimes sent you temporarily blind with its potency.

Now he was on guard, outside the hut that was used as the armory.

"Who's that?" Roused from his thoughts, Xavier was sure he'd heard the sound of someone walking, feet crunching on ice.

"Who's movin' there? I'll chill you, you shithead bastard!"

He stifled a coughing fit. It might be Zimyanin himself, trying to catch guards out, sleeping on the job. Less than a month ago Nevada Kenny had been caught by the Russian. They'd found him the next morning with a straight blade through his cock and balls, driven clear into the wooden wall of the hut, held upright by the knife.

"Who's that?"

Xavier looked around, swinging the barrel of the M-16 from side to side. There'd been a flurry of snow about a half hour ago, and the frozen ground was dusted white, shimmering in the silver light of the sailing moon.

The noise wasn't repeated, and the man leaned back again, pressing himself into the doorway for some protection from the slicing wind.

Ryan was still holding a second stone, but he replaced it quietly on the ground. The throwing of the first one had told him all he needed to know about the watch on the armory—a single man, nervous, possibly drunk.

Who could ask for anything more?

XAVIER FELT another cough coming on, and he grabbed a length of rag from his pants pocket to try to muffle it. The sensation always seemed to start just at the back of his throat, then slide down into his lungs.

He felt a tap on his shoulder and he spun, nearly pissing himself in shock. There was a tall man standing there, real close, half smiling. He wore a dark coat, and Xavier noticed that there was something wrong with his left eye.

"Shit! I never—"

"Just wanted to ask something."

It was all very ordinary and Xavier didn't feel in the least threatened, though part of his mind was beginning to wonder just who the fuck the stranger was.

"Sure. What?"

There was a fearsome, jarring blow to his genitals, so savage that it actually lifted him clear off his feet. Pain lanced through the sec man, burning into his throat, the shock almost stopping his heart. The carbine slipped from his hands, but he didn't register the sound of it clattering on the rocks.

Ryan took the blaster and laid it gently to one side.

The guard was on his knees, thighs spread, mouth open as though he were trying to shout a warning. Nothing was further from the truth. The only thing happening in Xavier Hutson's brain was a total preoccupation with a suffocating agony. Bile surged up, gouting between his lips, mixed with bright arterial blood from his ruined lungs.

Ryan stood back, watching the man fall slowly forward onto his face, surprised to see him hemorrhaging as a result of the knee to his groin. He stooped down and pressed his index finger to the side of the sentry's throat, feeling for the pulse and finding none.

"Have to tell J.B. about that," he said quietly to himself, dragging the corpse out of sight around a corner of the hut.

The door to the armory was held secure by a single padlock. Ryan quickly found a rock of suitable size and shape, and sprang the lock open. The windows were all shuttered from the outside, so he closed the door behind himself and switched on the flickering overhead lights.

He breathed in the familiar scent of gun oil and grease.

There was a triple row of carbines, all held in place with a long chain running through the trigger guards, locked at either end. Half a dozen assorted scatterguns were bolted into a steel cabinet on the far wall.

Ryan was surprised at the low level of security that Zimyanin maintained in his armory. With his sec men clearly outnumbered by fifteen or twenty to one, any rebellion among the slave workers could threaten the hut filled with weapons.

But he guessed Zimyanin knew what he was doing. From everything that Ryan had seen, the captives were so cowed and exhausted that a rising wasn't very likely to happen.

In a drawer, there was a jumble of handguns, thrown untidily together. On an impulse he picked out one for Kate, quickly dry-firing it, listening intently to the sound of the action.

It was the Charter Arms Undercover Model, which held five rounds of .38-caliber ammunition. The steel-framed revolver was one of the lightest ever made, weighing in, Ryan recalled, at about seventeen ounces. Its small size made it the perfect hideaway gun for the young woman to carry.

Shelves on the long wall of the hut held boxes of all sizes of ammo. Ryan took a handful of .38s for the Undercover, and filled three 15-round clips with 9 mm rounds for his own SIG-Sauer. He also slotted bullets into the half-empty clip on the P-226, giving him a total of sixty rounds.

It crossed his mind to use a slab of old and sweating ex-plas to blow the whole place apart, but it wouldn't help any in rescuing Dean, except as a diversion.

Since his son was already working on his shift in the mines, there wasn't much point in doing anything in the open air.

The escape, when it came, would have to be initiated from the shafts and tunnels, rather than outside in the admin complex.

Ryan turned the lamps off again, then eased open the door of the armory, squinting into the moonlight to make sure there were no more sec men around. The snow was falling once more, covering the pool of blood and vomit by the entrance. He carefully clicked the padlock shut, smearing a little mud over it to hide the fresh scratches on the brass.

As an afterthought, Ryan quickly dragged the dead body from its hiding place and left it on the ground in front of the door.

"Guessing's not so good as knowing," he whispered as he made his cautious way back to the sleeping hut.

He could've filled a book with the sayings of the Trader.

THERE'D BEEN A LONG intense discussion among the senior sec men on duty during the night. Should the major-commissar be awakened?

If so, who would do it?

If not, who would explain why when the Russian was up and about at dawn?

In the end a majority thought he should be woken up. Then it was down to the drawing of straws to determine the lucky man selected for that honor.

The knock on the door of Zimyanin's quarters was hesitant, but it still brought an instant response. "Who is there?"

"Cliff Roberts, Major-Commissar."

"What do you require of me?"

"Dead man at the armory."

It was way below freezing, but Cliff Roberts was perspiring, waiting in the corridor, hearing the sound of movement from within. The door opened and the barrel of the Makarov pistol probed toward his face.

"Dead? A sec man?"

"Hutson, Major-Commissar."

"How?"

Roberts swallowed nervously. "We checked him over. No wound. No bullet. Not a knife. Not strangled. I looked at his neck myself."

Zimyanin was out in the passage, standing uncomfortably close. "You did well. The corpse has been stripped?"

"Sure has. I asked around, and it seems Hutson had a real bad cough. Used to spit red. There was blood by the body, frozen on the ground. You reckon that he might've sort of coughed and choked?"

Zimyanin nodded slowly. "It seems a possible conclusion, does it not? No wound?" He spotted the hesitation. "No wound, my man?"

Roberts swallowed, wondering who'd sucked all the air from the corridor. "I saw his... His balls looked kind of swelled up, Major-Commissar. Others said it didn't mean shit."

"The armory?"

Roberts was on safer ground. "Still locked. Blasters all still chained. Doesn't look like it was a raid at all, Major-Commissar."

"But his balls were swollen, were they? Interesting. You've done well, Sec Man Roberts."

"Thank you, Major-Commissar."

"I'll come and look. But first arrange for a girl to be sent here now. Make sure she's been washed."

"A girl? Sure, sure, right away."

Gregori Zimyanin went slowly back into his room to wait. He felt a sudden need for sexual relief, to ease his mind.

There was something wrong. Nothing he could yet prove, but there was an intruder at work in his demesne, burrowing in the thick walls.

He could feel it.

Chapter Thirty-Seven

They worked for another ten-hour shift in the depths of the sulfur mines, cold and wet, trying to save themselves from too much labor. Their plan meant that they'd try to link up with Dean's working party the next evening, which could mean starting on another twelve-hour shift immediately afterward.

Ryan was worried that his killing of the sec man might have brought an extra check, but there was no sign at all of Gregori Zimyanin, and the day proceeded normally.

As they'd filed into the noisome tunnels, they'd passed Dean's shift leaving. Ryan had looked desperately for his son, hoping that he might be able to send him some kind of a sign. But the yellow-slimed figures all looked identical.

The snow had stopped, and the morning felt appreciably warmer. The river was running in full spate, brown and thick, topped with a tumbling creamy froth. Before they'd even been marched into the shelter of the tunnels, it began to pour with rain.

"Shaft Four, Level Two" was the order. "And watch for slips. Couple got buried last night. Two women. So much shit fell on top of them they'll stay there for years.''

THE MAZY WILDERNESS of the vast mines made it absurdly simple to slip away again. Picking their moment when one of the sec men was in another part of their section, they simply walked off from the noise and the lights.

Ryan deliberately didn't go too far away. It had reached the point where they'd taken an irrevocable step. If a sec man caught them now, they couldn't afford to be trapped and taken back. Both of them carried their blasters tucked into the front of their belts, ready for action.

All they had to do was find somewhere to keep as dry and warm as was humanly possible.

And wait.

THE DAY DRIFTED BY. Ryan tried hard not to keep looking down at his wrist chron, but he still couldn't believe that only four or five minutes had crawled past since his last glance at the digital dial.

Every now and again one of them would stand and move around, trying to keep the blood circulating and fighting off hypothermia.

Ryan managed to sleep for a few snatches, waking finally at the distant sound of whistles and shouts marking the end of the shift.

"Not one of my best days," he commented.

"Want me to warm you some?"

He shook his head. "No. Got to get someplace we can look out for Dean. Tag on the end of his line and then spring the lad."

Kate looked at him. "I've never known a man like you, Ryan Cawdor, and that's the truth."

He smiled and kissed her once on the cheek. "You're something, Kate."

Less than four hundred yards away, on a parallel passage, three levels above Ryan and the young woman, two electronic red eyes glowed venomously in the darkness.

DEAN HAD DECIDED that he'd have to make a break for it. Now that he knew that his father had come for him, it seemed his best plan was to try to sneak away from his work shift and then try and link up with Ryan. He was puzzled that he hadn't seen J.B., Doc, Krysty or Mildred. Or especially Jak Lauren.

But the boy guessed that the others were probably holed up in a base somewhere, possibly close by the gateway.

Today they'd been told they were going to be down on Level Five, Shaft Eight, which was one of the deepest working faces in the entire complex. The boy had caught a conversation between a sec man and one of the senior overseers. For some reason, Zimyanin had personally ordered this particular group to go down into what was widely regarded as one of the most dangerous sections of the mine.

Despite his young years, Dean had survived long enough in Deathlands to have an instinctive feel for situations.

And he didn't like the feel of this one.

So, he'd decided to make a break for it as soon as he had a chance.

ON THE PREVIOUS DAY Ryan had noticed that a gallery ran high around the top of the vast chamber, just inside the main entrance. Virtually all of the working parties began their day by passing through there.

Now he led the young woman toward the vantage point.

They doubled on their own tracks, hearing the sound of feet moving toward them, and found a narrow passage where they hid, out of sight of the quartet of sec men that pounded by.

Once the sound of the tramping boots had faded into the distance, they proceeded toward their destination.

"Keep low."

The gallery was wooden planking, suspended on a network of thick ropes, swaying and dipping as they stepped onto it. It was a good hundred feet above the glistening floor of the chamber, shrouded in shadow, like the complex web of some gigantic spider.

There was only a single rope to hang on to, and Kate fell behind Ryan, calling out her distress.

"Can't."

"You can."

"Frightened of falling."

"Stay where you are." He turned around to check her position. "Just keep low, Kate, and stay quiet. We'll get out the same way, so you're safe."

She hunkered down on hands and knees, struggling not to peer between the rotting slats of wood to the floor below. Already the first of the groups of slave workers were thronging through on their way to their shift locations.

Ryan ignored her, concentrating on trying to spot Dean. Because of the assortment of torn clothes and furs, it was a difficult task.

"Gaia, help me," he said through clenched teeth.

He'd once asked Krysty how her powers of "seeing" worked, and she'd simply replied that she didn't know. All she'd said was that she never consciously strained to use the mutie skill, that she kind of switched off and allowed her subconscious to point her in the right direction.

Ryan breathed slowly, letting his eye roam freely around the echoing cavern beneath him, trying not to control what he was doing.

"Dean," he said.

He followed his intuition, concentrating on the small figure in the dark maroon jacket, the hood thrown back to show his mass of black curls.

At that precise moment the boy looked up, past the dizzy maze of thin ropes and cables to the hanging bridge far above his head.

For a split second, father and son stared into each other's faces.

Ryan turned to Kate. "Come on."

Chapter Thirty-Eight

With a movement of his flattened hand, fingers spread, Ryan warned his son not to make any approach, or let on that they knew each other.

He and Kate had moved quickly through the throng of workers, heads low, careful not to make eye contact with any of the sec men.

He'd watched to see which tunnel Dean's shift entered, and in less than five minutes he and Kate were safely tagged onto them, grabbing at a pair of shovels from a pile at the top of the first ladder. The guards were oblivious to the extra two workers.

Dean was second in the column of sixteen men and women. Ryan gradually eased his way closer to the boy, pushing a place or two toward the front as they stopped for each fresh descent into new levels of the mine.

There was far more water around than at any other time. It ran down the walls of the vertical shafts, gathering in slick pools of golden mud along the centers of the passages. Twice they waded through fast-flowing streams that appeared to come out of bare rock and vanish somewhere lower down.

After descending four ladders, Ryan was only one place behind Dean, with Kate jostling at his own elbow.

"Kind of wet today, kid," he said.

"Sure is, old man," Dean replied, not even turning to look at his father.

"We goin' deeper?"

"One more drop."

"You okay?"

"Been better."

A guard drew closer and spotted them talking. "Shut up!"

Ryan waited until they were at the bottom of the swaying ladder. "Got to move quick. Russkie knows me from way back."

For the first time, Dean glanced at him. "Your eye! Is it so's he won't pick you?"

"Don't ask so many questions. Just be ready to move fast."

"Her?" He gestured with a thumb toward Kate Webb. "With us?"

"She's been helping. When we run, she runs. Name's Kate."

Dean nodded to the young woman. "Hi."

Once again, a sec man walked toward them, and Ryan tensed himself for trouble. But this time it was something different.

"Listen good!" Every head turned slowly toward the guard. "Been some falls around here. Bad ones. So watch where you step and how hard you dig. The rain on top and a double-fast thaw's making it even more sodding dangerous. So, you been warned.''

After delivering the information, the sec man went to the ladder and climbed rapidly up to the next level, leaving the work party completely unattended.

RYAN QUICKLY EXPLORED the shaft, finding to his disappointment that it was closed off, with the single exit up the same ladder that they'd come down. It was obviously a new work area, with no other passages leading out.

He passed the news to Dean and Kate.

"So, what do we do?"

"Either climb to the next level, but that's risky, or wait for the end of the shift and try to drift away from the end of the line."

Dean shook his head. "Dangerous."

"We've done it before, son. Sure, it *is* dangerous, but it looks like the best chance there is."

The rest of the workers were becoming more and more suspicious, watching Ryan's wanderings, and the hurried snatches of conversation with the young boy and the skinny woman.

Finally a tall man with a ragged white beard went crabbing over to Ryan. "Hey, mister?"

"What?"

"We got to shift tons of dirt or we get flogged. Or worse."

"Yeah?"

"So, you and—"

"Not pulling our weight. That what's worrying you, is it?"

The man saw death in the single, cold eye and he shuddered. "You got to understand, mister, that it ain't fair if—"

"Sure, sure. Made your point. We'll do some digging for you."

A sheer face stood fifteen or twenty feet high, its muddy surface pitted by shovels, streaming with freezing water. Ryan and Dean went to join two other men, while Kate stayed with the rest of the group to fill the buckets that swayed up the long greasy ropes toward the distant processing plant.

There was no warning of the fall.

One moment Dean was standing between the other two workers, with Ryan busy shoveling about ten feet to the right. The next moment the face dropped away, bulging out, releasing a wave of pent-up slurry that knocked Ryan off his feet and sent all the others into a screaming tangle of arms and legs.

Tons of thick mud gushed into the cavern.

Ryan's mouth filled with the stinking ooze, and he fought for his life, struggling with blind desperation to get back onto his feet in the semidarkness.

The initial tide eased, and he managed to claw himself upright, fumbling for his shovel. He wiped his good eye clear of the mud and looked around frantically for Dean.

But the boy had vanished under the wall of earth, mud and water.

"Get help! Kate, call the sec men. Shovels, here, now!"

Ryan could see a pair of feet protruding from the fall, with one torn boot. But he knew it wasn't his son and he ignored it. He started to dig frantically, working with such desperation that the shaft of the shovel snapped like a rotten twig and he dropped to his knees, burrowing with his bare hands into the semiliquid mass of watery mud. He fumbled among the jagged hunks of rocks, feeling for some contact with the boy.

There was the noise of feet on the ladder, and someone bellowing orders, shouting for everyone to get out before the whole place caved in.

"There's folks trapped!" Ryan called, his groping fingers suddenly touching something soft and yielding, flesh within cloth.

"Do as you're..." the sec man began, hesitating as he saw Ryan scrabbling in the yellow muck, heaving out a limp, helpless little body.

"Dean," Ryan said, shaking the boy, heaving him the right way up. The boy's head lolled on his neck, and a trickle of blood seeped from his left eye. But he still breathed.

Kate was behind him, shoving fingers into Dean's open mouth, scooping out gobbets of filthy slime, freeing his airway. The boy coughed, arms flailing as Ryan gripped him tightly in his arms.

"Leave him be," the sec man ordered. "We'll get him up top."

"I'll carry him," Ryan insisted, not even looking at the guard.

"I said leave him."

"Don't you..." He half turned, glimpsing the rifle butt as it went crashing into the side of his skull, just in front of his right ear.

The adrenaline was screaming through Ryan's body, forcing him away from the chasm of blackness. He reached out for the sec man, fingers clawing for the pale, staring face. But the M-16 swung down a second time, and he toppled over the brink into darkness.

Chapter Thirty-Nine

Kate was back in the hut, with the survivors of the shift. They'd been allowed to return early, trudging through the teeming rain, already turning once more to sleet as the temperature dropped back below freezing.

Three of their working party had died in the fall, and one had been shot by a sec man when he wouldn't stop screaming about his broken thigh.

On the specific orders of Gregori Zimyanin, Ryan was held prisoner in a small room at the back of one of the sec huts. His wrists were manacled behind him, and he lay on the cold stone floor. Blood caked his face and the side of his head from the beating the sec man had given him.

The Russian hadn't yet visited him, preferring to devote his attention to the serious cave-in in the low-level shaft. The whole of that section of the mine was closed off.

"Send them in to clear it."

"They won't go, Major-Commissar."

"I fear my hearing has become afflicted. I thought I heard you use the word 'won't' to me."

The sec man had felt his bowels turning to water and had pressed his thighs together, trying to clench the muscles of his buttocks. "We gave a good thrashing to two of the lazy dogs, but the rest still wouldn't go down."

The Russian had sighed. "I believe in the pragmatic world of real politik."

The senior guard had blinked. "What?"

"We must move more slowly. I will investigate myself and judge the danger. Then I will talk to some of the older members on the shifts. Persuade them that the hazard has abated."

The sec man had seen some of the Russian's methods of persuasion. One of his first jobs when he enlisted had been to scrub the splattered blood from the ceiling of the 'persuasion' room.

DEAN WAS UNCONSCIOUS. He'd been taken away and was in another room of the same large hut as his father. Zimyanin had looked in briefly on his way to check the damage to the mine, standing for several long seconds at the bedside of the young boy.

A woman was trying to clean all the clotted mud and blood from the lad's scalp, wiping away at the chalk-white face.

RYAN WONDERED whether his skull might have been fractured. It ached, and every time he tried to move, a ferocious stab of fire raced behind his eyes and injected acid along his spine.

He was furiously angry at himself, angry at his own futile, destructive anger.

Once he'd plucked Dean from the swamping mass of yellow mud, he should have slipped quickly away, ready to try to carry out the rescue on some other, safer day.

But he'd allowed the choking mist of rage to fill his brain. Now he was a helpless prisoner.

Dean was safe. One of the sec men had been kind enough to tell him that. It had been the same guard who'd told him that Zimyanin had asked for him to be held safely.

Ryan didn't know where Kate was, or what she might be trying to do to help. Or, whether there was anything at all that she *could* do to help.

KATE'S UNDERCOVER .38 was buried in the middle of her straw mattress. The best plan she'd been able to think up meant that the blaster wouldn't be much use, and would certainly get discovered.

It was the middle of the evening when the slim young woman crept from her hut and picked her way through the drifts of fresh snow, moving quietly toward the part of the complex where both Ryan Cawdor and his son were being held.

DEAN COULDN'T SEE out of his left eye. There was a jagged cut just on the brow, and heavy bruising above and below the socket. The flesh was so puffy that the eye had swollen shut.

The woman who'd cleaned him had clucked sympathetically at the sight, shaking her head at the deep purple bruises that mottled the boy's upper body.

"Poor chicken. Lucky to be living."

"How was I saved?"

"Someone off your shift dug you out, then a shit-eating guard clubbed him down."

"Where is my... Where is he now?"

"In the river, like as not." The woman had paused. "Though I believe someone said he was took and chained up. For the Russkie to see him."

"The Russkie seen me?"

"Only for a moment, chuckie. But he might come back anytime, so's we'd best fix you as good as possible. Got some black cloth here. Make you a patch for that left eye of yours. Like that?"

The boy smiled. "Yeah. Be double good."

ZIMYANIN PAUSED halfway down the trembling ladder. The opening to the tunnel above him was ringed with the anxious faces of a group of his sec men.

He smiled at them. "I trust the water is not too inclement to facilitate bathing," he said.

The circle of pale watchers vanished.

He carried on down to the bottom, standing with one hand on the ladder, ready to move fast, sniffing the cold, damp air.

The danger was there.

The Russian could almost taste it.

All around him, the sides of the shaft seemed to be flowing, the earth like sticky honey, slow-moving. He could hear water running, somewhere farther down the passage. His boots were covered in rippling slime, almost to his knees.

He looked up and shouted. The faces of a couple of his sec men reappeared.

"Buckets and ropes. It must be drained first. Then send the older men from the day shift down here to dig it clear. Shoot the first one who draws back and hesitates. And the second and the third. In time, you will find a man who will be content to dig rather than die."

As he began the wearisome climb up to the fresh air and the falling snow, Gregori Zimyanin was conscious of an overwhelming need to possess a woman. But first he might revisit the young boy who'd been injured and the man who'd been beaten after he'd rescued him.

Then a woman.

When lust came to the powerful Russian, it became almost impossible to resist. He was halfway up the third of the series of greasy ladders and he had to pause, adjusting his breeches to accommodate the sudden, thrusting erection.

KATE HAD FOUND a guard who'd promised to let her in to see the prisoner. All she had to do was be nice to him for a few minutes.

"Then you'll let me see him?"

"He your husband or what?"

"Sort of."

"Come around back here, out of sight of the Rus-skie."

She followed him, hunching her shoulders against the fine, driven snow. The sec man stopped in an alcove that had once been a side door but was now barred off. He beckoned to her.

"On your knees."

"What? Don't you want to go somewhere inside so we can do it properly?"

"Just get down and get it out for me. Open your mouth and stop talking. Quick." He slapped her hard across her frozen cheek, his fingers leaving a flaring, livid mark on her skin.

She cupped her hand inside his trousers, squeezing gently, trying to make it end more quickly. But he held back, thrusting between her frozen lips, almost choking her. When he finally came, Kate attempted to pull away but he grabbed her by the back of her neck, pressing her against him, so that her senses were swamped with the rancid smell and bitter taste of his sweating body.

She stood up, gagging, as the guard zipped himself and pushed her aside, before taking up his position again.

"Can I go in now?" She hawked and spit into the snow, stooping and taking a mouthful of the clean whiteness.

"No."

"What?"

"I said 'no,' didn't I? Just fuck off, or I'll cut your throat."

Kate stared at him. "You promised."

He grinned. "Yeah, I did, didn't I? So what? Changed my mind." He laughed. "Tell you what."

"What?"

"Some of my mates might like you to do it for them. Later tonight. You come around again and get that little tongue and lips ready. And then I'll definitely take you in to see that one-eyed bastard."

Kate half turned away, then suddenly changed her mind, putting on a slack-faced grin. "Honestly and truly?"

"Sure. Cross my cock and hope to die."

"I'll be back," she promised, as she turned toward her dormitory hut, intent on retrieving her revolver.

THERE WAS only a small light bulb in the room where Ryan was being held. Zimyanin was preoccupied with his sexual needs, as well as the worry about the way parts of the mine were becoming unworkable.

The Russian stood in the doorway, staring at the chained man on the floor.

"You displayed courage, I am informed." Ryan didn't answer him. "But also stupidity. The one is set against the other, so you are both lucky and unlucky. You understand me?"

"No, Major-Commissar, I don't."

Once again, there was the faint stirring of the layers of thick gray dust in the far-off rooms of distant memory.

"If you had not been stupid, I might have allowed you to go free. So, you are unlucky." Zimyanin laughed. "But there is, the, how do you say it? The other side of the coin. To resist a guard would have resulted in severe unhappiness and a cessation of breath. So, you are also lucky. Tomorrow you will work again. You agree with that?" Ryan didn't answer. "Well, you do not disagree."

The door slammed and the key turned in the lock, leaving Ryan alone once more.

DEAN WAS in one of the cleanest beds he'd ever seen, with relatively white sheets and three blankets. A small fire smoldered in the grate, though the inside of the windows was still coated with a rainbow sheet of ice.

The woman had left after giving him a bowl of thick fish stew, with sliced mushrooms, all heavily salted. The boy had devoured it to the last drop, wiping the inside of the dish with the remains of the three generous slices of fresh bread.

There had been a small shot glass of colorless home brew, which brought tears to the boy's eyes. The woman had whispered that it had been sent, special like, on the orders of Major-Commissar Gregori Zimyanin himself.

Now Dean was dozing, lying on his back, one arm thrown up across his face, covering the worst of his visible injuries.

The door opened slowly, the movement disturbing the sleeping boy. He squinted out, seeing the pock-marked face of the squat Russian peering at him. Dean started to sit up, but the man waved a gloved hand at him.

"Lie still and rest, young Master Goode. I have just come to—"

There was a voice from outside the room, a sec man, muttering something to Zimyanin. Dean could only catch a few words, something about a pair of girls being ready in the rooms.

The major-commissar nodded impatiently, throwing the boy a snatched smile. "Duty calls and I needs must go." Dean sat up, blinking from under the black patch over his left eye.

For a moment the Russian stared at him, face blank of emotion. His mouth opened as though he were on the verge of saying something, then the invisible sec man spoke and Zimyanin turned quickly away, slamming the door shut behind him.

ONE OF THE GIRLS lay unconscious in a corner of the bedroom. She had ragged blond hair, though most of it was missing from the right side of her scaly, infected scalp. Blood oozed from between her thighs, and there were savage bite marks across her belly and breasts. A dark bruise covered most of her right cheek, and blood seeped from nose and mouth.

At her side was a piece of ragged black material that had once been her blouse.

Her friend was moaning, kneeling on the bed, face pressed to the blankets. Zimyanin was standing on the floor behind her, ramming himself into her from behind, enjoying her panting and cries. He was holding the girl by the back of the neck with his iron fingers, squeezing harder at each thrust.

This was good. So good, taking away all his worries about the earth falls, about the mysterious deaths that kept occurring around the mine and about the identity of the young Will Goode and his captive rescuer.

Everything would be resolved once his passion was spent and his mind clear again.

He was muttering to himself in Russian, breathing obscenities as he drove harder and harder into the woman. The bed rocked back and forth, rattling against the outer wall of the hut.

Out of the corner of his eye, Zimyanin noticed that the young woman on the floor had recovered consciousness, sitting up, touching her various injuries with trembling fingers, reaching for the scraps of material that lay beside her.

But he was nearing his third climax of the evening, feeling his stomach muscles fluttering, closing his eyes.

He gave a great roar of pleasure, fingers tighter, leaning on top of the shaking, weeping woman.

The Russian opened his eyes.

Inches away from him was the face of the other girl, a wad of black cotton covering her left eye, like an eye patch.

Like the eye patch over the left eye of Will Goode.

Like the one the American, Ryan Cawdor, had been wearing.

Over the left eye, like that of the prisoner who'd rescued Will Goode.

"Fucking father and fucking son!" Zimyanin screamed, snapping the woman's neck in a spasm of blind rage.

Chapter Forty

Krysty watched the pillar of dust as it moved steadily toward them across the flat New Mexico desert. The others were all back at the homestead for the evening meal.

Christina Lauren had been baking, the clay oven in the yard servicing a constant flow of bread and blueberry muffins. Jak had slit the throats of a brace of chickens, plucking and gutting them, then jointing them for a rich stew with sweet potatoes.

Now they all sat out on the porch, looking toward the sky-toppling column of gray-brown.

Krysty shaded her eyes as she stared at the dust cloud.

"Lot of people," she observed.

Jak blinked. His white hair was splashed with red from the western sun. He narrowed his pale eyes, but his vision was always poor in good light. "Could be maybe some Mescalero with cattle or horses?" he suggested.

"Moving slow," J.B. offered. "Doesn't tell us anything."

"Get us some trains every now and again. Like the old times when the settlers came through in big ox wags." Christina moved toward the door. "Anyone want some coffee?"

"A mug of your best java would be most welcome," Doc said.

J.B. and Mildred also took up the offer, but Jak and Krysty turned it down.

"Your hair looks just about ready to burst into flame," Mildred said, smiling.

Krysty nodded. "It's the sun does it."

"You all right?"

"Sure, thanks. Just worried about Ryan. Where he is. What he's doing."

The black woman stood and joined her. "If Ryan can't make it, then nobody can. He's just about the most surviving man I ever met."

"I try to see, but all I get is cold, black and wet. And danger all over."

From the low hills behind the house, they all heard the distant crackle of lightning. Most evenings there was a spectacular chem storm, with the lightning ripping apart the pink-purple clouds, while the thunder made the earth shake.

"He'll make it."

She looked across at the Armorer, who was staring toward the west. The light flared off his spectacles, making it impossible to see his eyes.

"Sure. When?"

"We agreed, Krysty. If he's not back in time, then we go after him. One way or another, we'll bring him here."

"One way or another? You mean breathing or cold, J.B.? That it?"

"You know he'll return."

Christina came back out on the veranda, holding an old telescope that was covered in light brown leather and had a small brass focusing screw on the side.

"Been watching from the bedroom," she said. "That dust."

Jak looked at her. "What?"

"Lot of people coming this way. Wags. Moving slow. Won't get here until first light tomorrow. Unless they come in the night."

Krysty sensed the disquiet in the woman's voice. "We'd best get ready for them," she said. "One way or the other."

Chapter Forty-One

Zimyanin had his Makarov pistol in his hand, cocked and ready. He stormed out into the blizzard with his favorite Dragunov sniper's rifle strapped across his broad shoulders.

He bellowed for sec men to accompany him, without giving them any explanation of where they were going or what was happening. By the time he reached the hut where Ryan was held prisoner, he had eight of his guards trailing after him.

The snow was already lying way over the ankles, piled higher in drifts, three and four feet deep against exposed walls.

Visibility was down to less than twenty feet, and Zimyanin wasn't surprised not to be challenged.

But when he saw the open doorway, swinging in the strong wind, the black hall with inches of snow lying inside it, the Russian halted, holding up his hand as a warning to the others.

"Wait!"

The group of men, all carrying M-16s, gathered around him. It was close to midnight, and the slave-labor camp seemed to be sleeping.

"The man who saved the boy," Zimyanin shouted. "He is a most dangerous criminal element. A man who could free himself from the strongest—what is the word? Strongest gulag. He has, I think, escaped. We must find him. Must."

"Just one man, Major-Commissar?"

The cold eyes turned to the speaker, who took two stumbling steps backward, mouth closing like a steel trap.

"Two of you around the back. Four go to the room where the injured boy is kept. The rest come with me. How many men should be here?"

"Three, Major-Commissar."

"Then where . . ." He stopped as one of his guards suddenly reappeared around the side of the building. "What? Why haven't you gone to the back of—"

"They're just . . ." He pointed with his hand.

"Who?"

"Three that was on guard."

"Chilled?"

"All blasted through the back of the neck. Close up. See the burns."

Zimyanin took several rapid, short breaths. "Go on around the back."

"Want to see them?"

"No. I have seen the corpses of the stupid many times. Do as I say. The rest come with me."

But he knew what he would find in the room where Ryan Cawdor had been held prisoner.

THE DOOR HAD OPENED slowly and in the half-light Ryan had been able to see a hand, wearing a leather gauntlet, come into the cell, holding a large-caliber pistol.

It was an image of death that he'd often seen in his darkest dreams, and he tried to get to his feet, ready to take any last chance that might present itself.

Then he realized what kind of gun the hand was gripping—the .38-caliber Undercover that he'd stolen from the armory for Kate Webb.

"Ryan?" she whispered.

"Yeah."

"I got the key to let you out."

"The sec men?"

She was kneeling, fumbling with the key, dropping her gloves on the floor. "Deal was I'd suck them and they'd let me see you."

"And?"

"First time I did what he wanted and the bastard wouldn't keep his word. Said come back and do it for his friends."

Ryan could feel a cold wind blowing from the open door. He tried to move around to make it easier for the young woman to free him. The only good thing was that, in the brawl and the confusion of the cave-in, nobody had thought to search him. The SIG-Sauer and the panga were still safely hidden under his heavy clothing.

"Yeah, go on telling me."

"Three dumb fucks. Stood there. I said to get their cocks out ready and line up. Stood there. Pathetic little maggots, in the cold, around the side of the hut. Drew the blaster... Got it."

He shook the chains off his wrists, freeing himself completely, drawing his own automatic.

"You reloaded your blaster?"

"No."

"Do it."

"Now?"

"Yeah. How many you fire?"

"Three."

"Chilled them all with three rounds." Ryan was impressed.

"They near shit themselves. One bullet back of the neck. I made the shits kneel in front of me."

"Didn't hear a sound."

"Blowing a blizzard outside."

"You did real well." He grabbed her and gave her a quick kiss on her cold cheek.

"Now what? Rescue Dean?"

He shook his head. "Be more guards. Zimyanin could come anytime. Best is get outside and hide up. Then save the boy when they don't expect it."

He moved past her, glancing into the deserted corridor. Since he hadn't heard the bleak execution of the three sec men, it was safe to assume that nobody else had.

The snow was whirling into the passage from the black night beyond. Ryan walked slowly and peered around the door, but it wasn't possible to make anything out more than thirty feet away.

"Shelter," he said to the young woman, who followed him into the storm with a stumbling, coltish grace.

They vanished into the blizzard.

Less than five minutes later, Gregori Zimyanin came roaring up.

"I KNOW THAT YOU ARE the son of Ryan Cawdor."

"Who's that?" The dark right eye, the left one still covered by a patch, brimmed with innocence as it stared up at the Russian.

"Listen to me, pretty youth, and listen to me very well."

Dean had seen much wickedness in his ten years of life, had very often been frightened. Though he was trying with all his might to conceal it, he'd never met anyone who scared him like the powerful, bald-headed Russian.

"I know who you are. I know your father. We have... met socially. I will kill him when I see him next. I want to rip out your heart and devour it, so bitter is my hatred for you, little Master Cawdor. But, you will be good, Master Goode."

"How?"

"By remaining here alive."

"My father'll kill you first."

"Bravely spoken. You have never hunted the white Siberian tiger, have you? No, I believe that the reply will not be in the affirmative."

"No."

"A cunning beast. But it can be trapped by offering it something that it wants. Perhaps a tender young goat."

Dean looked at the man. "You think my father'll come to save me, then you can catch him?"

The large head nodded slowly, the eyes hooded and blank. "It is not beyond the realms of possibility, Master Cawdor."

"I'll cut my own throat first."

Zimyanin smiled. "Bravely spoken, tovarich. If I had a son, I would wish that he showed such bravery in adversity. But I had thought of that. A sec man will watch over you as tenderly as an apple-cheeked *babushka*. When the trap is sprung I will have the tiger flayed alive and hang its skin upon my wall. And you may watch, Master Cawdor."

"Go fuck a dead rat, shiftface."

But the Russian was already halfway out of the door and the insult was wasted.

THE TIGER WAS LESS than a quarter of a mile away from his hunter, squatting with Kate in a low-roofed concrete hut that had once provided primitive shelter for the workers when blasting was taking place. It had no door, and the snow was already filling the rectangular opening.

On their way to the hiding place they'd heard something of the sec alarm. Ryan guessed from some of the yelling that Zimyanin might finally have figured who Dean was, and that Ryan was there to spring him.

Ryan had his arms about the young woman, trying to minimize the extent that they were exposed to the elements.

"We goin' to try and hide up again in the mines?" she said, having to raise her voice to ride over the screaming of the blizzard.

"No. Russkie'll figure we're going to free the boy. But we're not." He paused. "We're going to free everyone else."

Chapter Forty-Two

Jessco Shannon lay on the floor of the hut, hands clasped to his stomach. The 9 mm round that had put him down didn't hurt very much. There was a numbness across his lower abdomen, and he could feel warmth around his groin.

The powerful blaster hadn't made the thunderous roar that he'd expected, more like the sound of someone farting after a good meal of beer and chili. That made him grin.

But it was still a puzzle. He and everyone in the hut had been awakened by the tall man with the bloodied face, who'd stood there with snow matting his long black hair.

Jessco couldn't remember all of the talk, something about them going outside into some blizzard and running away into the mountains. But everyone knew that was just about the same as putting a 10-gauge into your mouth and pulling the trigger.

The man had pointed at Jessco and told him to get out and start running.

"I said he was crazy as a shithouse rat," he muttered to himself, noticing that he seemed to be the only one left in the dormitory.

Then there'd been that farting noise and the next second Jessco was flat on his back, staring up at the damp ceiling with its big loops of colored electric wiring.

The warmth was turning into fire and he moaned, wishing he was back up in the Shens in the isolated holler with his sixteen brothers and sisters, minding their own business before the sec men had come and lifted them to this icy, godforsaken wilderness.

"My daddy knew more tap steps than anyone in the whole of Deathlands," he whispered.

Jessco then became involved in the dark mystery of his own passing.

RYAN MOVED QUICKLY from hut to hut, repeating the same performance.

Kate stood by the door, holding her own blaster, while the one-eyed man tugged everyone awake. He talked fast and hard, not giving anyone a chance to even think about what he was saying, intent on simply pressuring them out of their huts.

The mass escape of most of his workers would cause Zimyanin some serious problems. He'd have to send his sec men out into the storm to herd them all back again, which, would mean fewer guards watching over Dean.

A couple of the huts proved stubborn, and Ryan had to gut-shoot men to persuade the rest that he wasn't joking.

It wasn't something that Ryan particularly liked doing, but the Trader used to say that you couldn't make a stew without having to cut some meat.

ZIMYANIN HAD ONLY JUST returned to his own rooms, intending to have a hot shower and a change of clothes, when the sec guard knocked and brought him the unwelcome news.

"All?"

"Most all. Not the workers already on the night shift, Major-Commissar."

"But... You are informing me that one man has released everyone!" He had stripped off to the waist. His muscles stood out like bars across his shoulders as he fought to prevent himself from ripping the messenger's face off his skull. "Where were the..." But he was almost choking in rage and he couldn't go on.

"The sentries?" Seeing he wasn't about to get an answer, the man stumbled on. "They was most about here, them not in the shafts. You said they was to guard the boy in..." Zimyanin turned around and the sec man fell silent.

The Russian nodded slowly, again and again like a child's toy. "I had ordered this. The son of Ryan Cawdor. He will raise a revolution among the workers, I think. They cannot hope to live in this weather out in the... No. Rebellion. Put extra men on the armory and send all that can be spared to hunt down these ragged fools as quickly as possible. Before they can become organized."

"What about the boy, Major-Commissar?"

"Two in the room. Watch for the child seeking to harm himself. And two more—no, make that four more—outside. I will come myself as soon as my ablutions are completed."

The man saluted and left the room, pausing in the narrow corridor to wipe the beads of sweat that were streaming over his forehead and cheeks.

IN LESS THAN AN HOUR, most of the escapers had been recaptured and returned to their huts. One or two had been shot by frustrated and frozen guards, and one sec man had put a bullet through the throat of one of his comrades, mistaking the looming shape in the white-out conditions.

But there were still at least fifty of them somewhere out in the blackness.

Zimyanin was in a vicious mood. The disturbance was worse than he'd hoped, with sec men rushing around like headless gophers. There was a temptation to simply let the fleeing slave workers go, in the certain knowledge that most would be dead within twenty-four hours. To have to send off hunting parties through the gateway to replenish the labor force by fifty or more was also going to be time-consuming.

And where was Ryan Cawdor?

If he'd managed to lead the fifty absentees to a good hiding place, they could represent a serious threat to the security of the whole mining complex.

The Russian stalked around the admin compound, resisting the urge to go out himself into the valley beyond and try to hunt down the one-eyed man.

The other nagging worry was of Cawdor going into the tunnels with these missing fifty and, perhaps, linking up with the trackies.

Zimyanin glanced up at the sky. The wind seemed to be easing a little, veering to a more westerly direction. It meant that the shape of the bowl of mountains that gripped the river and the valley gave more protection from the blizzard.

And the snow was easing.

DEAN HAD THE COMFORT of feeling his beloved turquoise-hilted knife, still hidden in the small of his back. If the Russian had left him with only one guard, the boy would have tried to butcher him.

But with the two poker-faced sec men standing on either side of the locked door, each holding his carbine ready for action, the chances were down to zero.

The bruising was still coming out, but Dean kept trying to move, flexing and tensing muscles beneath the blankets, doing everything he could to stay ready for the moment.

He didn't know what Ryan would do, when he'd do it or how he'd do it.

But he felt a diamond certainty in his heart that his father would try.

Chapter Forty-Three

Ryan stopped in midstride, hand going to his forehead.

"What?" Kate whispered.

"I just got a sort of flash of... of Krysty and the others, kind of a 'seeing,' like she gets."

"What was it? What'd you see?"

He shook his head. "There was flames, blood and thick black smoke. The smoke came down like a heavy curtain and I couldn't see no more. I mean any more. Nothing."

"So, what does that mean, Ryan?"

"Don't know. Fireblast! It was kind of bad, but it could..." He looked at her, puzzled. "Might mean nothing at all. Let's go get the boy saved. That'll mean something."

IT WAS PITCH-DARK, with the sec lights glinting off the hard white ground. Shadows were knife-edged, and the air was so cold that Ryan and Kate had to keep holding their breath as they moved to avoid betraying themselves.

Guards scampered by, heads down against the wind, ignoring the two figures that lurked in the darkness.

Twice Ryan saw escaped prisoners being recaptured, bludgeoned to the snow by rifle butts, blood spilling, black on white.

There was no problem identifying the building where Dean was being held.

A quartet of sec men huddled together by the main door, nervously looking around them. A tiny ruby light glowed as they passed around a cigarette.

Ryan considered the chances of taking them all out with the silenced P-226. The range from where he and the young woman were hiding was less than fifty yards, and the light wasn't bad. But the men all wore dark clothes, only the silver uniform circles glittering against the coats. It was hard to identify individual targets with any certainty.

He could definitely send them all off on the last train to the coast, but not without short odds on one of them being able to yell a warning to the rest of the camp.

"Most these buildings got a side or a rear door?" he asked.

Kate nodded. "We could circle behind the power plant."

He hesitated. One of the guards had moved apart from the others to stub out the cigarette in a flurry of orange sparks. For a second or two all four made separate targets, but the moment passed.

"Let's try it," he said.

Behind them, in the lee of the tallest of the surrounding mountains, was the huddled bulk of a massive building. Its windows were long broken, doors ripped off hinges.

"What's that?"

"Think it's where all the old machines for the mines are kept, from before sky-dark. Cody went in there once. Said it was a death trap of rusting platforms and rotting ladders."

Ryan stared at it, a plan half forming in his mind.

FOR THE PAST HOUR there'd been shouting, with the occasional burst of gunfire. At first the two sec men in the room with Dean had been uneasy, going to the side window to peer warily out.

But they'd gradually relaxed, deciding that looking after a ten-year-old boy wasn't such a bad chore compared with being out in the postmidnight chill.

Dean had got into the bed, using the blankets as cover to draw his own slim knife, readying himself for whatever might happen.

The rap of a pebble against the glass made all three of them start.

"Put out the light."

"Could be the one-eyed bastard the Russkie warned us all about."

Another small stone tinkled on the window, the sound barely audible. The taller of the sec men flattened himself against the wall and sidled around until he could squint into the darkness.

"Woman."

"What?"

"Young slut. Think I know her. Got black hair and tiny tits. Standin' there like she wants some help from us."

The other man moved to join him. "I'll fuckin' give her some help." He grabbed at his own groin in case his friend hadn't understood him.

"You and me both." He looked behind, pointing a warning finger at Dean. "Stay there." He eased the window up a few inches, biting air pushing its way into the room.

"Could be a trick."

"Russkie didn't say shit about a woman. She just ran like the others and now she's gotten cold feet and wants in."

"More'n her feet cold."

"Warm her."

He slid the window wider, leaning head and shoulders out, eyes fixed on the slight figure of the girl.

"Hey, you come here," he called quietly in case the other four sec men heard him and came around wanting to cut themselves a piece of the buttered bread.

Ryan erupted from the blackness like an avenging angel of bloody death, grabbing at the man's lank hair, holding him steady for the fraction of a second it took to slit through the pulsing carotid artery at the side of his throat. He heaved at him with all his strength, so that the dying man slid unresistingly out of the open window.

The other guard stared in total disbelief, his rifle held in slack fingers. He was standing by the window, his legs apart, back to Dean.

Ryan had expected the other sec man, who he'd been watching through the window, to come to see what had happened. Or to move to the door. Either way, Ryan was ready to take him. He hadn't planned on the guard standing stricken, rooted to the spot, out of the line of fire for a clean shot at him.

"How did..." the guard muttered, his mind slipping into clinical shock.

The blow from behind tipped him into the abyss of dark madness. It had come from below, something striking him with unbelievable force between the legs, driving into his genitals, a hideous metallic grating against the point of his pubic bone.

The breath fled his lungs and his cry of shock wasn't even audible to Dean, who crouched behind him, the turquoise-hilted knife firm in his right hand. Warm blood ran over his fingers, across the back of his hand and up his lower arm.

"Come in, quick," the boy whispered.

Ryan's head appeared over the sill, peering into the room, seeing a macabre tableau.

Dean's blade was still buried high in the sec man's groin, pressing him up onto the tips of his toes. He'd dropped the M-16 on the floor, and his arms were spread wide, fingers bent into tortured claws.

The guard's eyes were staring wide and blank, his tongue protruding from his bloodless lips. Poised in helpless agony, he was frozen into immobility by the vicious attack.

Ryan pushed the muzzle of the SIG-Sauer under the man's throat, angling it upward, and squeezed the trigger once.

The sound of the explosion was muffled by the silencer, and by the man's flesh.

A chunk of skull, scalp and hair exploded against the ceiling, followed by a gout of pale blood and gray-pink brains.

"Let him go," Ryan said, and Dean withdrew the knife, wiping it quickly on the blankets before quickly resheathing it.

The body dropped like a sack of watery meat.

"There's more at the front."

"I know. Four of them." Ryan beckoned for the young woman to join them, helping her to climb in through the window and sliding it shut behind her.

"You got me out the earth fall?"

Ryan grinned. "Thought you might have changed. But you still ask too many questions. Yeah, I did. You okay to move?"

"Try me."

"He got a handgun?" He pointed at the sec man's corpse.

"Yeah. Browning Hi-Power, 9 mm. Can I take it?"

"Too much for you. Still, better than nothing. Make sure you—"

The boy grinned. "Brace my wrist. I know that."

"We could go out the same way we came in," Kate suggested.

It looked like nobody had heard them butchering the two guards. Ryan glanced outside, seeing the way was clear. "Yeah, why not?" he said, starting to open it.

Then they all heard the outside door open and boots clatter along the passage toward them.

Chapter Forty-Four

"Coming in!"

"Sure," Ryan said, steadying the pistol at the center of the door.

"It's colder than a Nogales gaudy and—"

The bullet hit the new arrival just below the breastbone and a little to the left. The hollowpoint round spread and tumbled, ripping his heart to rags.

The sec man's feet flew out from under him, and he crashed down on his back in the narrow corridor. His blaster skidded away and rattled against the half-open front door of the hut.

"Fireblast!" Ryan motioned for Kate and his son to get out of the window, while he dropped to one knee, steadying his right wrist in the classic shootist's position.

He shot the first sec man through the lower stomach as he rushed in, deliberately avoiding knocking him into the others. If he didn't take out all three then he'd failed.

The second man managed to snap off a single round at Ryan, but the bullet struck the door frame and angled away into the wall.

Five out of the six sec men were down, either dead or dying. Once the last one was chilled, then they could have a clear run to hiding without the dogs baying at their heels.

The final guard charged in after his colleagues. His combat boots slipped on the gray ice and he fell sideways.

Ryan snapped off two quick rounds, one of which nipped a slice of flesh from the back of the man's left calf. The other missed completely.

Then he was off and running, ignoring the blood that was soaking through the leg of his pants, filling his boot. He'd dropped his M-16, but he was screaming at the top of his voice, like a stallion under the gelding knife.

Ryan couldn't get to the door for another shot over the dead and dying. He holstered his warm blaster and climbed quickly through the open window at the rear of the hut. Kate and Dean were waiting for him.

"Head for that big building over there," he said. "Zimyanin'll be here in less than five minutes. With moonlight on this fresh snow he could pick us off at a half mile with that sniper's rifle he used to carry. Got to hide up."

IT WAS ALL that Major-Commissar Gregori Zimyanin could do to hold on to the tattered rags of his fleeing sanity.

"The boy gone and all dead!" he bellowed, eyes looking clear through the wounded sec man who'd brought him the unwelcome message.

"All but me, Major-Commissar," he replied, hoping for some kind of grudging praise for his escape.

"All dead," the Russian repeated, shooting the guard through the center of his chest.

THE SENIOR SEC MAN wasn't absolutely sure he'd heard the Russian's command correctly.

"All of them, Major-Commissar?"

Suddenly Zimyanin was filled with enormous good humor. "Yes, my good chap. Execute every single worker not in the mines. It will take an hour or so. Then all of the available beaters...sec men, can join the hunt. It will be great fun if the weather remains satisfactory, will it not?"

"The shift in the tunnels?"

"They will stay there. After we have caught Cawdor and his mewling brat, then we shall reorganize the remaining serfs into two half shifts. And you will lead search parties to replace those who have given their lives for their beloved leader. I might raise a memorial to their loyalty."

There was a distant smile on the pocked face that made the sec man wish he could find a very deep hole to creep into until this even more terrifying madness had passed.

"See to it. Execute them, then bring all the men to where the sport has taken us."

"Where's that, Major-Commissar?"

"The trail in the snow will quickly provide us with the answer to that riddle, my comrade," Zimyanin promised, chucking the sec man under the chin.

RYAN HAD SEEN similar sights in other places in Deathlands, normally on the edges of the ruins of the larger villes, where power and industry had ridden in tandem. But the huge rusting towers of machinery were a new experience for Dean and for Kate.

"Was it some sort of religion?" she asked, standing stricken with wonder in the main entrance hall.

"Must've been to build blasters. Is that what it was for, Dad?" Dean craned his neck, peering upward.

"Turbines and generators to work these mines in the old days, way back before the long winters came along."

"We hiding here?"

"Yeah." Ryan looked around, not displeased with what he'd found. The building was truly enormous and must once have housed some of the processing equipment as well as the power plants. It was a maze of corridors and levels, where three armed people could comfortably hold off a hundred. In the end the weight of men and blasters would triumph, but it would be at a terrible cost and take a lot of time.

And a lot of time meant a lot of chances to escape free.

"Could be worse," Ryan said.

"IS IT SURROUNDED?"

"Not really, Major-Commissar."

"Not really!" Zimyanin shook his head in mock bewilderment. "That sounds rather as though my express orders have not been followed. Is that correct?"

"Not ... I mean that we don't have enough men to cover it completely."

The Russian smiled. "Of course."

"It's real big."

"And I had thought it so tiny it would fit into the hand of a child. No, I am merely jesting, my dear fellow."

"And the back runs clear up against the face of the cliff."

The smile vanished like the sun behind thunderclouds. "Can they escape us that way, do you think?"

"There's a path that leads up and around the valley. Trackies use it."

"You have men covering it?"

"Sure. Yeah. Course. Right, Major-Commissar. Men with rifles watching the back."

"There are no tracks leading out again?"

The sec man smiled. "Thought of that. Checked real careful. Got a breed ... part Chiricahua Apache from the deserts. Went right around."

Zimyanin managed another smile. "You've done well. Had you failed me I would have heated a ramrod until it glowed white, and then I would personally have inserted it, slowly, into your body. They would have heard your screams even in far-off Mother Russia."

The guard swallowed hard. "Want us to close in or just sit tight?"

Zimyanin glanced at the sky. "Still three hours to first lamp."

"Light."

"What is that?"

"You say 'first light,' Major-Commissar. Not 'lamp.' That's all."

"Ah, I understand. I am grateful. I am always eager to add to my poor store of knowledge of the English tongue."

"You was sayin' about there being three hours until... dawn."

"I was. And I think that you and the rest of the sec men should wait and watch. The rest will join you once the killings are done." Even as he spoke, he could hear the sound of regular, spaced single shots, coming from the living quarters. Zimyanin smiled as he thought of another joke. Living quarters. "They are dying quarters, are they not?" he said.

"Sure are," he agreed blankly. "So, we all sit tight. Go in when we got enough men?"

The Russian's brain was racing like a flywheel that's lost its controlling governor. "You will simply wait for a further order from me."

He spun on his heel and began to walk toward the cathedral bulk of the massive building. The noncom guard called after him, asking where he was going.

"Where? Elementary, my dear man. Cawdor and I have things to settle. I am going inside, and I might be some time."

His heels ringing on the icy snow, the short, powerful figure disappeared into the looming entrance of the power plant.

Chapter Forty-Five

They had all heard the clatter and shouting as the thin line of uniformed sec men got into position around their hiding place.

Ryan left Dean and Kate huddled together on a high gallery at the heart of the rambling complex, going himself on a swift and urgent recce.

He squinted out unseen through the smashed windows. Twice he could easily have picked off members of the Russkie's attacking force with the SIG-Sauer, but that would have shown his hand too soon. Better to wait and use surprise and doubt as primary weapons.

He counted twenty men, all with rifles, containing a thin perimeter. In the distance he could also hear the regular sound of shots being fired, a sound that spoke of organized killings. Ryan could hardly believe that Zimyanin was taking out all his own workers, just to have a better chance at him. But that was the only sensible and logical explanation.

Apart from the far-off echoing shots, the sarcophagus was still. Once Ryan thought he heard a faint sound, a metallic scraping, like knives being dragged against a stone floor, but it wasn't repeated.

ZIMYANIN HAD BEEN TRAINED as an ambitious young man in the arts and crafts of street fighting, dodging in and out of gaping doorways, checking hollow cellars and roofless attics, working in a combat team, each man supporting the next.

Then, as an officer marked for promotion within the sec force, he was sent to hone his skills among the empty boulevards of the largest ruined ville, a place that had changed its name so many times over the centuries that it was now simply called "Grad."

There he'd run alone, given a Makarov and a single round of ammo, with a saw-edged knife, sent among the young gang packs that ran in the ice-slick streets. They were teen killers known as "werewolves," eager to scent out and destroy any stranger on their turf.

After all that urban training, promotion had finally come—to the far-off northeast, where only a narrow strip of frozen sea separated Russia from the States of Deathlands, where a ville might be a hundred miles from its neighbor.

Zimyanin had always resented that obscure posting, unaware of how many enemies he'd made in the security hierarchy, men who feared the stocky young man with the pockmarked face, shaved head and the flat eyes of a psychotic killer.

There was a piece of paper in a filing cabinet in Moscow that held the details of the major-commissar. One question asked where he should be sent. The handwritten answer said simply "As far away as possible."

Now, at last, Gregori Zimyanin had the chance to use those distant skills in urban combat. He picked his way silently through the accumulated rubbish of more than a century, the rifle snug across his shoulders. The 9 mm Makarov PM in his right hand probed at the air in front of him with all the cautious delicacy of a cobra's tongue.

His pulse was up a couple of points, the adrenaline racing through his body like the most delicious elixir.

It was going to be good.

Cawdor was a dangerous opponent, but he was crippled with the boy. And, from the tracks, the young woman who'd been seen with him.

Zimyanin had tried to put himself into his enemy's mind—best to tuck up the baggage somewhere safe, and then try to watch out for any threat himself. Which was exactly what Ryan had done.

THE SIGHTS AND SOUNDS of the building when it had been running full-out were impossible to imagine. The generators, crushers, conveyors, graders and processors must have been deafening. Even now, stepping carefully through the darkness, Ryan found his head filling with awe.

He stopped on one of the upper galleries, kneeling behind some tumbled display paneling, staring intently into the whispering depths below him.

It was a relief to think that the young woman and his son were relatively safe.

He didn't think that Zimyanin would attempt to rush the place during the night. The Russian was fight-wise enough to know that, even with the filtered moonlight, his men could take a devastating body count in the lethal maze.

But he might send in one or two of his best sec men. Or even come in himself.

Ryan felt the hairs at the back of his neck prickling with anticipation. Something was moving down below him—a shortened shadow, scuttling like a dancing crab, with a hideous, silent elegance.

"Zimyanin," he breathed.

DEAN CLASPED THE CANNON in his hands, ears straining at the stillness. He glanced a couple of times at the pale young woman sitting opposite him, looking toward the smaller doorway. She was holding her five-shot snub-nosed revolver in her lap, right hand on the butt.

Kate caught the boy looking at her and smiled, teeth white in the gloom.

The boy wondered if she'd be any use when it got time to draw the ace on the line.

Ryan had picked one of the smaller control rooms, high up under the roof, on the side of the building nearest to the cliffs. His order to them had been very simple.

"If it's me, then I'll warn you. If it's not me, then blast away. Hesitate and you'll be chilled. Both of you."

Dean waited. It had never occurred to him for a moment that their chances of escaping from the building were so slight as to be nonexistent. His father was in charge, so it'd be fine.

ZIMYANIN WAS AS HAPPY as he'd ever been in his entire life, enjoying an elation of spirit that was almost sexual in its power.

This was what he'd been born for.

To hunt a worthy enemy, man against man, with death waiting in the shifting shadows for the loser.

He licked his lips, eyes darting from side to side, taking the greatest care to keep a watch out for any sound or movement above him. That was what his grizzled old instructor had knocked into him.

"In buildings you can get chilled from behind, in front or to the side. Even from below. Four times out of five it'll be from above. Remember that, Zimyanin."

Gregori had always remembered the warning.

A man in flight would instinctively seek higher ground. He'd stake his life that Ryan Cawdor would be somewhere in the concrete layers above him.

"I *do* wager my life," he breathed, smiling to himself.

Like a panther picking its way over black velvet, he began to climb silently toward the upper levels of the vaulted building.

RYAN SAW THE RUSSIAN again, on the farther side of the main power room, above the rusting turbines, each a hundred feet high. The dark figure was climbing toward a tottering gantry that would bring him into the highest floors.

Over the past few days, since he'd left Jak Lauren, and the rest of his friends, Ryan had been vaguely aware of a change in himself. His life had been a number of differing periods: the frightened, tormented child; the teenager who'd run alone, become hardened to killing, learned the craft of death; the man who'd matured with the Trader, covering the land; then, the leader of the small group, and lover of Krysty Wroth. Now the father of Dean.

Somehow, the days in the bitter cold around the sulfur mines had revealed a harder and more brutal persona. Without Krysty and the others to temper his violence, Ryan could see that he'd slipped toward the ice-hearted killer he might so easily have become had his life not been different.

It was a thought that disturbed him.

In his inner soul, Ryan couldn't shake the uneasy feeling that he'd known all along that Zimyanin would come after them, and that he'd left Dean and the girl up in their aerie as a bait for the Russian.

He began to move through the dusty complex of rooms and passages, his heart filled with the excitement of the chase.

Ryan become the ultimate hunter, the terminator, the bringer of death.

NEITHER OF THEM said anything.

Kate brought her blaster up very slowly, pointing it past Dean, toward the rectangular silhouette of the doorway. He'd heard it as well, and was half turned, his Browning Hi-Power drilling into the blackness.

It was a regular, steady sound, like someone scraping a handful of chisels over stone. It didn't sound like feet.

There was a hesitancy about the noise, as though the man weren't sure of where he was, or what he was doing there.

It stopped.

Dean pressed his back against the wall, sliding up to his feet. Opposite him, the young woman had done the same.

Finger to her lips, Kate inched toward the door, ignoring Dean's attempt to stop her with a warning wave of his hand.

She peeked into the passage.

And was decapitated by the killer sec droid.

Chapter Forty-Six

It had been tracking with an infinite, programmed patience, twice seeking the watery sunlight of the open hillside to recharge the fading solar batteries, waiting until relays were tripped and it was able to move once more into the blackness of the tunnels.

Its sensors kept it moving, following the traces of the double helix that had been imprinted into its circuits.

Once it had only missed the human by a scant hundred yards, finding itself the wrong side of a crevasse, unable to get across. Ladders presented an almost insurmountable obstacle to the lethal robot, though its insensate drive to kill had led it to make clumsy attempts on a couple of the simpler climbs.

Now it was close. Its vents sucked in the air, analyzing it, tasting the spectroscopic presence of its target. But it was also ailing. Hundred-year-old circuits were beginning to falter, giving microsecond delays in important relays, distorting information, making it hesitant.

But it still found the act of killing absurdly simple.

The knived fingers were long and powerful, and had remained razor sharp. The young woman's slender neck parted like a mouth opening in a sigh. Her skull toppled heavily to the floor, spouting blood everywhere.

Dean closed his eyes and screamed at the top of his voice.

Ryan heard the high, thin scream of white terror and began to run toward it.

Gregori Zimyanin heard the high, thin scream of white terror, smiled, and began to run toward it.

AFTER THE FIRST MOMENT of mind-rocking horror, with hot blood splashed into his face and eyes, the boy ran for his life. He'd barely glimpsed the metal creature that stood swaying gently in the doorway, its carapace clotted with steaming blackness. All he'd noticed was the twin ruby eyes, drilling in his direction.

Dean was out of the other door, arms pumping, unbalanced by the heavy automatic in his right fist. Never for a moment did he think of turning to try to use it on the apparition.

The gantry shivered under his pounding boots, and chunks of corroded iron peeled away and fell clear to the first floor.

To his left the hanging walkway had already collapsed, giving him only two options—straight ahead or to his right.

Ahead of Dean someone was moving fast toward him.

Shaking like a leaf, the boy dropped to a crouch, leveling the Browning, finger on the trigger.

"It's me!"

"Kate's dead. A fuckin' droid took her head clean off."

Ryan was nearly there, at the joining of the wavering gantries. Beyond his son he could make out something advancing, with a grating, inexorable step.

"Fireblast!"

"Can we stop it?"

Ryan put an arm on the boy's shoulder, feeling the shocked trembling. "Could try. Best steps we can take are fucking long ones."

"Where?"

"That way's broke."

"This one isn't too safe. Feel it moving, and bits fell off it."

Ryan watched the slow, shuffling progress of the robot closing the gap. "Best is the way I came. We can get into another part of the building..." He glanced over his shoulder. "There's someone..." Then he recognized the burly figure, silver circles gleaming on the lapels of the dark coat. "It's the bastard Russkie!"

Zimyanin had spotted him at the same moment, pausing and unslinging his rifle, which was able to hit a man clean through the forehead at a thousand yards in the hands of an expert.

The major-commissar was less than eighty yards away from Ryan and the boy.

"Chill him, Dad!"

The android was about sixty paces from them, moving in its usual unhurried way, its knife blades clicking and whirring against each other, almost as though it were eagerly anticipating the ultimate success of its mission.

The whole gallery was swaying, cables singing and more pieces flaking away from it. Ryan's intention to empty a mag of the SIG-Sauer in the direction of Zimyanin was too risky, a small, partly hidden moving target in near darkness.

"It's over, American friend," the Russian called, bringing his blaster to his shoulder.

"That way," Ryan said, pointing to the dark-shrouded gallery to the left. It meant running directly toward the advancing sec robot, but Ryan and Dean were closer to the aerial crossroads.

"But you—"

"Fucking move, boy!" Ryan shouted, pushing him, turning and snapping off half a dozen rapid rounds toward the Russian. The bullets sparked off the iron rails and floor, shrieking into the black vault around them.

He didn't wait to see whether he might have scored a lucky hit, racing after the slight figure of his son, trying to ignore the looming android, its long arms extended toward them.

The handrail on the right side broke away, almost tipping him over the edge, and he stumbled, nearly dropping the SIG-Sauer.

Dean ducked around the corner, Ryan close on his heels. He risked a couple more shots at the sec droid, hearing the metallic clang as one of them hit it on the chest armor. Combined with the rocking of the gantry it was enough to make it fall on its back, sounding like a load of scrap iron being dumped into a storm cellar.

Part of Ryan's attention noticed the crack of the high-powered rifle as Zimyanin tried a couple of shots at him. But the hopeless results immediately showed the Russian that the conditions were impossible and he laid the gun down, drew his pistol and started off after his enemy.

"It kind of splits both ways, Dad."

"Go right."

Behind him, he could see the droid battling back to its feet, fighting for balance as the whole structure swayed, threatening to collapse. Zimyanin was thundering toward him, face split into a crazed smile.

"Knock it over the edge," Ryan shouted, "or it'll chill us all."

The Russian hesitated a moment, a moment that saw the hunter robot regain its equilibrium, head turning toward Ryan, knives flashing in Zimyanin's direction.

There was still enough time for him to go back, leaving the droid to pursue Ryan and his son, but the major-commissar was shaken by the encounter, seeing his nemesis vanishing into the safe blackness. Zimyanin went after him.

The killer sec droid followed them.

"Broke off!"

Dean had turned around, facing his father, who had just arrived at the T-junction. Ryan looked the other way, seeing that it, too, was snapped off, leaving only rusting jagged ends of metal, hanging out a hundred feet above the floor of the building.

The only possible way out was back again, the same way they'd just come, along the narrow, teetering walkway.

Toward the droid.

And, much closer, toward Gregori Zimyanin.

The Russian saw the dilemma and paused, hanging on to the single rail with his left hand. His laughter rang out above the void. "End of the line, ladies and gentlemen. All change here for the terminus of the line."

The boy was close to the broken end of the walkway. Ryan and Zimyanin were barely thirty paces apart, both hanging on against the pendulum swing of the gantry. The droid was about twenty paces behind the Russian, moving slowly toward them.

"It'll chill all three of us," Ryan shouted. "Unless..."

Chapter Forty-Seven

"Unless what, Cawdor?"

"Truce!"

"Agreement between gentlemen, involving a temporary cessation of hostilities?"

Ryan was ready to shoot at Zimyanin, despite the erratic movements of the dangling walkway and the dreadful light.

"We all try, we can mebbe chill the bastard. No chance for a man alone."

The Russian glanced behind him at the leisurely approach of the sec droid, moving with a lethal, inexorable sense of purpose.

"Agreed," he yelled. "Until the monster is destroyed, we are companions. After—"

"After is after. Come on!"

Ryan was virtually certain that the androids had been programmed in some way he didn't understand to hunt him down. Him and only him. Anyone who got in the way was chilled, but if Zimyanin simply kept out of the robot's path he'd probably be safe.

That was something that Ryan kept to himself.

"GET DOWN AND HANG ON, Dean," Ryan ordered.

"I got my blaster as well."

"More danger to me than that son of a bitch, rocking around like this. Do it, please."

The sec droid had stopped at the junction, its head turning slowly from side to side as it took in the situation. To its left was a spur that ended in dangling wires and emptiness. To its right were the three humans. Its night-scope vision hummed as it appraised what it saw.

Its determined subject, another humanoid, shorter and heavier, another humanoid, shorter and lighter.

All were grouped close together.

Its central gyrosystem was working overtime to keep it balanced as the ground beneath the lower support stabiliziers moved to external parameters. Despite the age of its controls, the droid was still functioning well.

It was ready to complete the mission.

"Why not shoot it down?" the Russian asked.

"Tried that on another one. About as close to indestructible as I've seen. Arma-piercers'd put it away."

Zimyanin nodded. "Perhaps I can knock it over the side."

Ryan considered that one. It had a number of attractions to it. "Got that hammer hand and knives. Comp-fast controls. Hit you before you reached it."

Now that all four protagonists were briefly still, the swaying of the overhead catwalk had slowed, almost stopped.

Ryan glanced sideways at Zimyanin, noticing that the powerfully built man kept smiling, his lips pulled back off his teeth in what seemed a nervous reflex. But the smile never touched the dark obsidian chips that were his eyes.

"You believe that this thing is faster and stronger than I?" Zimyanin asked, rubbing at his chin with the muzzle of his Makarov.

"Yeah."

"Let us see."

The Russian began to edge toward the android, which watched intently. When he figured he was close enough, Zimyanin dived toward the steel knee joints of the robot, hoping to break its balance and shove it over the edge.

One arm stretched with a hiss of gears, the hammer fist clubbing down. Zimyanin tried to roll and dodge it, but it struck him on the right wrist with the sickening, unmistakable crack of splintering bone. The pistol whirled into space, landing eventually with a sonorous clatter on the ice-covered concrete floor below.

Ryan leveled the SIG-Sauer and fired four aimed rounds at the head of the android, trying to take out its vision. But the red specks of crystal were less than a third of an inch across, carrying thousands of optic fibers. The bullets whined harmlessly into the blackness, making the robot stagger slightly, giving Zimyanin a chance to crawl back to safety.

He was moaning and cursing, cradling his right wrist in his left hand.

Ryan didn't say anything, taking the moment to slot in a fresh magazine.

The momentary scuffle made the gantry sway again, and a twenty-foot length of girder snapped off and plummeted down in a spray of orange rust. One end of the walkway dropped nine inches with a heart-stopping jar. The sec droid rocked, arms flailing, feet shuffling to keep upright. Its head revolved silently through three hundred and sixty degrees, returning to stare at Ryan.

Somewhere near the roof there was the flat sound of a cable strand breaking.

"Only chance," Ryan said. "Rock the fucker clean off."

"Hey, hot pipe, Dad!" the boy whooped, ignoring the imminence of death for all of them.

"Let us commence," Zimyanin agreed through gritted teeth.

He clung on with his left hand to one of the frayed supporting wires, starting to sway back and forth. Ryan and Dean picked up the measure, both hanging on to upright supports.

The sec droid responded by moving against the rocking motion, steadying itself with the hammer hand, its knees creaking with the constant effort of maintaining its position.

The gallery rocked faster and farther, the corroded hawsers that kept it in place straining and screeching. A fine rain of fiery rust fell on the heads of Ryan, Dean and Zimyanin.

Outside, the eastern sky was showing the very first glimmering of the cold dawn.

"Faster, brothers. On, my droogs! Heave and heave and heave again."

The Russian was roaring with laughter, head thrown back, his bald head gleaming in the dim light.

The excitement was contagious, and Ryan found himself bellowing out in time with Zimyanin, sending the fragile walkway swinging faster and higher. More chunks of rotted metal tumbled away, and they could all hear the wires twanging under the intolerable pressure.

"It's losing it!" the boy screamed, his face flushed with the effort and the danger.

The droid was beginning to stagger. In a desperate attempt to steady itself it seemed to be using some kind of electromagnetic force through the feet. There were sparks fountaining from the rusty iron grid, tumbling like a fall of golden rain into the blackness below them.

Now it was employing both its upper extremities to fight to keep itself on the gantry, but the hammer was clumsy and the steel knives simply sliced through the old, rotten wires.

Ryan's plan was working.

"Da...da...da...da..." the major-commissar chanted in rhythm, kicking with his iron-toed boots.

The sec droid was losing it.

Ryan's head was whirling, his vision blurred by the sickening motion, but he could still see that the metallic killer was staggering.

The whole building felt as if it were breaking up around them.

There was an endless clattering of falling metal, and the air was filled with motes of rust. The walkway dropped with another deadly jolt, as one of the main cables disintegrated.

"All fucking right!" Dean saw the droid slipping, losing its fumbling hold on the handrail, its feet sliding, claws grating.

Its programming wouldn't let it give up, not even on the very brink of extinction. Feeling itself starting to fall, it powered toward Ryan, arms elongating, knives rotating.

But Gregori Zimyanin was in the way.

The murder machine toppled into him, one hand hitting him a glancing blow on the right shoulder. The knives slashed at his leg, cutting a neat circle from his coat, going on to slice through the remaining strap on the Dragunov rifle.

Hanging on for grim life, Ryan witnessed an astounding display of physical strength and courage by the Russian.

Fighting against the powerful servomotors, he gripped the droid by its neck in his left hand, tucking his feet under it and kicking hard.

Ryan heard ribs go as the robot clubbed its steel hammer into Zimyanin's body, but it was already off the ground, unable to find any traction. With a grunt of agonized effort, the Russian heaved the creature up and over the rail.

Ryan never heard it hit the floor. The air was filled with the sound of other cables snapping as the aerial walkway broke apart, one end coming away and falling vertically.

Above him, Dean was swinging like a lithe monkey, arms and legs wrapped around a stanchion, saving himself from dropping.

Ryan himself swung his right arm around a bent upright and felt it yield, then hold firm.

But Zimyanin was going.

Badly injured, his right hand useless, he slid away after the vanished sec droid, gathering momentum, feet first. Ryan watched him, expecting to see him vanish over the jagged brink.

But his left hand still functioned. Incredibly the Russian swung there, hanging by the one hand from a frayed cable, unable to help himself up.

For several breathless seconds, nobody spoke.

A MILE OR SO AWAY, in the airless deeps of the old redoubt, a pair of crimson eyes clicked on in the blackness.

GREGORI ZIMYANIN LAUGHED, a quiet, ruminative chuckle.

"So, Yankee, this is it."

"Looks like it."

"How is the . . . the truce?"

"Until we beat the droid. And we beat it."

"I beat it, Cawdor. The honor of victory is mine, is it not?"

The building was silent. The jerky pendulum movement was gradually slowing down.

Ryan finally answered the Russian. "Guess you did it, all right."

There was pain running ragged through Zimyanin's voice. "What is honor, Cawdor? And do you have it? Will you let me fall or will you help me to ascend? Which?"

With only one effective hand, and other crippling injuries, the Russian couldn't possibly climb back to safety without help. Nor could he hold on long enough for help to come in from outside the thick-walled building.

Within a minute or so he'd lose his hold on the rusting strands of the cable and plummet to a sickening death.

Ryan knew what the Trader would have done, knew what he should do.

He began to crawl slowly down, a gloved hand reaching out to help Zimyanin.

"No, Dad."

He heard the click of the Browning's action behind and above him.

"I promised, Dean."

"I didn't. I'll chill him. I swear on my mother's death that I'll chill him."

"We had a truce."

"Until that steel bastard was negatived. It's gone. The truce is done. He's done."

The boy's voice was steady. Ryan glanced up, seeing the heavy automatic held in both hands, Dean keeping his grip on the stanchion by wrapping his legs around it.

"Pull the trigger and you could get thrown off."

"I know that, Dad. My chance. I'll take it."

Zimyanin laughed again. "His father's son, is he not, Ryan Cawdor?"

"Yeah, he is."

The round, pocked face stared up, a pale sphere in the gloom. "I would not want one so young to carry so heavy a burden." Something that could have been a smile flashed across his face. "Goodbye, Cawdor, and your boy."

The hand opened, quite deliberately, and Major-Commissar Gregori Zimyanin fell to his doom.

Nothing in his brutal life equaled the manner of his passing.

Chapter Forty-Eight

In the scant three seconds before his body impacted with the stone floor, Zimyanin succeeded, left-handed, in drawing a silver-hilted, leaf-shaped throwing knife from its sheath. He hurled it up at Ryan Cawdor with a scream of maniac laughter.

It missed by a good twenty feet and tinkled down to the concrete four or five seconds later.

DEAN LED THE WAY up the web of hawsers and thinner wires to a ladder gallery that ran around under the roof. From there they managed to pick a route down onto the safer levels below. Getting out and onto the mountain wasn't difficult.

The guards were unsettled, the word passing that Zimyanin had gone into the cavernous building over two hours ago, and nothing was known since.

Someone claimed to have caught the sound of gunfire, and someone else said he'd heard cries that could have been laughter, pain or sorrow.

One of the sec men, armed with an old Kalashnikov AK-47, fired a burst at two figures he saw making their way around the rim of the canyon, keeping ahead of the rising tide of sunlight. But it was at extreme range and he didn't think he'd had much success.

If they were escaping slave workers, then either the cold or the trackies would certainly pick them off.

IT WAS still bitingly cold and Ryan and the boy hurried through the redoubt and into the gateway chamber, with its walls of dark, dark brown armaglass. Ryan pressed the button that should return them to the last destination used by the mat-trans unit, praying hard as he did so that none of Zimyanin's sec men had used it since their previous jump.

Dean had the heavy Browning tucked into his belt, face split in a great grin. "Going home again, Dad," he said.

The jump mechanism was already triggered, the disks glowing and the air seeming to become thicker around them. Ryan could hardly hear his son's words through layers of gauze.

But he managed to nod and smile.

THE MORNING WAS scorching hot. There was a light wind, carrying the sharp scent of sagebrush to their nostrils as they stood together, drawing in deep breaths of the New Mexico air.

It hadn't been a bad jump.

Dean had been sick, Ryan had suffered a small nosebleed. But now they were out of the claustrophobic depths of the ruined redoubt, only a few miles away from the homestead where they could both have a good hot bath to wash away the stinking yellow taint

of the sulfur and ease the exhaustion from their
bruised bodies.

"A good meal. Eggs, potatoes and some thick-sliced
ham."

Ryan put his arm on the boy's shoulders. "And
sleep for a day and a half."

"Sure, then . . ." He paused, shading his eyes as he
stared across the land. "What's that, Dad?"

"Dust storm, or—"

"Looks like smoke." Dean sniffed. "Yeah. You can
actually smell it. Burned wood and a kind of scent like
charred meat."

The column of dark smoke rose and curled, high
above the desert, until it vanished.

It came from the direction of Jak and Christina's
home.

Ryan felt his heart shrink into cold marble.

"Come on, Dean," he said quietly. "Best go take a
look."

Behind them in the redoubt's heart, the walls of the
silvery armaglass that formed the gateway chamber
were beginning to fill with a pallid mist, and the disks
in the floor and ceiling were starting to glow.

Someone had triggered the mat-trans mechanism
and was in the process of making a jump.

Someone.

Something?

These heroes can't be beat!
Celebrate the American hero with this collection of never-before-published installments of America's finest action teams—ABLE TEAM, PHOENIX FORCE and VIETNAM: GROUND ZERO—only in Gold Eagle's

Available for the first time in print, eight new hard-hitting and complete episodes of America's favorite heroes are contained in three action-packed volumes:

In **HEROES: Book I**   July $5.99   592 pages

ABLE TEAM: Razorback by Dick Stivers
PHOENIX FORCE: Survival Run by Gar Wilson
VIETNAM: GROUND ZERO: Zebra Cube by Robert Baxter

In **HEROES: Book II**   August $5.99   592 pages

PHOENIX FORCE: Hell Quest by Gar Wilson
ABLE TEAM: Death Lash by Dick Stivers
PHOENIX FORCE: Dirty Mission by Gar Wilson

In **HEROES: Book III**   September $4.99   448 pages

ABLE TEAM: Secret Justice by Dick Stivers
PHOENIX FORCE: Terror in Warsaw by Gar Wilson

Celebrate the finest hour of the American hero with your copy of the Gold Eagle HEROES collection.

Available in retail stores in the coming months.